D1559628

In the Beginning

Church Mouse
Musings at
Historic St. Peter's

Sandra Voelker

IN THE BEGINNING
FINLEY'S TALE - BOOK 1
Copyright © 2018 by Sandra Voelker

Printed in Canada

ISBN: 978-1-4866-1531-5

Word Alive Press
119 De Baets Street, Winnipeg, MB R2J 3R9
www.wordalivepress.ca

WORD ALIVE
—PRESS—

MIX
Paper from
responsible sources
FSC
www.fsc.org
FSC® C016245

Cataloguing in Publication may be obtained through Library and Archives Canada

This book is dedicated to my Robert, my husband, my love.
I treasure the way you are, especially that you give and receive God's grace, through Christ
our Lord, cheerfully, thankfully, and persistently. You give me strength to do the same.

"I would be happy just to hold the hands I love."
—Gordon Lightfoot

GREETINGS!

I have a tale to tell, and you are cordially invited to follow my tale. Nevertheless, before launching forward, it is best that I quickly introduce myself to you since I am a stranger, someone with whom you are completely unacquainted. Newcastle is my name, Finley Newcastle. I am honoured to be a church mouse at Historic St. Peter's Church, located in Oswald County, where I delightfully work and reside while jotting down actual experiences and observations. My tale uncloaks heaps of knowledge about the wide panorama of parish life that only those on the inside witness. Recorded are triumphant joys and blessings, the ups and downs, sometimes with various annoying kerfuffles that more than ruffle delicate human being's feathers.

My given name, Finley, happens to be an old-fashioned, but not cast-off, Gaelic male name that means "fair-haired warrior." The "fair-haired" description of me is spot-on, but the "warrior" implication is not even a wee bit applicable, as it fails to portray or depict my personality or demeanour. I am not brave. I am pleased to admit to you that I have never found myself smack in the middle of a fight, physically or verbally. I am a peacemaker, a peacekeeper, and unquestionably not a warrior. Because of that, I have never needed to bury the hatchet with anyone, thankfully having successfully avoided squabbles, rhubarbs, or skirmishes that come filled with tempestuous dramatics long before the kettle ever gets settled.

When selecting my first name, my fine and loving mother, Lilje Morgenstern-Newcastle, thoughtfully contemplated between two names that were on the top of her list, Finley and Finnegan. Much later I learned that mother settled on the name Finley because she was concerned about possible ramifications the name Finnegan might bear on my future, knowing that it would be dubbed with the ungentlemanly nickname of Iggy, a silly, unsophisticated, unpolished, lowbrow shortened form of Finnegan. My "mum" had faith and conviction that I would grow up to be a genuine Finley who is gallantly courageous, perceptive, and considerate, continually in pursuit of a no-nonsense way of life. Many times throughout my upbringing she assured me that I would come to possess lionhearted attributes that would be essential in handling any situation that I might come across throughout my lifetime. Even though the name Finley is of true

Scottish origin, it somehow reminded my mother of her Viking roots. Her abundant memories growing up in Norway's extreme geographical landscape of fire and ice genuinely matched the way she lived her life. The tender side of my mum often recalled to me her favourite childhood pastime of gathering wildflowers from the mountainsides as she took adventuresome hikes along the deep fjords near her family's dwelling. The "fresh air life" that she lived, the *"Friluftsliv,"* seemed to be in each and every deep breath she took, day after day of her life. My mother was a bona fide one-of-a-kind loving and captivating individual. (Now I will let you in on a little secret. Just between us, my middle name is Tweed. I have no inkling as to why I was endowed with this kooky name. Just mentioning the name generates thoughts of an English gent arrayed in a humdrum homespun herringbone crumpled jacket and slacks that smell of tobacco due to smoking a vintage bent-applewood pipe. Long ago I came to grips with my middle name and made a willful intention to never make use of it. However, I do admit that it feels almost inspirational to get that off of my chest. So, thank you kindly for listening to me and I trust that you will help me keep the name Tweed on the hush-hush.)

Newcastle, my surname, derives from my father, the stout and strappingly strong Ellis Newcastle. He was born at a brewery by the same name located in Newcastle upon Tyne in north-east England. I am exceedingly honoured to be born into the Newcastle lineage. Keeping a close check on my humility helps me to stay well-balanced. Because the Newcastle name carries an aristocratic association with it, if I were to leave my pride unchecked, it could easily go to my head and skyrocket out of proportion. I have found that prioritizing modesty and humbleness is the best path to take, producing the opposite of pridefulness. I believe that St. Augustine described pride as "The love of one's own excellence." I prefer to perpetually focus on others, finding out what I can do to be of service to them, as well as contributing to the world by doing my part to see that the earth remains in tip-top shape.

Many of my relatives reside at a brewery in England. I have aunts, uncles, first cousins, second cousins, third cousins, first cousins once-removed, first cousins twice removed, second cousins once removed, step-cousins, half cousins, cousins-in-law, distant cousins, and, of course, "kissing" cousins that were all born at the brewery. There are so many relatives in my large extended family that I could have a gigantic chart kept up-to-date by a paid administrative assistant to keep them all current.

Perhaps remembering names is a source of distress for you and causes embarrassing emotional strain and anxiety in public, simply because you cannot recollect someone's name. Just tell me about it, because I used to wrestle with that same hiccup. But, luckily, I've found a helpful tip to remember someone's first and last name. The tip is to immediately make some kind of association with it, just as I have done for you with my name, and chances are you'll remember it. Having just fully explained the origin of my name to you, hopefully you will remember that I am named Finley Tweed (remember, hush-hush, on that one, please) Newcastle. Now that I've said this, I am no longer a stranger to you, but a new acquaintance.

I am in the process of completing an aspiring goal that has been on my bucket list. For one full year I am recording the events and happenings at Historic St. Peter's Church. English is my second language, so the words I select will not always be elegant or eloquent, flowing fluently from a polished silver pen. At times you may wonder where my tale is going or even when it will take flight, but please keep in mind that I am a mouse, meaning that the unfolding of my tale will differ greatly from what a human being would write. I'm telling you this so you don't presumably expect my words to steadily glide along the pages of my journal like those from some of the great writers of the world. However, with my basic, but ever-broadening English language skills, I have tried my best to articulate clearly everything I record while on duty at Historic St. Peter's.

Due to the time I have spent residing and working at Historic St. Peter's, my thoughts are completely absorbed when it comes to observing human beings, and in particular, church parishioners with all of their attention-catching and thought-provoking actions. Even though I am still at a pioneer level of discovery about what makes people behave the way they do, I was inspired to begin my tale after I came across an unused or unloved journal that was resting on the bottom shelf of the church library at Historic St. Peter's. The journal pleaded with me to pick up a pen and begin writing. Being brand new, this journal had to have been abandoned by someone who does not have journaling on their own personal bucket list. Whoever owned it temporarily must have been too timid or terribly afraid to re-gift it. So, they donated it to St. Peter's Library to get rid of it. I clung to it and claimed it as my own, or more correctly, to temporarily borrow it from the church library for one full year.

The cover of my journal has a lovely depiction of an antique church organ that features J.S. Bach playing one of his musical masterpieces. In the painting Bach appears to be not only a master of his own original organ music, but also is a master at filling up every single square inch of the petite organ bench that he is sitting on due to his full-sized derrière. But, that is not of importance. Of greater importance are his brilliantly creative musical works that he masterminded during his lifetime, the dimensions of which are far more vital than the width and breadth of Bach's buttocks.

My focus is to record the goings on of one liturgical church year here at Historic St. Peter's. (Many of the parishioners have nicknamed the church St. Pete's or HSP.) By writing down everything as honestly as I possibly can, I guarantee you that you will not be snowed under with tall tales, fairy tales, or fish tales. Tales like that, especially fish tales, seem to brag, exaggerate, and stretch the truth so far that while listening to them you almost feel you need to pick up your phone and place an order at a take-away fish and chips shop, the type of establishment you know that carefully seasons the fish and chip basket with just the right amount of sea salt, tossing in a few plastic sachets of tartar sauce and malt vinegar. After placing your order, you might be able to endure the torture of having to listen to someone tell an entire fish tale in detail from head to tail. I will not do that to you, but in an honourable and quality manner I am composing *Finley's Tale*, a factual true-to-life tale. You will be presented with events and occurrences that will cling to you and easily wrap around you like a comfy fleece blanket. It's similar to the way clear plastic food wrap surrounds and protects a bowl of tasty leftovers by tightly clinging to it for the purpose of keeping it fresh, ready to be enjoyed later on. You are invited to cling to my tale, *Finley's Tale*, by following and embracing my writing. If my tales end up being excessive and unrestrained, that is because life sometimes gets involved, messy, and complex. No matter what, I will tell the truth truthfully and I will tell it like it is.

I am appreciative of you, the reader, for deciding to spend your precious free time following my tale. While reading my journal, my hope is that all of your woes will be gone while you put your feet up and unwind with this journal. Hopefully you will enjoy the news revealed to you in which I will try to convey what "church life" is really actually like.

The dear members of Historic St. Peter's seem to savour their time spent together as a congregation, whether it is in worship, at the coffee hour, or at special events as well as social settings. I notice that parishioners seem to live their lives with special meaning and purpose, with Jesus Christ as their cornerstone. Their faith lets them look to life eternal and not just at their earthly life. The members of St. Pete's are gracious and full of compassion for the homeless and the sick, especially going overboard at Thanksgiving and Christmastime. They also seem to be made up of a wide variety of personalities. Not only are there beige-coloured, bland people who are often referred to as the "regular" members because they follow the rules or do what is expected of them, but there are also the extra-ordinary and the extra-odd ones. Some are financially well-off, some not, with most of them falling in the category known as in-between. There are the high-maintenance ones who are time-demanding, all-consuming, and often impatient. There are people of every age, not just the old and the young. Somewhere I heard the phrase "people are people" just as "mice are mice," and I know that there is a truism in that, but they also vary a bit from that notion here at St. Peter's. Something appears to be unique about them, much like what is mentioned in the Holy Bible found in 1 Peter 2:9 where it says, "But you are a chosen people, a royal priesthood, a holy nation, God's special possession, that you may declare the praises of Him who called you out of darkness into His wonderful light." That Bible verse contains words of value like chosen, royal, and holy for believers, let alone that they are called God's special possession. I think that God must really love and cherish His people. Occasionally some of the things that the members do around here are hilarious, but it will only double the delight of my recording those events, and triple your joy in hearing about them.

I invite you to stay with me and my journal to see how the church year unfolds. God bless you!

Your newest friend,

Finley Newcastle

(F.N. for short)

Monday, December 1

ON THIS HAPPY MONDAY MORNING, I AM DELIGHTED TO SHARE WITH YOU SNIPPETS about my beloved wife, my Ruby. Ruby lives up to her gem of a name in every way. The Burmese Ruby located in the National Museum of Natural History in Washington, D.C. weighs in at 23.1 carats, but is of far less value to me than my Ruby. I have no idea how much Ruby tips the washroom scale, but she wears every single bit of it very well. She is remarkable, a precious gem, just like the other three precious gemstones: the emerald, the diamond, and the sapphire. Unfortunately, Ruby and I haven't been able to have a baby, so it is just the two of us in our family. Sometimes we worry about our future as there will be no one to visit us when we are elderly, a big downside of not having had any little ones.

Ruby and I were the very first mice to reside at St. Pete's. A few other families followed our lead and are living happy and healthy lives here. We are a tight-knit mouse village community. Our mouse membership grows slightly faster than Historic St. Peter's people membership. Perhaps it is due to the fact that we adopted and fully take to heart, strength, and mind their well-crafted missional song, "All Are Welcome Here." Our village wholeheartedly sings the welcoming song at each mouse gathering. Parishioners occasionally sing this in church on Sunday mornings. From hearing it sung several times, the mice were able to learn it by rote in the English language. The words of the song reveal a concept of there being big open arms that embrace all newcomers. It is so welcoming that it almost makes me cry. It is like hearing the words *bienvenue* (French), *herzlich willkommen* (German), *bienvenida* (Spanish), *kuwakaribisha* (Swahili), *powitanie* (Polish), and *velkommen* (Norwegian) all spoken simultaneously, similar to what occurred on the Day of Pentecost. The song really tugs at the heartstrings of the mice residing in the village. I am not certain if the current words on the outdoor signage at church are related to the welcoming song, but I have to wonder. This is what the marquee currently says, "We're not perfect, but you are welcome here!"

After Ruby and I moved in last fall, we discovered that we needed to get smart quickly. It was essential that we become proficient in the English language, at first for safety reasons, but later on to lead to our understanding of what human beings are like, which helps to make sense of all that goes on in a church setting. To develop our verbal skills, we listened from behind the scenes as people spoke. To develop our reading skills, we studied the Sunday bulletins that had been dropped on the sanctuary floor. We sharpened our pronunciation skills by practicing speaking with each other. We soon figured out that people language is far more intricate and knotty than the spoken and written word alone. The fascinating part for all of us mice has been to watch people's facial expressions and gestures as they wildly and assertively try to get their points across. The desire to attain fluency in English has led to the development of a weekly ESL (English as a Second Language) class that Ruby and I team-teach to the residents of our village. Due to that, most of our mice will shortly be bilingual. The little mice continue to be the fastest learners.

Most likely you are puzzled about what we do with our time, spending all of it at the church. Simply put, there's a lot going on here and many things happen every single day. It's the truth. In the beginning of our life here at HSP, parishioners would arrive on the premises and the mice were filled with fright. After much effort, we've faced the mighty giant of extreme fear and trembling, thinking that we might have won the battle. We often have unwanted situations, but we have enough strength and smarts to immediately find safety. The first step for the mice community was to become familiar with every single inch of the building so that we could quickly slide into hiding places when trouble arose. We often think of verse 41 from Luke 10, "Thou art careful and troubled about many things." Realizing that it is normal to be nervous and afraid, we try our best to calm down. When we're safely hidden, a well-trained team of mice goes out and about as scouts on the lookout for the possibility of potential danger. The team's job is to listen carefully to people's conversations, return to the village, and report their findings. Our village prides itself on staying current at all times, mindful that there is potential for danger daily. After all, this is our home, our favourite place to be, treasured by each one of us. We are fully aware that this is a wonderful community for the mice to raise their offspring and we want to continue to reside here. By being aware, we know if our village is in any danger.

Attached to Historic St. Peter's is a clergy house, which is similar to a manse or a rectory. It is called a parsonage and is home to the current parson, Pastor Osterhagen and his family. The parsonage is connected to the sanctuary by a very long and beautifully enclosed windowed breezeway. Ruby and I have access to the parsonage as not long ago we found a hidden passageway which we keep concealed from all the other mice. Most every evening after the Osterhagens are sound asleep, Ruby and I run as fast as possible down the breezeway, slip through a small crack under the Osterhagen door and arrive in the parsonage, ready to consume a late night snack of minuscule nibbles and crumbs found on the floor either underneath their dining room table or in the corners of the kitchen floor. We find these gleanings to be gourmet treats that are waiting for us alone, a feast of various types of foods.

Pastor Clement Osterhagen, his wife Aia (pronounced I–ya), and their four-year old daughter Gretchen have been at Historic St. Peter's for nearly two years. All three have a sparkle and twinkle about them that gives off a message that they are delighted to be here with the members of St. Pete's, enjoy living in the parsonage, and like to discover what's in Oswald County. Pastor and Aia recently found out that they are expecting their second child, but they have not yet told their good news to anyone at the church. Aia is a foodie, so when she feels like cooking she will prepare recipes from her international cookbook, making meals a real adventure. Clement never knows what Aia will prepare for their supper as there is no predictable pattern. The only pattern is supper on Friday nights, which is pizza. Because of her increased hunger, Aia is very talkative about how much or how little food that she has consumed, trying hard to avoid eating for two throughout the upcoming months.

NOTE: It might be helpful if I tell you some basic information before you read any further into my journal. The most recognizable mouse, of course, in the entire world is Mickey, who even has a star on the Hollywood Walk of Fame. All mice think that he has done really well for himself. Generally speaking, we are all a lot like Mickey in that we are good looking, smart, personable, quick, and strong. We are simply tiny little earth dwellers and nature lovers that are a bit reluctant to interact with humans. After observing Clement, Aia, and Gretchen, the mice community thinks that people are amazingly wonderful. The entire mice village has developed so much regard and respect for the Osterhagen Family. We think they must be the most important people in the whole world.

ADDITIONAL NOTE: The mice at St. Pete's are careful about being neat and tidy by daily cleaning our homes. We recognize that we are living in God's house. A unique priority in our mice village is practicing and perfecting cleanliness. In order to do that, each mouse has to take responsibility, to stand on his or her own four paws and persistently clean up many times a day. We are aware that most humans are repulsed by mice and their mess, which is mind-boggling to our community. If we leave any tracks or trails we are at a great risk of being discovered and eliminated, so our village is tightly united in safety, safety being our top priority. "Safety First" is the mice village theme song that we sing at our meetings. It has a stately, majestic tune and is written in four-part harmony.

When I have some spare time I will write down our theme song and include it in my tale so that you can sing it, maybe even memorize it, as "Safety First" certainly applies to both mice and men.

When Ruby and I travel to the Osterhagens late at night to nibble on tiny morsels of food that are almost unseen to the human eye, we only touch the floor in the dining room and kitchen. We do not wander about the house, climb on counters, or get into anything. We leave no trace of our presence. We do not need to break into their packages of food. We are quite content with the crumbs that fall from their table. That way we don't get detected and, besides that, things become a little neater. I wanted you to know this or your imagination might tell you that we leave a big mess everywhere we go. Unlike the other mice we have known, our mice community is so clean that the Osterhagens, along with the parishioners, do not even know that we exist. Also, Ruby is a little bit of a neat freak. I'm so thankful that she has a knack for immaculateness, because life is better that way.

On a recent late night visit to the parsonage, I noticed an empty beer bottle on the kitchen counter. It was probably parked there until it was to be added to the recycle bin in the garage. For a moment it took my breath away as I noticed the label was printed with my surname. Having told you that I hail from a very long line of Newcastles with relatives still living at a brewery in the UK, I immediately felt linked to Pastor Osterhagen in a zany sort of way. Right then and there I told Ruby that Historic St. Peter's is graced with a man of quality, a real keeper. Very soon I will write to one of my cousins to request that Pastor Osterhagen become a member of the Newcastle Society. When I receive positive confirmation from the Society, I'll somehow let Pastor know that he is now a honourary member of this aristocracy. I am convinced that Osterhagen and I are now bonded, fastened together by the Newcastle name.

Since the Osterhagens are spell-binding people, Ruby and I are considering moving right next door to them in order to keep current on their day-to-day lives. It would be like watching a soap opera every single day, "church-style."

At 11:30 p.m. Ruby and I travelled to the parsonage for our snack. We were extra lucky tonight because we stumbled across a chocolate-covered raisin. The coating transformed a Playne-Jayne raisin into a very pleasing confection. As we chewed, we quietly discussed the precise spelling of "Playne-Jayne," thinking that it might actually be spelled "Plain-Jane." We were open to the idea.

– F.N.

Tuesday, December 2

EVEN THOUGH IT IS TUESDAY, LET ME SPELL OUT WHAT SUNDAY MORNINGS ARE LIKE AT St. Peter's. Each Sunday Ruby and I are filled with mountains of awe-inspiring wonderment as we appreciate the fine organ music. Because of our richly rewarding experience, we have become regular Sunday morning attendees at church. Having found a passageway into the tummy of the church organ, we have selected the best place for us to listen to the music. Our experiences are as splendid as if we held season tickets with grand-tier seating at an opera house.

However, it was no opera last Sunday morning when Dirk Klanderman filled in as substitute organist. The quality of music dove downward to the murky depths of the deepest dark sea. Dirk also displayed an attitude of audacity when he showed up unprepared. Obviously he was playing through music for the very first time during the actual worship service. So many sour notes and chords were produced that it resulted in parishioners complaining. Ruby and I decided that if Dirk is asked to play the organ again we will simply skip church. Ruby overheard Pastor Osterhagen privately tell Aia that he will not invite Dirk to play the organ again at St. Pete's. Aia agreed with him. Ruby and I suspect that Dirk is lacking knowledge regarding organ stops, seeming to have zero mastery over what the combination of organ stops will produce. We are aware that it takes vast knowledge to know how and when to use the 32' Contre Bombarde, the 2' Night Horn, the IV Sharp, and the Koppel Flute, just to name a handful of organ stops. Because inappropriate use causes feedback in hearing aids, that Sunday the hearing aids broke out in various forms of crying in which they whistled, chirped, and squeaked. Matthew 11:15, "He who has ears to hear, let him hear," appears to be a rather ill-suited Bible verse to explain the hubbub experienced the day Dirk was the fill-in organist.

At 11:30 p.m. Ruby and I travelled to the parsonage and snacked on a kernel of home-made caramel corn along with a morsel of a dropped leftover. We were not able to identify exactly what it was, but we both found it lip-smackingly delicioso.

— F.N.

AIA WAS PERTURBED THIS MORNING. HER ACTIONS WERE WITNESSED BY SILVER-BIRCH, one of the most genuine and graceful mice in our village, who also has a lot of curiosity. Zipping down the breezeway with Gretchen in her arms, Aia burst through the study door to enter Pastor's office, motioning for him to hurry up and hang up the telephone. He ignored her plea, as this was an important call from Bishop Fillmore regarding how to handle the private matter of a couch potato that works in the district office. Clearly Bishop did not know what to do, or what not to do, but talked about it and appreciated Clement's advice. Concluding the telephone call with a prayer asking God for help and guidance, Bishop must have felt better. Listening to Clement pray, Aia joined in by holding Gretchen on her lap and folding their hands together. After lifting her own hurting heart to God she became composed and less anxious. During this time Silver-Birch waited discreetly outside Pastor's office door hoping to discover the reason why Aia was so ruffled and upset. After Aia had a chance to speak, Silver-Birch's sky-high curiosity became satisfied as to why Aia was so aggravated.

Aia took a big breath and calmly explained to Clement the unexpected visit she had just had from Agnes Toppler, whom Aia now has nicknamed "The Blabber." Agnes had arrived at the parsonage bearing a Christmas plastic platter filled with snicker doodles and rum balls all wrapped up in Santa Claus printed cellophane, tied with a big red bow. Pastor wondered what was wrong with that, as he thought it was generous of Agnes to give them a gift and appreciated her thoughtfulness. Aia told him that the cookies were not the problem. The problem is that every time Agnes stops at the parsonage, for whatever reason she concocts, she suddenly needs to use their washroom. Tears fell from Aia's eyes while saying that Agnes must have seen the discarded pregnancy test kit in the washroom wastebasket, which results in Agnes being the first person at church to find out their baby secret. Aia emphasized that it is their good news, something that she hoped to keep completely private. Explaining that within minutes Agnes would blab to everyone that Pastor and Aia are expecting their second child, Aia complained that this is one downer of living in a pastoral fish bowl. Pastor gently smiled at Aia telling her that at least this time Agnes, "The Blabber," will be spreading the truth. Aia took a couple of big breaths and then agreed with Clement, saying that he was right. Silver-Birch told us that after Clement's kind words Aia stopped acting like a baby and the tears came to a stop.

The mice community notices that Pastor has been working very hard lately. It's not just Christmas preparations, but everything else. There is the annual report and directory to produce in January and much of that cannot wait until the New Year to be accomplished. Also, all of the shut-ins need a visit which takes up hours of Pastor's afternoons. He has been asked to deliver a mini-Christmas cactus to each one of them, purchased by the Ladies' Guild. That's fine, but babysitting the plants until they are delivered isn't easy.

At 10:30 p.m. Ruby and I frolicked cheerfully down the breezeway to the parsonage where we delighted in finding a roasted-in-the-shell sunflower seed on the floor underneath the kitchen step stool.

— F.N.

Friday, December 5

Pastor Osterhagen arrived at his office this morning with his mind set on getting a lot of work done. There are a few December weekdays that are quiet at the church and that is helpful because it gives him time to think, plan, pray, and do his work. Today appeared to be that type of a day. Ruby heard Clement tell Aia that he was looking forward to accomplishing his work. All was fine until Vern Moore showed up and interrupted him, clearly in need of some pastoral care about his personal problems. Vern was candid with Pastor that he would rather receive words of wisdom from a professional counsellor, but he won't go to one because they charge a hefty fee. Vern told Pastor that it is far thriftier to tell him his problems because pastoral care is free of charge – free for Vern, that is.

Vern suggested to Pastor that they take a short walk downtown to The Sugar Bowl to enjoy a cup of coffee. Mentioning that they could sit in a corner booth, Vern insisted that the discrete location will provide them with the freedom to talk candidly by being remote from any eavesdropper. After they arrived at the diner and ordered coffee, Vern ordered a slice of The Sugar Bowl's specialty, Loretta's Pecan Pie, along with a scoop of French vanilla ice cream. After that he launched into his current personal problems revealing them all to Pastor. When the cheque arrived, Vern slid it over to Pastor and sincerely thanked him for listening to him and also for treating him to pie and coffee, telling him that he already feels better and that they should do this more often, perhaps once a week. We understand that Clement doesn't want to spend money or time in this way. He must only have wanted to pay $1.50 for his own coffee and call it quits. The total bill, including tip, put him $12.38 in the hole.

Aia's friend, Annette Dixon, happened to be at The Sugar Bowl with her cousin and overheard Pastor's and Vern's entire conversation. After that she went home and called Aia to tell her everything that she just got wind of. Ruby and I notice that every time Clement spends money on parishioners and Aia finds out, she plunges into the story of how Katie Luther was wise to hide from Martin what little worldly goods they possessed. Their monetary treasure consisted of a few silver goblets and a pair of candlesticks. Martin, led by his far too generous heart, often gave away their wealth to those who said that they were in desperate need and who begged him for his help. Ruby mentioned to me that being the recipient of a silver goblet or candlestick must be far more valuable of a gift than a single slice of Loretta's Pecan Pie, ice cream, and a cup of coffee, and that Aia should just quiet down and not boil over about $12.38 going down the drain.

Pastor Osterhagen listens, guides, but, most importantly, prays with the people that he tries to help. But every single time he tries to pray with Vern it doesn't work out. Vern does not have the ability or patience for prayer. As soon as he sees a prayer on the horizon, he suddenly jumps up and says that he has to get home to where the real problems need to be solved. To hinder a prayer today, Vern diverted Pastor's attention by criticising him for spending money on their family pull-along camper. Pastor Osterhagen quipped back by telling Vern that he would be able to afford a camper, too, if he didn't spend so much money on women, drinking, and gambling. That unfortunate conversation happened after Pastor got stuck with the cheque at the restaurant. At that point, it was obvious to Annette that Pastor was upset and in need of some pastoral care himself. When he returned to the church, one of our village mice, Prairie-Rose, happened to be hiding behind the lost and found box. She heard Pastor come close to spilling out the details of his encounter with Vern to big-ears Chuck Brownton, the church janitor. Even the mice community knows that would not have been a wise move on Pastor's part as Chuck comes equipped with elephant-sized listening ears, but when it comes to confidentiality, he has absolutely zero skill, not even a dab of ability to keep tight-lipped. Clement went home instead, unloaded to Aia everything that had just occurred. Ruby and I were so proud of Aia for helping Clement recover and to feel better. Aia also tried to come up with practical solutions so that Vern and the coffee, pie, and ice cream incident would never ever be repeated.

At 11:30 p.m. Ruby and I travelled to the parsonage and snacked on one dropped shoestring potato stick. While we ate, we quietly visited about the possibility of moving in next door to the parsonage. The vacant spot is a medium-sized storage area that has all of the amenities that we fancy. As luck would have it, there is a small hole in the dining room wall that will enable us to listen to the Osterhagen's conversations, which should be abundant because they talk a lot about everything. Most likely Clement and Aia do not know about the hole. Their china hutch sits in front of it, covering up most of the opening, but there is enough of an opening so that we can see into the parsonage. Ruby and I are certain that this is, by far, a step up in real estate from where we are currently residing in the church basement. The two of us brought it to a vote and it passed unanimously. Our plans are to move next door to Pastor, Aia, and Gretchen tomorrow. The last thing Ruby and I talked about tonight was to discern exactly what a pecan is as we are unfamiliar with them. Putting our thoughts together, we broke the actual word in half, which resulted in two little words, pee and can. We must not be on the button as both words are certainly not ingredients in the popular pecan pie that is baked and served daily at The Sugar Bowl.

— F.N.

DURING THE WEE HOURS OF THE MORNING A HANDFUL OF VILLAGE MICE VENTURED INTO one of the holy places at St. Peter's that is referred to as "the sanctuary." After yesterday's delivery of twenty-four poinsettias from Serena's Floral Shoppe, these mice were inquisitive to see the festive Advent/Christmas display in "the chancel," the holiest place at St. Pete's. However, eagerness dissipated when the mice eyeballed the poinsettias. Even though they were in costly golden planters that were either made from real gold or perchance fool's gold, the plants themselves were already wilted with their leaves dropping and plopping on the floor. Assuming that the plants arrived in tip-top condition yesterday, the mice expected that they would be showing their Christmas Spirit with lipstick red and forest green foliage. The mice concluded that the condition of the wilted leaves is due to the sanctuary's chilly, almost arctic temperature. They unanimously agreed that tossing all twenty-four of them out would make the sanctuary look far better. In other words, no flowers would be better than dead flowers. In thinking about it, I now recall Pastor Osterhagen telling Aia about the grumbling done by one negative goat at the last Voters' Meeting, Herman Jenkins. His actions were far from being a gent when he spoke in detail about how sky high December's utility bill would be if the sanctuary was kept higher than 50 degrees Fahrenheit. Since Herman's explosion, the members keep their winter gear on every minute they are in the church building. Because of this, the two-hundred-plus plastic coat hangers at HSP are rarely used. If coat hangers have feelings they must be hurt and assume that they are just taking up space. It is evident that most members do not want to tangle with Herman, so they keep away from touching the dial on the thermostat. Members have been whispering to each other the stern correction that they would receive if Herman were to discover one of them raising the thermostat. The mice are aware that poinsettias are tropical plants that originated in sunny Mexico which require warm temperatures in order to sustain their beauty. Several mice commented that after one brief and chilly day at St. Pete's the poinsettias are already wilted, sad, and grumpy, which is a downright shame. In less than twenty-four hours they must want to transfer to another church because their needs are not being met at HSP. But, maybe if people see the look of the poinsettias in worship this morning, they will work together to warm things up. Poinsettias just might be like people in that the temperature of relationships is very fragile and is best handled with warmth plus prayer.

Throughout the nine o'clock Sunday School hour today, the dress rehearsal for the Children's Christmas Program was held. Excitement, plus anxiety, filled the air as final improvements were made for the performance of the pageant, "A Children's Christmastide," that was held during today's worship service. Miss Jeanette, the Sunday School Superintendent, was noticeably having misgivings about the whole thing. At the first sign of trouble, Winter and Green, two mice in our village, noticed that Miss Jeanette went to the office and called her parents, begging them to please step on the gas and get over to the church to help her supervise the commotion. Her mother, Cookie Grey, must have been in her nightgown, robe, and slippers when Miss Jeanette called. Most likely she was situated in her recliner enjoying the warmth of both her morning cup of coffee and their gas fireplace. I tell you this detail because when Cookie arrived, Winter and Green noticed that she did not have her normal "put-together" look about her. Also, Jeanette's dad, Eldon, had offensively bad breath, as he must not have had time to do his brush, floss, and gargle routine. Winter and Green said that the pandemonium can all be blamed on three "dedicated" Sunday School teachers who skipped last week's rehearsal to selfishly go shopping at the nearby outlet mall, all without informing Miss Jeanette that they would be absent. As a result, the three teachers did not have the first idea what was going on. Ruby and I agree that they made a poor decision, as they should have been in attendance last week to help their classes with their section of the program. It made us wonder if those three women were raised right.

The Osterhagens arrived at Historic St. Peter's this morning in a cheery mood to witness the true Christmas message presented by the Sunday School. Gretchen looked adorable in a little red dress and black patent leather shoes. Aia looked smashing in a soft red sweater, black slacks, and rhinestone jewellery. Clement topped his clerical shirt with his best black sport coat. This little family, this little holy family, stood smiling in front of the decorated Christmas tree for a Christmas photograph. Ruby heard them say at breakfast that they intend to get a family photo today to include in their annual Christmas card, a greeting that will travel far and wide to family and friends.

Pastor's family is the only family at HSP that is not related to any of the members. Entire family histories are at Historic St. Peter's and that means many generations have called this place their church home. Sadly, Pastor and Aia have often mentioned that they feel like they are not at home here. But they have a home in each other, and now their little home is growing. Hopefully the parishioners do not yet know about Aia's pregnancy, that is, if Agnes "The Blabber" has kept it on the Q.T. For now, Pastor and Aia treasure that gift all by themselves. Sometimes they feel so eaten up and used up by the demands of the church that it benefits their mental health to keep something back, to not let the church find out everything about them. Time will come for revealing the baby news later, close to the time when the pregnancy becomes visible on Aia.

The Sunday School program appeared to go smoothly. The children knew their speaking parts, sang their carols, and did not get lost. It was a hoot to listen to and observe a group of five boys singing "The Little Drummer Boy" as they played their empty coffee can drums (a very inventive use for coffee cans) by using a pair of chop sticks to produce the sound. The only Sunday School participants that got lost in the Christmas program were the three Sunday School teachers that cut out on the rehearsal the prior Sunday. Looking downright embarrassed of their own performance, they did, however, overcome it by wearing their recently purchased splashy Christmas attire. Parents and grandparents were ever so proud of their families and worked overtime snapping their cameras. The children portraying Mary and Joseph stood shoulder to shoulder as they tenderly took care of the baby doll, definitely honoured rolls to be chosen for. After it was over, the Christian Education Committee gave every child a take-home lunch sack that contained an orange, an apple, a few pieces of chocolate, and a candy cane. Many said that it was a great day at Historic St. Peter's. Several mice noticed that the parishioners seemed to leave church today taking with them the gift of a genuinely warm memory.

After shaking hands today, Pastor and family hurried down the breezeway to return home for lunch. Their methodology when they arrive at home each Sunday is to follow the "Hand-washing Hygiene Guide." This technique washes off trillions of germs that they receive from other people's hands. Clement, Aia, and Gretchen plan to stay healthy all winter and are aware that keeping their hands impeccably immaculate is the first step in achieving their goal.

After the microwave finished reheating their food, the little Osterhagen Family sat down together, held hands and prayed, and ate their meal. Today they were having Saturday evening's leftovers that consisted of oven fake-fried chicken, rice pilaf, and smashed carrots. At two o'clock this afternoon Clement headed off to lead the chapel service at Loving Arms Nursing Home. After supper tonight, he attended the council meeting held in the church library, arriving home very late and all keyed up.

At 11:30 p.m. Ruby and I travelled to the parsonage and found a tiny sliver of Gretchen's candy cane. After that treat, our breath was so cool and incredibly fresh, we kissed for a very long time.

– F.N.

THE ANNUAL LADIES' CHRISTMAS GATHERING WAS HELD AT ST. PETE'S TONIGHT IN Woolcox Hall, hosted by a group of women in the church that refer to themselves as the "M & M's," which is a short form of the words, "Meet & Meditate." Just lately they made a decision to upgrade the name of their group by changing it from "The Young Ladies' Circle" to the "M & M's." This was done because the group members are no longer young ladies but are in their late forties, fifties, and early sixties. They chose to come up with a fresh, colourful, and sweet name. The "M & M's" seemed like the perfectly quintessential choice.

Tonya Lorenzo is the current president of the group having taken over the position from Kallie Sauer, who transferred from HSP to another church last year due to her attitude being exactly as sour as her last name reflects. Kallie left St. Pete's for three specifically sour reasons: She "was not being fed," "things aren't the same as they used to be," and "we've never done it that way before." Unfortunately, before, during, and after her departure, Kallie kept tutoring Tonya, her replacement, on exactly how to run the "M & M's" in the correct way by using a firm grip. One of our delightful young mice, Gooseberry, heard Tonya tell the other members of the "M & M's" that she respects and looks up to Kallie. She admitted that she finds it helpful to invite her out for coffee in order to ask her advice as she benefits from learning from her abundant expertise in the area of leadership. Tonya said that during those times she is able to gather up Kallie's advice for free by simply repaying Kallie's on-going curiosity with "what's new" at St. Pete's. Tonya says it is simple to pick up the church bulletins and newsletters, collect them for Kallie which enables her to keep informed as to the current happenings at St. Pete's, things she is missing out on. Because of that, Tonya told the "M & M's" that Kallie seems to be more current on "what's happening" at St. Pete's than the average member.

Most of the mice, along with the people at St. Pete's, notice that Tonya is a confident leader. Being the most well-dressed member of the "M & M's," Tonya power-dressed for the Christmas gathering tonight by wearing all black - an expensively tailored blazer, skirt, and high heels which enable her to stand up very straight, drawing extra attention to her fashion doll figure. However, the "M & M's" appear to shake like a leaf in her presence. We wonder if their thoughts are not welcome with her, almost as though she has appointed herself the "thought police" of the group. So far, no one has stood up to her or gone to battle with her about anything.

At the entryway to Woolcox Hall tonight each lady received a plastic champagne goblet containing a sparkling cranberry beverage. This was designed to be an imitation cocktail hour meant for mingling and for partaking in an amusing Christmas get-to-know-each-other game. Most of the ladies were engaged in finding their assigned place card on one of the dinner tables, discovering who else would be sitting with them at their table. The "who sits where?" decisions were all chosen in advance by Tonya. Some of the ladies seemed hurt that they would be separated from their family or friends during the meal and would have much preferred the seating arrangements to be first come, first serve.

For three continuous weeks there has been a sign-up sheet for this event. In addition, Tonya has made an announcement in church each week, saying that it was necessary for the ladies to sign up in advance so that the "M & M's" will have an exact count of attendees. Tender, loving, and sweet hearted Gooseberry cried when she heard Tonya speak to the elderly twin sisters, Esther and Elsa Baldwin, when they arrived at the church. As they were trying to walk in the door with Esther carrying a goulash hotdish and Elsa bringing in a crystal bowl containing cucumbers with dill, they were turned away from the event by Tonya. Tonya explained to them that there were no places for them to sit because she was not aware that they would be attending the gathering, emphasizing that their names were not on the sign-up sheet. After that occurrence, there was constant buzzing among the ladies about how badly they felt for the Baldwin twins. Someone said that they saw tears in Esther's eyes right before the sisters turned around and left the building. When Gooseberry explained all that she had witnessed tonight to Ruby and me, the three of us came to a logical conclusion. The deduction was that there is a "disconnect" between the kind and warm words of the "All are Welcome Here" song and Tonya's cold-hearted actions. Perhaps the true meaning of that song has not sunk deeply, or at all, into Tonya's heart and mind. Gooseberry revealed that Tonya's behaviour displayed a string of "un" type actions. There were unloving, unfair, unaccepting, unapologetic, unfriendly, unembraceable, unchurchly, uncompassionate, unneighbourly, let alone unashamedly unwelcoming behaviours. The "All Are Welcome Here" tone of graciousness that St. Peter's cherishes was simply vacant in Tonya and must have taken a remote trip to Timbuktu, which actually is an existing place in Africa. Tonya also unpleasantly reminded the twins as they were leaving, to be certain to sign up early for next year's gathering and then they will be welcome to attend the event. Gooseberry said that she suspects Tonya just might become uncomfortable when she thinks back at how unkindly she treated Esther and Elsa.

Pastor Osterhagen arrived in Woolcox Hall when it was time for the meal, prepared to give tonight's dinner prayer, which he had been asked to do. Even though he was there, Tonya stepped up to the microphone and read her written out dinner prayer that included the word "just" at least seven or eight times. She said words like, "We just want to thank you, Lord," "We just want to ask you, Lord," "We just need you, Lord," "We just want to praise you, Lord," and "We just want to say another thank you, Lord." After hearing that, Pastor Osterhagen "just" went back to the parsonage. Ruby peeked through the slit in the dining room wall and saw Pastor reading out loud his dinner prayer that he had written down for the ladies' gathering. After that he enjoyed a bowl of bean soup generously topped with oyster crackers.

The Christmas meal featured a delicious potluck as everyone was asked via the weekly bulletin to bring something extra special and fancy to contribute to the meal. By observing what's on the potluck table, one is able to conclude what the popular recipe currently is in the area by counting how many bowls or casseroles there are of that one particular type. This year there were five bowls of Napa Cabbage Salad, the type that is made yummy with crunchy almonds and sesame seeds. People's dishes are scrutinized. Sharon Nash learned her lesson last year when she brought a gourmet relish platter containing fancy pickles, caper berries, and Italian country olives. When Lenore Norris saw what Sharon brought, she mentioned that she did not contribute something home-made, remarking in a catty tone that her contribution was the lazy-lady way to attend a potluck. The dessert table was much larger than the table with the hot food. Instead of small paper plates for the desserts, there were dinner-sized paper plates that were printed with Christmas stars. The reason for the large dessert plate is that most of the women take a larger amount of dessert than the hotdishes and salads.

Between dinner and dessert, all women gathered in the sanctuary for an Advent devotion led by Tonya Lorenzo taking on the role as if she were a pastor. Some of the other "M & M's" read the lessons, passed out individual candles with paper guards for the singing of "Silent Night," and collected an offering for the homeless. Last week Tonya asked Pastor Osterhagen if he could provide an Advent devotion that they could use at the Ladies' Advent service as she couldn't find one. He agreed to provide her with one. Clement spent time creating and writing a beautiful devotion for the service, but when it came time to use it, Tonya told him that she didn't need it because she had come across a devotion that had not been used in a very long time. She was convinced no one would even remember it. During the reading of the prayers, she read a prayer out loud asking to bring an end to the war in Vietnam. Obviously she did not read through the script ahead of time, or she did not know that we are no longer in 1975. Gooseberry mentioned that she didn't look very professional when she said that. Many of the ladies giggled when that happened and talked about Tonya and her mistake afterwards.

When the Advent devotions were finished, most of the ladies were happy campers due to the marshmallow feeling they felt in their hearts while singing "Silent Night" in the glow of candlelight. After that they returned to Woolcox Hall to feast on items from the dessert table. We mice thought there is something incredibly sweet about a worship service with only female voices singing but something not incredibly sweet about ladies eating way too many sweets.

The final part of the evening was the kitschy gift exchange where wrapped packages were opened and displayed one at a time to the sound of cheerful laughter. Many of the ladies have been on a search to obtain a chintzy item when they go on thrift store adventures throughout the year. If they can find a really good one, it will bring out an abundance of laughter. Among the gifts this year was a ceramic rolling pin wall decoration that read, "For Use on Cheatin' Husbands." There was a bright pink floral thong in size XXXL. An ivory-coloured flower vase had a counterfeit sticker adhered to the bottom of it with the hand-written words, "Royal Doulton, Ascot Blue, Made in England." That brought out a lot of chuckles as it was obvious that the vase was not a treasured collectable. There was even a container of fart-covering spray, a real novelty item. One glitzy-wrapped box contained a four-pack of toilet paper, a box of herbal tea, and a can of baked beans and was labelled: "Holiday Detox Kit." The giver of that gift had crossed out the word holiday and replaced it with the word "Christmas." I reckon that whoever did that was emphasizing that the word "holiday" is too commercial and materialistic and attempted to switch the focus to the religious, faith-based part of Christmas. An oversized mug that said, "Happy Retirement! So Long Tension, Howdy Pension!" brought out whoops of laughter, too.

After Ruby and I finished hearing the details about tonight's event from Gooseberry, I asked her how she got her beautiful name. She told us that when her father and mother lived in an old farmhouse root cellar, they would often go upstairs to the kitchen after the farmer and his wife were in bed to see if they could find a bite to eat. One day the farmer's wife prepared Gooseberry curd, a choice artisan preserve that is not widely available in stores, except maybe in

Ireland. Her parents happened to spot a droplet of Gooseberry curd on the floor, just underneath the stove. Claiming that it was the best thing that they had ever tasted in their lives, they told each other right then that when they have a baby they would name the baby Gooseberry. Gooseberry told us that she has always appreciated her name because her parents didn't randomly pick her name. They must have known that common and popular names just end up blending in because there are so many of them. You must know what I am talking about, like nowadays when there are at least three girls named Jennie, Jessica, or Kayla in every single Grade Five class, the same issue applying to names like Kyle, Michael, and Ryan for the boys. To choose the name Gooseberry was special to them, distinctive and unique. Gooseberry said that is the story of how she got her name, mentioning that she is thankful that her parents did not give her one of the other berry names like Boysenberry, Chokeberry, Thimbleberry, Barberry, Nannyberry, Mulberry, Brambleberry, Cranberry, Lingonberry, Blackberry, Elderberry, Cloudberry, or Saskatoon Berry. Gooseberry did add that she would not have minded being named Raspberry, Blueberry, or Strawberry.

By 10 p.m. all of the ladies were gone so Ruby and I travelled to Woolcox Hall and snacked on morsels missed in the cleanup where we found bits of Napa Cabbage Salad, Christmas Stollen, Blueberry Slump, Buttercream Truffles, Mini-Brownie Pies, and several other desserts. While we nibbled, Ruby talked about how she would like to try a healthy detox plan and wondered how she could find some herbal tea. I assured her that both of us are already on a detox plan, as Aia prepares many of those foods that are well-known for their detoxing properties, like beets, flaxseeds and blueberries. I thought it was worth pointing out to Ruby that Aia brought the Blueberry Slump to the potluck and that she always doubles the amount of blueberries that it calls for in her recipe. Ruby thanked me for that information and encouraged me to continue being a life-long learner.

– F.N.

Friday, December 12

TODAY ONE OF THE VILLAGE MICE, JONQUIL, OBSERVED AIA AND GRETCHEN PICKING UP and cleaning up Clement's office, as they transformed the room into a place that is festive and Christmassy. Of course, the picking-up part of the job seemed to be much more wearisome, confusing, and majorly time-consuming than the clean-up part. Aia absolutely flew as she dusted Clement's desk and bookshelves, washed the insides of the windows, and vacuumed the carpet, all while Gretchen was at her mother's side and often asked, "Why are you doing that, Mama?" questions. After sprucing up the room, they decorated the office with a small-scaled holy nativity set and holly and ivy window clings that they purchased from Bill's Dollar Bill, the local dollar store. They placed a small plastic crystal bowl of assorted wrapped Christmas candies on the corner of his desk. The final touch was to spray the room with some Fraser Fir scented room freshener.

Gretchen was promised an all-important ride in the church wheelchair before lunch today. After securing Gretchen safely in the wheelchair with Clement's clergy cincture tied around her waist, Pastor and Aia took turns pushing their sweetheart far and wide throughout the building. They also enjoyed talking to each other while doing the healthy walking workout. Gretchen giggled constantly at the indoor Christmas sleigh ride that she was aboard while strapped in the church wheelchair.

After their walk, they returned to Clement's office for a winter indoor picnic. With the tea kettle plugged in and a blue-checkered picnic cloth spread on the floor, this little clergy family sat down, sang the simple table grace, "Come, Lord Jesus, be our guest, and let these gifts to us be blest. Amen," and ate their lunch. Today they brought with them the old, well-used wicker picnic basket that Aia inherited from her grandparents. It contained chicken salad sandwiches, pickles, and veggies. The food was savored, of course, because the work had been carried out and they were hungry from exercising. At first Gretchen only ate pickles, which appears to be her favourite food. With a little encouragement, she ate her sandwich. We mice notice that instead of going to the mall for a winter walk, the Osterhagens take a hike at church, traversing the hallways and the perimeter of Woolcox Hall. They often check their pedometers that are secured to their running shoes to see if they are nearing their goal.

The last time Ruby and I saw them today, Aia was pushing Gretchen in the wheelchair through the breezeway and Clement was carrying a small ladder that he borrowed from the church janitor's closet, which he said would come in handy when decorating the very top of their family Christmas tree. They talked with excitement about plans to decorate their "Tannenbaum" in a non-traditional, whimsical, fun, and unusual manner this year. They mentioned that they will do that fun project as soon as Gretchen awakens from her afternoon nap.

After the Osterhagens lugged their Christmas tree into the parsonage, Ruby and I glanced down the breezeway and spotted a three-inch piece of a pine branch that had accidentally fallen off of the Osterhagen's Christmas tree. We gathered it up and took it back to our place. Taking a quick trip to the Ladies' sewing supply room we found a red spool of thread and decided to borrow it for a couple of weeks. We were a bit particular in selecting the thread, as we wanted to use the colour red as garland for our Christmas tree. After we got back to our place, we were able to stand up the little pine branch and place its trunk in the centre of the spool of thread.

At 11:30 p.m. Ruby and I travelled to the parsonage and snacked on dropped crumbs of gingersnap cookies and holiday party mix. I suggested to Ruby that we should keep our eyes out for dropped popcorn at the Osterhagens and gather them to craftily assemble a popcorn garland, a simple, old-fashioned way to decorate our Christmas tree. Ruby doubted that idea would be possible. Last week she overheard Aia mention that in the future they are going to serve their popcorn in individual soup bowls along with a soup spoon, instead of eating it with their fingers, claiming that this practice will practically eliminate popcorn spillage on the floor.

– F.N.

Saturday, December 13

COMMEMORATING THE TOWN'S SOLIDARITY AND IN CELEBRATION OF THE CHRISTMAS season, the annual community "Holy-Day's Shine-on Parade" took place tonight with most local businesses, churches, and clubs participating in the procession. The only requirement for the parade was that all entries needed to be illuminated. The first prize was $500, second prize $250, and the third prize $100.

For premier parade viewing tonight, the mice community at St. Pete's positioned themselves on the basement window ledges. It is there that they observed the glorious lighted parade advancing slowly down the street. The mice found themselves to be in a far more comfy environment than that of the Osterhagen Family who bundled up and stood in the cold for the entire parade. The mice were ecstatic that not one human being was within St. Pete's walls. This freedom from being overheard by anyone allowed them to freely break forth into exclamations of oohs and aahs.

Last September Historic St. Peter's Christian Witness Committee had unanimously agreed to enter the winter parade contest. They decided that if they were to win a prize, it would be a bonus; if their entry did not win anything, still some good would come of it in the form of the church's exposure and publicity in the community.

The construction of a lighted float was far too overwhelming to even attempt, so the committee decided to make their entry super simple and Bible-themed. In costume were to be Joseph and Mary riding on a donkey to Bethlehem. Joseph was to carry an old-time kerosene barn lantern to light the way.

The donkey, Kiks (Danish word for biscuit, given that name because he is the same colour as a tea biscuit), behaved well and fully did his business just prior to the start of the parade. Two teenagers, Trish Guttermann and Jeremy Abrams portrayed Mary and Joseph, appearing humble and sincere, seeming honoured to have been chosen to represent the Holy Family. Jeremy got the honour since Kiks belonged to his family's livestock. Mary (Trish) was kindly asked to remove her bubble gum prior to the start of the parade as it would not look very "Mary-like" to be blowing bubbles. All of the mice agreed that Mary's bubble gum behaviour might possibly ruin HSP's chance of winning one of the prizes. It would be very noticeable to the judges if Mary was riding the donkey while blowing four or five-inch pink bubbles. One of our mice, Gigi, recalled seeing Trish blow a bubble similar to that size during a worship service not long ago. Gigi has since referred to Trish as "HSP's Bubble Gum Primadonna."

Immediately following the parade, Mayor Art Heddwyn announced the winners. Speaking into a microphone from the steps of the Oswald County Courthouse, Mayor Heddwyn asked Pastor Osterhagen to come forward to accept the $500 first place prize for Historic St. Peter's. The mice village was overjoyed that HSP actually beat out the $250 prize winner sponsored by the local lighting company whose entry was highly illuminated by generators that produced jillions of lights. The focal point of their entry was the whopping large snow globe where two fake deer were nestled in a tranquil wooded setting. The motorized deer moved their heads up, down, back, and forth while shimmering imitation snowflakes gently fell upon them. Several children were aboard this float tossing candy out to the crowd. The $100 third prize went to the eight committed members of the local birdwatcher's club, the B.Y.O.B. (Bring Your Own Binoculars) Birding Association. We have overheard at church that the birdwatchers have won third place the past four years. Each Birding Association member rode a bicycle with a fourteen-inch plastic lighted Northern Red Cardinal attached to the handlebars. Riding together as a group while dressed identically in their birding outfits that were topped with matching brown jackets, they were a seriously organized group. Hanging around their necks were their trusty binoculars that were encased with red and green blinking light bulbs. After the parade is finished each year the eight red illuminated plastic Christmas Cardinals can be seen lit up on the front yard of the local B.Y.O.B. B.A.

The mice added to the conversation that it is a good thing that our town has such excellent snow removal procedures, as Main Street was completely clear of snow and ice today which put safety first when it came to riding a donkey or a bicycle. Our mice village was incredibly proud of the people of HSP for taking home first place!

At 11:30 p.m. Ruby and I travelled to the parsonage and snacked on a tiny morsel of Norwegian lefse that was spread with butter and sprinkled with brown sugar that we found under Gretchen's place at the dining room table.

– F.N.

St. Peter's forty-three inch round Advent wreath has been suspended from the sanctuary rafters since the First Sunday in Advent, November 30. Bearing three dark purple candles and one pink candle, the wreath is surrounded by natural pine branches, each candle adorned with a matching velvet bow. According to the church liturgical calendar, "Rose Sunday" is the day to ignite the first two purple candles in addition to the only pink candle. Two weeks ago one inquisitive parishioner, Pinkie Weston, asked Pastor Osterhagen about the significance of the pink candle, which she noted is of a stunningly lovely "Persian Rose" shade. He explained to her that Rose Sunday marks the joyous anticipation of the Lord's coming to be with us on earth, rejoicing in our Emmanuel, God-with-us. Pinkie latched onto that bit of knowledge and proceeded to sign up on the flower chart to provide the flowers for today. Pinkie donated two floral arrangements that consisted of pink roses, baby's breath and ferns. The arrangements were elegant, formal, and pricy, looking more like they belonged at a June wedding. But all in attendance enjoyed their beauty as well as the magnificent fragrance that floated throughout the sanctuary. It was refreshing for everyone to see and smell just a bit of summertime in cold, mid-winter December. Pinkie obviously put a lot of forethought into this day. She even wore a pinkish rose coloured sweater and sat near the front to view the roses. The members all know her as a delightful, helpful, generous, and creative person that brings a smile along with a breath of fresh air wherever she goes. Ruby and I think that her parents gave her a picture-perfect name because when someone gives her a compliment a rosy blush spreads across Pinkie's face. She is in the pink of health and stays that way by teaching Yoga classes at the Community Centre several times a week.

Prior to worship this morning, a huge semi-trailer transport with a sleeper pulled up in front of HSP. Two mice in our village, Rainbow and Fiddlehead, were briefly stationed on the basement window ledge glancing outside to sneak a peek as parishioners arrived at church. It was then that they spotted a stranger, a mysterious truck driver. The newbie got out of his truck and walked into Historic St. Pete's. At that point, Rainbow and Fiddlehead scurried up the basement steps and hid behind the open door that leads to the narthex, a door that is rarely used but happens to never be shut. From that unseen position they heard the truck driver introduce himself to Pastor and vice versa. Fiddlehead remarked at our village meeting tonight that this truck driver possessed the artful skill of gentle-manly introduction, mannerisms that have almost fallen to the wayside. The truck driver's name was Justin Severin. Pastor and Justin visited with each other for a few minutes while Rainbow and Fiddlehead overheard their entire conversation. Justin wondered if he could leave his semi-trailer parked on the street right in front of the church while he attended today's worship service. Pastor told him that it would be fine and also warmly welcomed him.

Rainbow said that Justin looked like a classic truck driver dressed in "work duds" with an all-weather work-coat, denim work-jeans, sturdy work-boots, work-gloves, and a baseball cap turned backwards. Because Justin was passing through town with a full load, he was dressed in his work-gear, not church clothes, so he removed his cap and sat in the back pew, hoping not to look out of place.

After the opening hymn #809 was introduced by organist Josie Johnson, Justin began to sing with a deep, outstandingly clear singing voice. The quality of his singing immediately had an influence on the others in the sanctuary as they changed from being singers to quiet active listeners. Many of the parishioners looked like they were in awe of his God-given voice, noticing his immense lung power and his massive breath capacity. While Justin was singing all of today's hymns and the liturgy, Rainbow and Fiddlehead noticed that he could sing over and above everyone else in the congregation, including over the volume of the pipe organ. Both mice announced at tonight's meeting that Justin has far better quality pipes personally residing inside his chest than the organ pipes we have hanging proudly on the wall at Historic St. Peter's.

After the worship service was over, many people came up to Justin and thanked him for his exquisite singing, hoping that he was new in town and could attend St. Pete's every single Sunday. Many commented that his attendance would greatly improve the singing level at St. Pete's. Gretchen ran towards Justin, but she must have remembered her church manners that remind her to walk, not run in church, so her little legs did a hefty speed-walk instead. After catching up with Justin, she kindly asked him if he would sing her mama's favourite song, "The Little Brown Church in the Vale." Justin hesitated, but Rainbow and Fiddlehead overheard Gretchen tell Justin that her mama liked his singing so much today that she closed her eyes, something she always does when she hears especially beautiful music. She asked Justin to watch her mama, the lady who is standing right next to her daddy, and he will see her eyes go shut when he starts singing. Justin just looked at sweet Gretchen for a long moment. Rainbow and Fiddlehead thought they could see what he was thinking. Both had a hunch at what Justin's thoughts were. Fiddlehead whispered these words to Rainbow: "Where in the world did this precious, smart, adorable, and highly communicative little girl come from? She is the sweetest thing ever!" After the moment was over, Justin agreed to sing for Gretchen. When he started singing, all of the people in the narthex stopped visiting with each other and turned to watch Justin sing, listening to him sing about coming to the church in the wildwood. Gretchen and Justin looked at Aia, and there she was standing in the narthex with her eyes closed. When Justin finished singing, everyone clapped and gave him a standing ovation, but, of course that was a given, as they were already in a standing position.

After Justin sang Aia's favourite song, Josie played her organ postlude that was based on a festive rendition of the Huron Carol, "'Twas in the Moon of Wintertime," Canada's oldest Christmas carol, written in 1642. Ruby and I hummed the melody in the tummy of the organ. We talked about Christmas Eve at St. Pete's and how we are looking forward to singing about "Gitchi Manitou" sending angel choirs when Jesus was born "in a lodge of broken bark." It's an exquisite northern Christmas carol!

Before Justin left, Pastor asked him about why he happened to be a truck driver when he possessed so much excellence in his voice, that of being a first-class singer. Rainbow and Fiddlehead overheard Justin tell Pastor that in his younger years he was a professional singer and appeared on stage for many years. He said that something changed inside of him revealing that he wanted to be independent, to be his own boss. Justin said that he is now self-employed and that the benefits of that freedom far outweigh what he experienced in his younger years. Now he can be an ordinary person instead of one who experiences the pros and cons of being a performer. After that, Pastor Osterhagen shook Justin's hand and told him to stop by anytime that he is driving through Oswald County. Gretchen thanked him for singing and invited him to the family Christmas party that was to be held in Woolcox Hall, adding that he can sit with her and her parents. Justin declined her invitation by telling her that he needed to get back on the road. He assured Pastor and Gretchen that the next time he drives through Oswald County on a Sunday morning he will be back at St. Peter's. Gretchen hugged him goodbye and watched him as he walked out the front door of St. Pete's, after which she speed-walked to the window in order to watch him get into his transport truck, waving farewell to him. As he started off, Justin looked at Gretchen, smiled, and blew his horn with two quick beeps. Gretchen giggled and gave him the double thumbs up.

After worship, the parishioners gathered in Woolcox Hall for a family Christmas party. There was a punch bowl, Christmas cookies, tea, coffee and conversation. A flood of people attended the party, which definitively proved to the Woolcox family, once again, that it was a necessity that Lloyd Woolcox and family had donated a huge amount of money to build a spacious parish hall. The entire Woolcox Clan beamed with pride today at their hall. Their vision for building Woolcox Hall was to make it a large room with generous square footage. They refused to donate the money to build the hall if it wasn't going to be the size their family envisioned. Another stipulation was to have the parish hall named after them. The Woolcox family name has been present in every single generation of St. Pete's history, being founding members of the church. All the mice could barely wait for the parishioners to go home today so that we could enjoy our own family Christmas party in Woolcox Hall.

Cadence Davis, the musically creative director of HSP's hand bell choir, lost control of her temper today when she was unable to locate the shoe box that contains the white hand bell gloves. The box is always to be kept in the choir room on top of the grey filing cabinet. (A troubling bit of information that I need to reveal to you is that St. Pete's sporadically and mysteriously has items that disappear from the premises. No one has a glimmer of an idea as to who is responsible for this menacing and unwelcome thievery, but it results in many headaches to the Osterhagens and parishioners when it happens. This has been going on for decades, but the culprit, or the guilty party, is still at large. When thefts are discovered, blame falls straightaway on someone who has been marked with the nickname, "Gremlin." Even our mice community cannot figure out who is up to all of the wrongdoing even though we are steadfastly observant as we watch out for church property. We have kicked around and chewed over a few suspects, but to no avail.) Cadence simply intended to take the hand bell gloves home and send them through the washing machine so that they would be dazzling white for the hand bell choir's performance on Christmas Eve. One of our scouts overheard Cadence whisper swear words as she responded to the conundrum she was in. Emotionally she was *that* ruffled. We felt surprised, but mostly saddened, when Cadence did not choose a more imaginative and original manner to handle her words as she is a woman of creativity and resourcefulness. Be that as it may, we realized that Cadence must not be familiar with the vast language of substitute swear words or phrases. *What a bummer! What the heckaroni? What the bleep is going on? Jiminy Crickets! What the blankety-blank? Good Night, Nancy!* Or simply the sturdy, old fashioned fake expletive, *Good gravy!* would have been a far better manner of speech than the quick barnyard four letter words that she muttered. Please forgive me for being hypercritical and judgemental regarding this issue, but I cannot help it.

At 4 p.m., when the coast was clear, the village mice had our own party, filling up on delectable Christmas cookie crumbs containing a lavish amount of red and green sugar cookie sprinkles. Ruby and I didn't bother to go to the parsonage for a snack tonight as were bloated from our own village Christmas party. After we were tucked in bed, Ruby and I found it entertaining to discuss a paragraph that was included in today's worship bulletin brought to our attention by Desiree and Raine. These two mice are out-and-out intrigued by anything related to weddings, finding particular interest in the attire worn by wedding parties and their guests. Earlier today, Raine read the bulletin blurb to us as we listened to her princess-style, sweet-sounding voice: "Bridal Gown for Sale: Worn once, by mistake. Description: Size 10 white strapless sweetheart lace mermaid-style gown with a sweeping train. This bridal gown is for sale due to a regrettable error in good judgement when it came to selecting the groom. Unfortunately, the knot was tied, but, thankfully, it has been successfully untied. If interested, please direct your inquiries to Stephanie Zeiler."

– F.N.

Thursday, December 18

Since mid-August, Sid Slavik, a life-long member of St. Peter's, has not been attending worship. A few weeks ago, two mice overheard Pastor Osterhagen's telephone conversation with Sid. Because Pastor cares about him, he told him that he is there for him if he needs any help or would like someone to talk to. He was concerned as to how Sid was doing and kindly let him know that he missed seeing him in church. Without mincing words, Sid told Pastor that he will not be coming back to HSP. Admitting that he had a hankering to find another church, Sid told Pastor that he likes his new church much better because it is not so liturgical, also adding that there are many people in his new church that are about his same age. The mice felt very sorry for Pastor when he hung up the telephone. He knows that he cannot do one thing to stop Sid from leaving. After that incidence, the mice village gathered together and talked about what is the real reason behind Sid's leaving St. Pete's after sixty-seven years of being a faithful member. They suspect that Sid didn't give Pastor an accurate or fully truthful explanation as to why he's changing and improving his church membership, but waffled around his reasons to avoid admitting the truth.

Most of the mice remarked that they have observed that Sid has obviously been looking for the "right" woman. He's been searching for a long time, years, in fact. Sid has dated a few of the women at St. Pete's but none of them have seemed to be the "right" one for him. Because he has exhausted the pool of available women at HSP, his pool became a lot larger by attending another church. The mice concluded that Sid's leaving is not about church liturgy at all, but about finding the "right" woman.

Several of the mice that are early-risers heard the church door being unlocked very early this morning. Even though it was still dark outside, they scurried out to catch a glimpse of what was happening, as time flies by so fast and they do not want to miss out on anything. They saw former member Sid Slavik opening up the church door with his own personal church key. For years he was the proud bearer of a church key at the time when he helped cut the grass on the church property. Sid was given a key in case he needed to use the washroom while he was working outside. This morning the mice found out that he has never bothered to return the key. A couple of the mice said that any responsible grownup man should know better than to hog his key for so long. It's almost as cheesy as going to the library, finding the book you wish to read and tucking it in your backpack. Avoiding checking the book out enables that person to monopolize the book for as long as they desire without any chance of receiving an overdue notice or fine.

Carrying some red envelopes with Christmas stickers adhered to them, Sid quickly went to the location of the church mailboxes, or pigeon holes, as they are called, and inserted Christmas cards in sixteen member's boxes. The mice figured out that he was hand-delivering the Christmas cards in order to avoid purchasing sixteen postage stamps. After he left, the mice village discussed how sneaky his actions were, especially since he is no longer a member of St. Pete's. Their opinions ranged from calling him slippery, sly, and slick. One mouse called it "cheapskate behaviour" by avoiding purchasing sixteen stamps from the Post Office—after all, the P.O. needs money, too!

The mice decided, beyond a doubt, that it is fortunate that not one of the fine, sweet, delightful, and available ladies at St. Pete's happened to be the "right" woman for Sid. He is not worthy of any of them. If he wouldn't even spend a few dollars to purchase stamps to mail out sixteen Christmas cards, in all likelihood he would be a dating tightwad about spending any money on them. We wondered if the ladies of St. Pete's that dated him were asked to split a meal at a restaurant and also split the dessert, or heaven forbid, split the cheque. They might have even been asked to split a cup of coffee at the coffee shop, all made possible by Sid bringing along a disposable paper hot beverage cup in order to pull that split off. The mice concluded that awkwardly stretching a buck while dating is no subtle way to save money, but a *faux pas,* resulting in the woman not feeling precious and definitely not very special.

Our mouse intellectual expert and head librarian, Dr. Theodore Simonsen, suggested that Sid Slavik, who split from HSP, might enjoy living in a city in Croatia that is actually named "Split." Maybe he could find the "right" woman in Split who enjoys splitting everything with him. He probably could weasel a cheap flight to Croatia, saving himself a few bucks.

After all of the discussion about Sid's pinch-penny behaviour, I couldn't get the word "split" out of my mind. Through word of mouth I have heard of a treat that is called a banana split and I would love to try one sometime, especially the maraschino cherry, which Ruby and I would split.

At 11:30 p.m. Ruby and I travelled to the parsonage and found two dried yellow split peas on the kitchen floor. As I bit into my split pea, I cracked or split one of my back teeth. It is okay as it doesn't show when I smile. It does not alter my good looks in the least bit. After our treat, we split from the parsonage and went home to bed.

    – F.N.

Friday, December 19

THIS EVENING THE OSTERHAGENS ARRIVED AT HISTORIC ST. PETER'S FIRESIDE ROOM equipped with a bag of microwave popcorn, two bags of licorice (one red and one green), lemonade, and a video. It is "Bargain Night" at Windell's Theatre, two for the price of one, but too expensive to fit into the Osterhagen's budget considering the expenses of movie tickets, popcorn, drinks, plus a babysitter. We heard them briefly mention how they could cut down on the cost of going to Windell's by sneaking in their snacks using Aia's largest purse. That idea failed because there would still be the babysitter expense. Their video player at the parsonage is on the fritz, so tonight they used the church video player for a homemade "movie night."

The first thing Clement did in the Fireside Room was to ignite the gas fireplace, which added to the ambiance of the room, making it warm, comfy, and homelike. The first thing Aia did was to present Clement with her Christmas gift wish list. Clement read it out loud, chuckled, and then tucked it into his worn-out wallet. The list was written on a sticky note so we mice assumed it must have immediately clung to the currency that was residing in his wallet. Another thought we wondered about was if the currency in his wallet understood that soon it would be leaving the safety of his wallet in order to purchase Aia's gifts, soon residing in a new location that would be anyone's guess. Clement simply thanked Aia for her wish list.

Later on we found out that the first item on Aia's list was for a new video player, secondly, a six-pack of durable and soft cotton white socks, and thirdly, a colourful food processor in red, if possible. The mice have noticed that Aia mostly speaks in "threes," probably because she is a graduate of Trinity College. Clement also read out loud the footnote at the bottom of her Christmas list which warned him to purchase the food processor only if it is on a knock-out sale. Aia seemed certain that Clement knows where to purchase the socks and a video player, but suspects he does not know a fig about food processors. She assured him that if he purchases any of the wrong things, she will return the items after Christmas. Being that Aia's entire childhood princess storybook collection is now available on video, doubled with the fact that Gretchen will soon be interested in watching those films, and thirdly, if they have another girl, she will be interested in watching those films, too, a video player is an absolutely essential necessity. With a baby in her tummy, Aia emphasized that the food processor will be helpful for baby food preparation. Everything about Aia and materialism emits practicality, thriftiness, and usually, frugality. She steered Clement away from the idea of giving her a bottle of perfume for Christmas, which has been his go-to Christmas gift for Aia. Instead, she assured him that she will find many other ways to smell lovely, appealing, and alluring throughout the upcoming year.

After young Gretchen fell asleep, the grownup relaxation time began. However, both Clement and Aia seemed to have a lingering worry, an anxiety that a parishioner will detect lights beaming in the Fireside Room, drop in to see what event is going on, or worse, make themselves at home by watching the video with them, plus helping themselves to their snacks. At this point, a conversation between them ensued and centered on how they fear this very private moment will be taken away from them, talked about among others, or worst of all, their choice of film criticized. Some parishioners imagine that clergy and their families only watch Christian based movies, which we mice thought might be an understandable deduction.

It was an evening that sadly reminded Clement and Aia of how little privacy they have. After they returned to the parsonage, some mice gathered together and decided that we should not be so inquisitive to know every single detail about Pastor and family, figuring that they deserve some space in order to live a balanced life. Now we understand that they need that. Perhaps the parishioners should gather together and decide the same thing, too.

At 11:30 p.m. Ruby and I travelled to the Fireside Room and snacked on morsels of red and green licorice, a new taste thrill. We presume that it is a fancy red and green Christmas food that is only savoured during the month of December.

– F.N.

IT WAS DOWN IN NUMBERS TODAY AT CHURCH, AS EXPECTED, AS SUNDAY SCHOOL, BIBLE class, choir, and coffee hour are all taking a recess until the New Year. A humdinger of a snowstorm hit last night which produced wicked winds, lots of snowfall, and a Siberian-like temperature. It seemed as though most members embraced the opportunity to skip church today and stay home, turning it into a pajama, games, and movie day. In two short days they will return to attend Christmas Eve Candlelight and Carols. A favourite part of Christmas Eve for many is to witness the glowing beauty of dozens and dozens of burning candles during the singing of "Silent Night." Even people within Oswald County who are not members of St. Pete's look forward to attending HSP's annual Christmas Eve Candlelight Service.

The mice village watched the snow fall last night while we rested on the basement window ledges. At 6:45 p.m. we saw the neighbour from across the street turn his porch light on and open up his front door, letting his Norwegian elkhound, Thunder, outside. It was engaging to watch this attractive, rugged, frisky, sturdy, and athletic dog lap up this long winter's night by leaping about and frolicking in the fresh snow. Some of the moves Thunder made tonight almost resembled free-style dance that was choreographed naturally right there on the spot.

The beauty of the dreamy snowfall was indescribable, awe-inspiring, and majestic. While we watched it snow, the mice village talked about how we are all of one mind in the way that we think about snow. From conversations the members of St. Peter's had in church today, we ascertained that their view of snow differed profoundly from ours. The word "snow" seemed to be spoken of in the form of complaints and disapproval, as if snow is an annoyance, something they wish would permanently disappear. One of the elderly German ladies kept talking about the "Schnee" with a down-trodden look on her face while shaking her head back and forth. Ruby and I didn't have the first idea what she was talking about but figured out that it must be about the subject of snow. Our village analyzed and talked turkey about this topic further at tonight's meeting and concluded that mice and men must visually discern colours differently. The colour wheel created by human beings must be poles apart from the mice colour chart. Many parishioners referred to the "white powder" that had fallen last night, but the mice are certain that the true and exact colour of snow, according to the Official

Mice Colour System Chart translates from Mouse into English as "shimmering, perfectly flickering, pink-silver, twinkle-sparkle radiance."

The snowfall did not stop the oldest member of Historic St. Peter's from attending church this morning. At ninety-nine years of age, Palma Evenson acts like a fifty-five year old. Palma herself is a historic person, resides in a historic home, and has been past president of the Oswald County Historical Society for three full terms. There isn't a person in all of Oswald County that thinks she's a silly old thing because she is so knowledgeable and up-to-date on most everything, except gossip. If there are any questions about St. Pete's history, Pastor Osterhagen turns to Palma Evenson for the answer and gets far more than he ever asks for. Everyone respects her and takes her seriously.

Palma has always taken great pride and pleasure in the stupendous amount of aesthetic beauty of Historic St. Peter's, a fine example of church architecture which is a blend of Tudor revival and Gothic revival styles. One side of the church is half-timbered, which is the Tudor revival style. The arches with points at the top of the church are of Gothic style. Stone pieces surround the windows and other places. Located on Main Street, in a corner location, it is a spectacle of grandeur, impressiveness, and stateliness, plus it is superbly maintained on both the outside and inside. Historic St. Peter's long ago was just plain old St. Peter's, but after it became listed on the State Historical Register, the word "Historic" was deservedly added to its name.

Palma was in church today to celebrate Christmas, but most importantly, to avoid the Christmas crowd that will attend church on the twenty-fourth. She looks great, has straight posture and impeccably immaculate grooming, excellent hearing, and is personable and very conversational. But, it is during those close-up conversations that people notice her lip line. She has trouble painting her lipstick inside of that line. Perhaps she doesn't see as well as she wants people to think she does. (That could lead to a conversation about her vision while driving, but we'll save that chitchat for another time.) She still wears her trademark raspberry-coloured lipstick that arrives through mail order from a special store located in Vermont, I think, or someplace on the East Coast, the only known carrier of that particular shade. Perhaps her blush is also of that tint because its hue matches her lipstick perfectly. The mice think that Palma has chosen the picture-perfect colours and shade of makeup to flawlessly compliment her skin tone, but we differ from what people have named that colour. "Raspberry" is the human terminology for the colour, but, according to the Official Mice Colour System chart, the specific colour for her lipstick and blush are termed "awe-inspiring mountain crimson French raspberry." But, that's a very fine point that is not all that consequential. Nevertheless, I thought I would add it to my notes to share a bit of educational knowledge. That type of knowledge is similar to learning how many olives are harvested from the gnarled tree branches of the ancient olive trees in the Garden of Gethsemane each year. An estimated answer to that question would be quite good enough.

Many of the women at church talk about how they hope that they can age as well as Palma. Someone mentioned lately that she knows a little bit about Palma's daily beauty routine. She said that each morning and evening Palma cleanses her face gently with extra virgin olive oil and wipes it tenderly with a warm, not hot, wet baby washcloth instead of a regular washcloth. Perhaps that cleansing method has been Palma's best beauty trick. Cleansing the skin with oil as people did in Bible days has enabled Palma to continue to have amazing positive results on her face, evidenced by the fact that she has baby-soft cheeks without many wrinkles.

At 11:30 p.m. Ruby and I travelled to the parsonage and equally divided a morsel of a chicken finger and one spicy curly fry. We were briefly resistant to help ourselves to the food because of the high sodium content as we are continually conscious of keeping our sodium levels in check. However, with just one nibble of the delicious treat, the urge was so bewitchingly powerful that we slipped and fell into temptation and ate it all. Ruby reminded me afterwards that we need to put logic first by thinking before we eat. She also emphasized that it is not just about sodium consumption, but about calorie consumption, finishing her point with the overstated cautionary dieter's advice, "A moment on the lips, forever on the hips." Because of Ruby's words, I now feel that I am a roly-poly butterball, a jelly-belly walloping bundle of blubber, nothing short of a piece of bacon fat instead of the slim, trim, and agile adult male mouse that I envisioned myself to be. I feel so gloomy and downhearted that I might need to talk it over with Ruby. Perhaps that will not be necessary as things are always better in the morning.

– F.N.

Monday, December 22

ARMED WITH A BUCKET OF HOT SOAPY WATER AND SEVERAL OLD RAGS, ALICE OLEWIG turned up at church today ready to conquer the church grime that she sees right before her eyes. Alice has recently recovered from surgery to remove her cataracts, correcting her cloudy and decreased vision problems that are due to her age. Ever since her surgery she has been complaining about how filthy everything is at St. Pete's. This is all because her vision is crystal clear now and she is just noticing dirt she did not notice before her cataracts were removed.

Her primary volunteer cleaning project this morning was to wash all of the white cupboards in the church kitchen so that they would sparkle like new once again. Pastor Osterhagen heard someone moving about in the kitchen and went there to see what was going on. Unfortunately, he should not have done that because as soon as Alice saw him, she handed him a rag and told him to get busy and help her with this colossal cleanup job. Alice mentioned to Pastor that she has not had any complications from her surgery, so she has been able to return quickly to her regular life. She let him know that she spends a lot more time cleaning than she used to, admitting that it is hard to cope with things not being clean, adding that the church people are messier than they used to be. After a few minutes of washing, she excused herself from the cleaning project and told Pastor that he needed to tackle cleaning the remainder of the cupboards. As she was walking out of the kitchen she announced that she will stop by later on to see if he did a good enough job cleaning. Her final message to Pastor Osterhagen was that she could not do any more work right now because she was hungry and tired and needs to head home.

While Clement burst forth his thoughts to his listening wife, Aia interrupted him to nickname Alice Olewig, "Inspector Olewig." A moment after that, a real zinger flew from Aia's mouth which supplied an even more appropriate nick for Alice, that of "Inspector Olewig, the Anti-earwig Bigwig." Clement and Aia finished their conversation by recalling that Alice has a habit of starting tasks but fails to finish whatever she has undertaken, expecting others to be happy to pick up the slack. This is even evidenced by her hairdo. The front portion of her "do" is always combed, neatly fixed, sprayed in place, and very presentable, while the back of her hairdo is completely untouched and ignored. Once while Aia was in the ladies' washroom, Alice followed her in there and handed Aia a teasing comb and a hair pick asking her to spruce up the back of her hairdo.

Late this afternoon Alice returned to St. Pete's armed with a supply of hand-written index cards that proclaimed, "This is dirty. Please clean!" Equipped with her cards and a tape dispenser, she travelled throughout the building to adhere notes to dozens of various surfaces. Her notes were placed on tables, the guest book, walls, pews, windows, garbage cans, the pulpit, hymnal racks, mirrors, two step stools, doorknobs, along with umpteen other places. She even went so far as to tape a "This is dirty. Please clean!" index card directly on the little lamb's nose of the fifteen-inch detailed resin bust of "Jesus, Our Good Shepherd" that stands proudly on top of the church library bookshelf. Clement was so appalled by her trail of notes that he told Aia that Alice's ill-mannered behaviour is just plain rude, not just because of her expectations, but because of her timing. He emphasized that in the middle of the Christmas season the very last thing he has time to do is to take on church cleaning projects.

At 7:30 p.m. Ruby and I fell into bed. Today's theme at the Osterhagen's was all about cleanliness so we concluded that it was a good time for us to take a bath. Finding a half-full bottle of water on the floor in the youth room followed by much exertion and perspiration flowing from both of us, we accomplished tipping the bottle over, removing the cap, and spilling the water on the tile floor. Soon we became impeccably clean, but were utterly exhausted by the time we finished. Noticing that cleaning things takes a lot of physical energy we ended up coming to a conclusion. We now understand why so many people hire a cleaning service to do the work of keeping their houses in shipshape condition. That way they can save up their energy and then apply it to various pleasures like racquetball, bowling, or playing card games.

— F.N.

Christmas Eve ~ December 24

PASTOR CLEMENT ARRIVED VERY EARLY AT CHURCH THIS MORNING IN A SOUR MOOD which remained with him all morning and did not improve throughout the day, as far as the mice could tell. He cares very much about his Christmas Eve sermon and is fully aware that this sermon will be the last one that many of his flock will hear until Easter morning, The Resurrection of Our Lord, unless someone dies and there happens to be a funeral at Historic St. Peter's. Aia told him that in Christian love for others, please don't put into words the fact that some people don't go to church except on Christmas Eve and Easter Sunday. She said that they already know that and it will just hurt their feelings. Aia also added that caring and intelligent doctors don't need to tell their obese patients they are fat and desperately overweight because the patient already is aware of that. Clement thanked her and said that he would take her advice. He told her that he is thrilled and thankful to see all of the good people in church on Christmas Eve because he loves each one.

Clement has steadily, day by day, been working on his sermon. He has been revising it, praying about it, and losing sleep over it. The most helpful thing would be if he could be left alone to think.

On Christmas Eve, "Candlelight & Carols" is held at 5 p.m. In years past Christmas Eve worship used to be held at 7 p.m., but after a heated and lengthy discussion a couple of years ago it was changed to 5 p.m. The thinking behind this was that parishioners could enjoy a nibble at home before church, perhaps a taste of the shredded dried beef cheese ball, artichoke dip, those appetite spoilers commonly referred to as hors d'oeuvres. Families returning home after the service could plug in the Christmas tree, ignite their gas fireplace and be ready to enjoy an ethnic and festive Christmas Eve meal. The old schedule of 7 p.m. was just plain awkward and ended up putting a damper on the evening. The much improved new schedule gets everyone out of the building by 5:45 p.m. This way the parishioners can open up Christmas presents after supper, stay up very, very late and skip church the next morning, celebrating Christmas Day, first of all, by sleeping in. The only person to vote against the new schedule was Dacus Brown, whom some call "the church alligator." After Darla Bungard noticed his hand up high in the air to vote against the new schedule, she kindly invited him to spend Christmas Eve with her and Will at their home. The mice have noticed that Dacus is always alone and that he must not have anyone to spend Christmas Eve with. Tonight he looked like Darla's kind invitation brought him a lot of Christmas joy.

Scarcely ten minutes of uninterrupted time did Pastor have before Alan Smith, a certified electrician in town and dedicated member of St. Pete's, showed up at his office. Although extremely slim in appearance and actually of petite size for a man, citizens of Oswald County commonly refer to him as "Big Al." The title of "big" would be far more appropriate applied to his wife, Marsha, as she is a bit thickset but is always in a very jolly mood. Ruby suspects that Marsha is cheerful because she keeps her tummy satisfied, unlike some of the gloomy, skinny females at St. Pete's who convince themselves that a stick or two of chewing gum qualifies as a complete fat-free and calorie-free meal.

Al decided that this would be a choice day to accomplish electrical work in the church sanctuary. He had no appointments today because people were at home making their final Christmas preparations. Al told Pastor that he'd take advantage of this unusual free time to get the work at church accomplished. His goal was to improve the brightness and intensity of the lighting in the sanctuary. Until now, many members have not been able to read their bulletins during the sermon due to the muted lighting. Al told Pastor that the Property Director has been hounding him since last spring to get the work accomplished, but that today was his first opportunity to get at the project.

Pastor Osterhagen stopped his work due to a request by Al, and helped him move the towering Christmas tree along with a few poinsettias, because Al said that they were in the way. Al, anything but sheepishly, confessed to Pastor that he was kicked out of the house by Marsha for the day and told to return at 4 p.m. to get ready for church. She told him that she needed time alone in the house with him out of her hair to complete last minute Christmas preparations, including dressing up and working on her hairdo. After all, for Pete's sake, she has to look extra fine for church at 5 p.m. From the look on Pastor's face, we mice could tell that he secretly wished he could kick Al out of his church "home" right now so that he could accomplish his Christmas preparations, too. Pastor gathered his sermon and headed back to the parsonage while walking down the breezeway breathing heavily, using techniques he gleaned from the child-birthing classes he attended with Aia before Gretchen was born. He's noticed that deep breathing in and out seems to calm him down during anxiety. All the mice felt sorry for Pastor and said that Al's timing couldn't have been worse.

The mice in our village wondered what church members want to experience when they attend church on Christmas Eve. We came to a simple conclusion:

they want three favourite carols, a great, but short sermon, and to hold a lit candle during the singing of "Silent Night," with the first verse sung in German, the remaining two in English. They are also expecting to see a family with a newborn baby portraying the Holy Family. The live Mary, Joseph, and Jesus really can add a nice touch to the mood. Evan and Sarah Parker and their new baby girl, Zoya, portrayed the Holy Family tonight and were in centre stage during the reading of the Christmas Gospel and also during the singing of "Silent Night." That was the first time at Historic St. Pete's that baby Jesus has had pierced ears.

Determined to witness the glowing candlelight during the singing of "Silent Night," the village needed to be extremely safety conscious on many levels. Blaze, our most watchful mouse, was the first one to notice that tonight's ushers were helping to get everyone's candle lit on the main level, but did a very poor job of "ushing" when they completely overlooked the choir in the balcony waiting for light for their candles. One of the tenors, Char Reynolds (who long ago was a soprano) whispered to several choir members that the ushers must have given the choir the old heave-ho, or perhaps they might consider them to be chopped liver. Char solved tonight's predicament by pulling out her cigarette lighter from her purse, becoming the balcony usher. If Char was not a heavy-duty smoker, it would have been dim for those in the balcony. Seeing the complete beauty of all the candles alight, along with hearing "Silent Night," the entire mice village felt like each one had a holy night as well.

Mary Walden volunteered again to sing "O Holy Night," unabridged. As she neared the end, people noticeably grabbed tightly onto their pew cushions, hoping they were braced for the high, flat piercing notes. Mary was completely unaware that she was flying solo in another key. The mice agree it is sweet of her to volunteer to sing on Christmas Eve, just as she has sung annually since she was eighteen years old. She looks to be about sixty, so she'll most likely be at it for several more years.

Cadence Davis directed the hand bell choir in a glorious, heavenly version of "In Dulci Jubilo." Due to the fact that the hand bell gloves went missing, which was blamed on the church "Gremlin," Cadence requested all members of the hand bell choir to bring black mitts from home in order to portray a uniform look. Yes, everyone wore their mitts from home, but most did not own black ones. In sweet rejoicing the hand bell choir stepped up and proudly wore their mitts in a rainbow of colours. As they rang their hand bells, the colour show looked festive and fitting and most worshippers thought it was planned that way to make "In Dulci Jubilo" extra special. Cadence handled her disappointment and carried on with the show.

Instead of being led by the church organist, the singing of one familiar Christmas carol tonight was sung along with a pre-recorded video accompaniment of a gloriously sounding orchestra. The large screen that is positioned in the front of the sanctuary showed a tender and nostalgic old-fashioned horse-drawn sleigh ride that travelled happily through the crisp and untouched snowy deep woods. Excited passengers were aboard the sleigh keeping toasty under large-sized faux-fur blankets. Two big and sturdy horses pulled the sleigh and sported antique brass bells on heavy leather collars around their necks. Parishioners thoroughly enjoyed singing "Angels from the Realms of Glory" along with the video.

After worship tonight Herbert Lindenlaub waited for Pastor to finish greeting everyone and cornered him in his office. Herbert squawked at Pastor by telling him that the film was highly inappropriate for church because it showed the horses from the famous beer commercials. Herbert said, "How dare you show a beer commercial in church, let alone on Christmas Eve? Never, ever do that again!" That was witnessed by the two woodcarver mice from our village, Stickley and Teak, who took a gander from behind the filing cabinet in Pastor's office in order to see and hear the unpleasantries of Herbert's harsh words and his jarring facial expressions when he lambasted Pastor for showing the film. They heard Herbert indicate his seriousness about this when he said, "If you do anything inappropriate like that again on Christmas Eve, you will lose me as a member!"

After that, Stickley said that Herbert had the boldness to ask Pastor if he could borrow the video in order to show it at the Legion Club during their upcoming New Year's Eve party. He was certain that everyone at the club would thoroughly enjoy seeing it. Pastor handed Herbert the old-fashioned sleigh ride video and wished him Happy Christmas. After that, Stickley and Teak noticed that Pastor seemed thankful that Herbert Lindenlaub turned around and simply went away. Stickley and Teak stopped over to visit us in order to tell us what they had just seen and heard. As they were leaving, Teak mentioned that they each have a bit of work to do tonight to put the finishing touches on the woodcarvings that they are making as Christmas gifts for their girlfriends, Windy and Velveteeny. Stickley said he is almost done with carving and colourfully painting a totem pole from a small branch of a tree for Windy's gift. Teak needed to carve the remaining letter "e" onto a small wooden heart that he has carved for Velveteeny. At that point the word "Love" will be complete and Velveteeny will find out before her very eyes that Teak is completely smitten and in love with her.

Josie, the organist, played "We Wish You a Merry Christmas" for a postlude tonight. Some of the parishioners lingered back and sang along. Most people were all about celebrating the Christ child among us by hurrying home with intentions to make life very merry.

At 11:30 p.m. Ruby and I travelled to the parsonage and snacked on a dropped morsel of one of the Osterhagen's Christmas Eve hors d'oeuvres, a butter cracker. We heard them talking about their appetite spoilers at 3:30 p.m. while they sat at the dining room table. They talked about how yummy the warm crab dip tasted along with a variety of crackers, little smoky sausages in Tennessee barbeque sauce, and mustard pickled eggs. We really wanted to try the BBQ sauce from the heart of the Smoky Mountains, but we were out of luck and could not even find a lick of it.

— F.N.

THE GERMAN CHRISTMAS CAROL, "WHEN CHRISTMAS MORN IS DAWNING," OPENED the worship service today. The only mouse on duty at St. Peter's was Nimble, as most of the other mice were visiting the Land of Nod. Nimble is an early riser who is consistently wide awake, sharp-eyed, alert, and attentive during the morning hours, but by lunchtime is completely withered and spends the remaining hours of the day and night in deep slumber. Nimble, whose given name is Jim-Bob, was furnished with the nickname by our village due to the noticeable skills he uses during his most favourite summertime pursuit, chasing butterflies during the early morning hours. Nimble told the village that he even once spotted a Wild Indigo Duskywing, not exactly recognized as a bonny butterfly like the Blue Mountain Swallowtail, but good looking in its own right. Nimble's physical movements are quick and agile, while his mind possesses a tremendous aptitude for the power of observation. The merging of these two highly polished skills within Nimble has been of tremendous benefit to him, as well as our village (only during the morning hours), as he is swift to detect if we are in harm's way by keeping a sharp eagle-eye on what's going on.

Nimble reported to me that he observed many parishioners yawning throughout the worship service with their mouths wide open, some of them finding no way to suppress it. Christmas Day had only just begun and most people have already fallen victim to the annual Christmas fatigue. Having suffered from far too much Christmas, they are weary of celebrating and are feeling guilty for consuming vast amounts of calories, even admitting that they have had too many prolonged conversations with their relatives. Nimble overheard two parishioners mention that they were so wound up last night that they stayed up late and watched Christmas Eve Mass featuring the Pope on television. At the core of their conversation, one of them mentioned that he was so relieved that he is not Catholic, what with all of the doodads and gismos they have in their church, like holy water and incense.

After the opening carol, Pastor wished everyone, "Happy Christmas!" Next he proceeded with the Confession (unhappy) and Absolution (happy/what a relief) portion of the service. Nimble mentioned to me that it must be very, very healthy to be a Christian and to know that you are welcome to bring all your sins before God to receive true forgiveness, no matter what you've done wrong. He added that it must be a cleansing of the heart and soul which keeps faith fresh and alive. Nimble wondered, too, if that is why the song "Heart and Soul" is often played on the church piano after the worship service is over, but especially at times when the youth group meets. The mice assume that it is a Christian song. Often two youth, ranging in age from eight to sixteen years of age, will sit down together on the piano bench and clumsily play the song duet-style. We notice that even those lacking piano skills somehow can play that particular song, while trained pianists seem completely uninterested in the Christian "Heart & Soul" song.

Speaking of Confession and Absolution, Bonnie Blue Habberstadt was in church this morning. Cold-hearted Milla Van Camp said quietly to Norma Lind, "There is not a broom wide enough to sweep Bonnie Blue's doorstep," words which Nimble happened to overhear. What was even worse was when Milla referred to the numerous boyfriends Bonnie Blue has had by adding these mean-spirited words, "That girl has spent an awful lot of time in horizontal recreation." After hearing Milla's shockingly cruel and harsh words, Nimble was certain that gossip-monger Milla was the one who most needed confession and absolution faster than immediately. Perhaps Bonnie Blue will change her ways even if there was any truth at all to the scuttlebutt that Milla spilled to Norma.

After worship today the parishioners hurriedly left St. Pete's, possibly prompted by the alluring aroma of roasted poultry that had wafted into the sanctuary, a savoury smell probably similar to an aromatic French farm kitchen. This fragrant aroma must have whetted the parishioner's appetites making them impatient to enjoy their own Christmas Day dinners. This was because Aia was roasting two Rock Cornish hens in the church kitchen. There was "no room in the inn" at the parsonage kitchen. Streusel-Smothered Sweet Potatoes and Cowboy Corn Casserole already were occupying that space in the oven. Early this morning, we watched Aia prepare a copycat Cordon Bleu recipe for the hens which were seasoned with rosemary, butter, and Herbs de Provence, an ever-so-savory sounding recipe.

Aia told Clement that she briefly thought about writing down the recipe for Copycat Cordon Bleu Cornish Hens and giving it to Bonnie Blue, but after logically thinking about it, she changed her mind. To her ears Bonnie Blue and a recipe from Cordon Bleu might be a good match, due to the blue factor. She further told Clement that reheating frozen entrees such as lasagne and corn dogs are probably a closer match to Bonnie Blue's cooking style. From visiting with her several times, Aia has figured out that Bonnie Blue has little interest in the latest cooking shows or magazines. Aia, however, is an enthusiastic recipe collector and ventures out to prepare most any recipe, as long as the ingredients can fit into their weekly grocery budget. For her, excitement explodes when it is time to prepare and taste foods. After all, gastronomy includes a far broader scope of food than some mama's creamed chicken and vegetables spooned over baked refrigerator biscuits from a tube. Most of the time, the three dishes Aia prepares do not exactly match, but Aia is convinced that the meal tastes better that way, similar to the best potluck you've ever attended where nothing matches.

Special meals at the Osterhagens are planned in advance, especially meals that have a foreign flair. Ruby and I have watched Aia select a country and prepare traditional foods that match that country. She has spent time researching articles and books to gain some knowledge about that place. When she has prepared an ethnic meal, Aia will say to Clement and Gretchen, "Welcome to India!" (or Africa, Wales, China, or Iceland). At that point the three Osterhagens sit at the dining room table, hold hands and pray one of the many table graces that they have memorized. At these meals they experience a fun taste and learning adventure as Aia contributes knowledge from her research to the conversation. Little Gretchen happily tries everything because at age four she has already been exposed to many diverse foods. She can even wield a child-sized pair of chopsticks with a flourish when Aia presents chow mein for supper. Occasionally, Clement and Gretchen sit at the table, open up a can of kipper snacks and a box of crackers and share a fish snack together. The mice think that no other little North American girl consumes kipper snacks, smoked oysters, and fresh steamed mussels, and enjoys them like Gretchen does. Our village has concluded that Gretchen is an amazingly diverse child, welcoming food adventures of all sorts.

After worship this morning, Christmas bells rang out loud and clear from the church carillon heralding, "Joy to the World! The Lord is Come." Some families were singing along in the parking lot as they walked to their cars.

The church was hushed and motionless the remainder of the day except for the running games that took place in Woolcox Hall. Only one mouse, Wheeler, was stationary as he was on duty to keep score as to which mouse could run the fastest.

At 11:30 p.m. Ruby and I did not travel to the parsonage because we saw that Pastor and Aia were sitting at the dining room table enjoying a pre-midnight snack. We heard Aia mention how much she was enjoying the aura of the candlelight, revealing to Clement her reason as to why she has stopped lighting taper candles at suppertime. She said that as soon as she lights the candles, Gretchen stands up on one of the dining room chairs, draws in a big gust of air, which inflates and puffs up her cheeks, and then releases a big breath to extinguish the candles, a sight that is hilarious to watch, but ends up being messy because melted wax flies all over the table. Aia mentioned to Clement that they will be "candle-less" for a few years before they can enjoy the ambience that candles provide. Ruby and I were a bit bewildered about her word choice, puzzled over whether or not Aia accidentally used the incorrect word. We wondered if what she really meant was to use the word "Candlemas," a feast holiday that happens to fall on February 2, something that is somehow connected to the *Nunc Dimittis*. Perhaps we were mistaken, or worse, it led us to wonder if Ruby and I are both exhibiting early symptoms of becoming hearing impaired.

– F.N.

AGAIN THERE WAS LOW ATTENDANCE IN CHURCH, ONCE MORE DUE TO A SNOWSTORM. Snow started falling at suppertime last evening and it continued dumping buckets throughout the night. There were telephone calls back and forth between Pastor and HSP's Chairman, Bill Tiederman, as to whether or not the Sunday worship service should be cancelled. Many events and church services throughout Oswald County had already been called off for Saturday evening and Sunday morning. By 9:30 p.m. they had to make a commitment one way or the other. They decided, even though the decision was mostly made by Bill, that Sunday morning worship would remain on schedule. Bill told Pastor to go ahead with it, adding that he hopes the volunteer in charge of snow removal would get the church parking lot plowed out in time for worship. Lastly, Bill told Pastor not to count on him and his family being in church tomorrow morning as he'd never be able to make it out of his long driveway.

Only nine people showed up for church this morning with four of them arriving on snowmobiles, all decked out in snowmobile gear. Cherelle, voted by the village to hold the honoured title of this year's Christmas Mouse, overheard the snowmobilers as they talked about how fun it was for them to arrive at church on their snowmobiles. The other two people live just two doors down from the church and walked to church wearing their hefty snow boots. They were dressed in jeans, sweatshirts, and big parkas. Pastor and family were in their regular Sunday clothes. Aia said if she had known there were going to be so few people in church she would have worn her old Trinity College sweatshirt and jeans and kept Gretchen in her fleecy Christmas-plaid pajama that she wore to bed last night. The organist couldn't make it "over the river and through the woods" to church, so Aia, a music performance and art double major from Trinity College, played the organ as Gretchen sat right next to her on the organ bench. The only way Aia could keep Gretchen's hands off of the organ keys was to keep her busy with a snack. Aia had a jar of processed cheese, saltine crackers, a plastic knife, a juice box, and a paper plate with her at the organ. While Clement was reading the lessons, preaching, praying, or giving announcements, Aia spent her time spreading crackers with fake cheese for Gretchen's treat. Later on she told Clement that she was thankful that she had the foresight to bring a few supplies along with her to church to keep Gretchen happy.

After church the two snowmobile couples said that they might see if The Sugar Bowl was open. That is where they enjoy California burgers, French fries, and coffee. The other two parishioners talked of walking home and eating crock pot hamburger soup and zucchini bread made from a bumper crop of zucchini that grew in their garden last summer.

Two of the most exciting words to a clergy family are "snow day." A snow day is especially beautiful if it happens to land on a Sunday. Aia said she had big dreams of today being a snow day. That dream was crushed last night when Bill Tiederman insisted that church not be cancelled. This would have been a perfect stay-at-home pajama day, a day to play games, read their books, make party mix, read to Gretchen, and make chicken chow mein for supper, as there was a bunch of celery in their refrigerator that needed to be used up. One unfortunate part about living at St. Pete's parsonage is that their home is connected to the church building by a breezeway. Even if it is a snow day they can always walk to church through the breezeway, not needing to go outside. The inclement weather never gives them an excuse to say that they are snowed in and cannot get to church as the other parishioners say when there is a snowstorm.

At 11:30 p.m. Ruby and I travelled to the parsonage and snacked on a dropped crumb of a fortune cookie. When we got home we talked about our ESL classes and decided that we don't need to lead more any ESL classes in the New Year, as most of the mice in our village are now fluent in English. We are proud of everyone and the effort that they have put into becoming bilingual. Perhaps later on we'll talk about holding a Spanish class. Spanish might be practical to know as well as English.

    — F.N.

Wednesday, December 31

AIA PACKED THEIR LARGEST SUITCASE THIS MORNING FOR THE THREE OF THEM TO SHARE which contained a change of clothing, pajamas, and most importantly, their swimming suits. Just as important to take along for their trip, Aia also packed a paper grocery sack with various snacks and drinks. Ruby overheard the three Osterhagens talk excitedly during breakfast today about their plans to drive to the next town and check into a motel that has an indoor swimming pool. Aia made the reservation several weeks ago as she concluded that it might be difficult to find an available motel room on New Year's Eve. They talked about going straightaway to the swimming pool after their arrival. Aia also mentioned that twenty-four hours from now they will have a whale of a time enjoying the motel's complimentary breakfast, which led Gretchen to inquire about whether their breakfast will be Cheesy Egg Bake, her favourite breakfast of all. Gretchen described the egg bake by indicating that it is her mama's fancy way to cook eggs, after which she indicated that it is probably also eaten by kings, queens, princes, and princesses that live in big castles using shiny golden spoons to eat their Cheesy Egg Bake.

Before ten o'clock this morning, Ruby and I saw the Osterhagens leave the parsonage, get into their van and drive away. Everything was immensely quiet at the church, so the mice had fun by playing hide and seek throughout the entire building, upstairs and downstairs. Ruby and I were spent from all of the merry-making and exercise today so we decided to skip staying up until midnight to say farewell to the old year and welcome the New Year. At 8:30 p.m. we wished each other "*Ovatxoi wmi yy moiniwxerp*" (Happy New Year in Mouse), kissed on the lips, and then sang the famously worldwide well-known New Year's Eve song, "Auld Lang Syne." The brilliantly written poetic and sentimental words by Scotland's Robert Burns definitely are a treasured gift to the entire world. As Ruby and I rested, we talked about how gifted of a man Robbie was, likely due to the excellent nutrition he derived from haggis consumption combined with the fresh Scottish air. However, we are not certain whether Robbie lived in the Highlands or the Lowlands, so we'll need to ask our village librarian to research that. But, the Highlands and the Lowlands probably both have a profusion of fresh air that invigorates and almost stings your nostrils when you suck it in, a far opposite from one of those cities that hosts smoggy pollutants. Ruby and I hope that Aia will someday prepare a Scottish meal so that we can experience a taste of what the master poet Robbie ate. If that ever happens, we will go outside for a bit of fresh air prior to taste-testing haggis, as it will clear out our heads and perhaps lead to poetry reading or a writing escapade.

    – F.N.

Friday, January 2

PASTOR OSTERHAGEN WAS SEEN ARRIVING AT HIS OFFICE THIS MORNING OBVIOUSLY IN A happy mood with a twinkle in his eye. He adores the twelve days of Christmas, today marking day nine, the "Nine Ladies Dancing" day. His demeanor is far different than what it was on December 25. After the anxiety of the Christmas services passed, he and his family began their own Christmastime. Many times, parishioners have asked Pastor on Christmas Eve or on Christmas Day, "How was your Christmas?," as if it was completely over. He simply smiles at them and shoots back with, "Thanks for asking. It's just beginning!"

Today looked to be a quiet day at HSP so Clement told Aia that he intended to accomplish a lot of work, but those plans were soon interrupted. He was barely able to make it to his office before the stoppage began.

Arriving at the church office, Darla Bungard found Pastor standing at the photocopier making copies for Sunday's Bible Study. She immediately began conveying plans for the upcoming chili competition that is to be held in Woolcox Hall, noting that the goal is to raise funds for St. Pete's current overseas mission project. Being that she is the head organizer for this event, she previously tried to set up an appointment to meet with Pastor, but he postponed the meeting until after Christmas. Darla arrived for their 10 a.m. appointment today, a meeting that Pastor later told Aia he had completely failed to remember. Proudly showing him the hand-designed posters and leaflets that were run off at Jay's Printing Shop, Darla added that she and Will "footed the bill" for that sizable expense.

One of our strongest leaders in the village, Wilder, heard deliberateness in the tone of Darla's voice as she spoke about the poster distribution. Wilder happens to possess a gift for numbers. His pattern is to travel to the church office once a week to study the weekly adding machine tapes that have missed the wastebasket and landed on the floor. From reading those tapes, he is able to give our mice village an account of the financial health of St. Pete's. Today he was positioned behind the wastebasket and was able to carefully take notice of all of the details concerning the chili conversation held between Pastor and Darla, with Darla speaking first, in the middle, and at the end, mostly doing all of the talking. Wilder reported that Darla was a shade apologetic for not showing Pastor a prototype of the posters ahead of time, but, of course, she was certain that he would really like them anyway. According to Wilder, Darla seems to be a "git-r-dun" type of girl, and proud of it, "just sayin'."

Her plans were to post the larger ones at various locations throughout town, while the leaflets were to be passed out at the bank. Every church in town has agreed to insert the leaflets in their church bulletin on Sunday, January 19. Grocer Dan has agreed to stuff them in every grocery sack at the checkout counters. Darla mentioned that she had purchased a display ad in the Oswald County Courier. Positioned in the dead centre of her poster is a big bowl of chili with a bold caption that reads, "Chili Eats Loud." At this point, Pastor was expected to praise her creativity and thank her from the bottom of his heart for a job well done, but Wilder noticed that he had trouble getting the right words out, so he said as positively as he could, "Great job, Darla." She received his praise and beamed. Later on Pastor told Aia that he knows that "Chili Eats Loud" is nothing but a derivative of the old Pennsylvania Dutch saying, "Bean Soup Eats Loud." Anyway, he let Darla proceed with her plans. The fundraiser is coming up soon, scheduled for Saturday, January 24. After Darla left the church office, he called Aia from his office as he needed a bit of therapy. Aia told him she understood that the poster is tacky, but that does not mean that the church will look sketchy simply because of a silly poster, and also that chili truthfully does eat loud, a natural occurrence from consuming beans. She urged him to remember that even royals and the president fart after eating chili. Aia's advice to Clement was to move on to more important things right away like coming home for lunch, adding that, ironically, they were having Rainbow Bean Soup and grilled cheese sandwiches for lunch.

Aia has a lot of savvy. She has figured out that people watch what time they arise in the morning. It usually is at seven, a little too late, but that is because Clement has evening meetings that make it difficult for him to unwind before he can fall asleep. However, one member, Bertie Koche, is on patrol every single morning at four-thirty driving around town to see whose lights are turned on. Bertie must have developed a "laziness chart" to measure and record what time people's lights come on in the morning. Aia suspects that Bertie is critical of them from the evil eye she shoots her way on Sunday mornings. To conquer this problem, Aia began rising at four-fifteen in the morning to turn on the living room and kitchen lights, going straight back to bed, curling up closely to Clement to warm up her icy-cold feet. She told Clement that she should have put a couple of timers on her Christmas list. The timers would save her hours of fretting about getting up on time. From the buzz in the village, the mice heard that Bertie herself only gets up that early because she wants to get all of her day's work done way before noon, as she takes a three-hour nap after lunch. The mice wonder if there is anyone besides Bertie in the whole world who hangs wash on the clothesline at four in the morning every month of the year. We all wonder what drives her to get in her car at four-thirty each morning in order to keep tabs on which people are the most industrious or hard-working, just because they get up way before they hear a cock crow.

At 11:30 p.m. Ruby & I travelled to the parsonage and snacked on a tidbit of chicken noodle hotdish that Gretchen accidentally dropped on the floor at suppertime tonight.

– F.N.

SUNG IN CHURCH THIS MORNING WAS "WE THREE KINGS OF ORIENT ARE," WHICH is evidently Gretchen's favourite song. She sang the only word she knew in the song, singing clearly and loudly. For her, it was all about the fermata, the extra-long hold on the word, "O." She sings the first word of the chorus, but not the other words, "Star of Wonder, Star of might, Star with royal beauty bright, westward leading, still proceeding, guide us to the perfect light." Gretchen held up her song sheet as though she could read the contents, singing with so much expression that she looked like a tiny Italian espressiva performing at an opera house. It appears that she was born musical, as she sings the F sharp and the A natural perfectly in tune. We notice that Aia nearly cried as she listened to her musical daughter sing, calling her "O Gretchen" the remainder of the day.

It has been three weeks since Agnes, "The Blabber," dropped in at the parsonage to deliver a platter of Christmas cookies. During church this morning, Aia seemed certain that everyone there knew that she is pregnant, thanks to Agnes squealing the news. Feeling ill-at-ease, Aia noticed that parishioners were checking out the size of her tummy. She found that to be foolish as she is down a few pounds due to morning sickness. Aia told Clement that she needs to make an appointment with her doctor to find out the exact due date. Soon members of the church will be fishing for that information. After church today, Aia told Clement that it would be best to announce their good news within the next month. That way the tummy-checking and whispering behind her back will stop. It seems that the parishioners are looking for concrete evidence that wise Agnes, "The Blabber," is spot-on.

At 11:30 p.m. Ruby and I travelled to the parsonage and snacked on a dropped morsel of poutine. My favourite part was the driblet of gravy, but Ruby preferred the melted cheddar cheese curd.

— F.N.

Epiphany ~ Tuesday, January 6

HSP's ANNUAL VILLAGE MICE MEETING WAS CONVENED TONIGHT WHERE ALL IN attendance strived to keep the mood good-natured without the complexity of twists and turns from various personalities in attendance. After gathering together for a potluck supper, we gently kicked around the past year, but sought to accentuate the highlights, the wow factors that happened among us. The meeting's agenda finished by focusing on future wishes and dreams, but also on some solid accomplishments that the village hopes to see come to fruition within the New Year.

One predominant feature under the agenda's "new business" tonight concentrated on HSP's sanctuary flooring. It happens to be the original "olden days" cinnamon-coloured hardwood floor. When visitors attend church they often remark as to how striking the wood is, as though the planks came from some ancient woodland. Our villagers respect the unspoiled traditional heritage connected to this floor that has been passed down from previous generations.

At the end of the day, just envision HSP's history where droves of people have come and gone in and out of the sanctuary. Each individual unknowingly has deposited dirt and dust particles from their shoes in the sanctuary's floorboard cracks. A fascinating study could be done on just the dirt particles left behind.

Because of respect and regard for Historic St. Peter's heritage, we are eager to safeguard the building from any state of dilapidation. However, there is a safety issue with the floor due to one discrete section that is not so durable. Our village is in a conundrum as to the reason why the boards in one zone are loose and wiggle a bit. During tonight's meeting, the village appointed a team of mice to delve into this clueless mystery. We await their verdict at the next meeting.

I feel ill tonight so I will crawl into bed right after I finish my writing, hoping to find that sleep will help me recuperate. Just lately, Ruby has become saddened as to the amount of time I spend at the end of the day recording my journal. She wants me to spend that time with her instead. I adore being with her, too, but this project is of momentous significance to me. I also realize that you are depending on me, as well, and I think it is good for me to spend quiet time working on my writing. But if I don't feel better soon, I'll ask my Ruby to kindly write in my journal to record what's happening at church. I know she will do her very best. I also am aware that there will be a different spin on the church news being written by another mouse, as it might showcase a more complicated point of view.

Ruby is a good wife and a very helpful one. She's also a beauty inside and out. She cannot help it that she wants me all to herself. She often tells me that she "married up," and I respond by telling her the same. The last words I said to my Ruby before closing my journal tonight were, *"Mqvw plv xxat,"* which means, "I love you," in the mouse language. She repeated the same words back to me. Oh, I'm thankful that we have each other, you know, like the phrase in the vows for holy marriage remind us of our promise, "in sickness and in health."

I am going to bed at 8:30 p.m., hoping to hibernate under my coverlet. Earlier tonight Ruby was so keen on having a snack that she travelled by herself to the sanctuary looking to find a dropped oyster cracker or a baby teething biscuit. Luckily, she did find a communion wafer that a communion assistant dropped on the floor during distribution this morning. She brought it back home and snacked on a few bites of that before I put down my journal and took an extended trip to Shangri-la.

– F.N.

Thursday, January 8

FOLLOWING BREAKFAST THIS MORNING, RUBY OVERHEARD CLEMENT TELL AIA THAT HE was in a flurry to get down to the gas station to fill the van up with gas. Last Saturday he mentioned to Aia that he noticed the wording on the gas station marquee that read, "Free T.P. on Thursdays with Fill Up." Mostly he emphasized that he intended to get down there before they ran out of their supply of toilet paper, as he didn't want to miss out on the free give-away. After ten minutes, Clement returned home from a successful mission, joyfully and proudly carrying a sixteen-pack of toilet paper in his arms. Because Aia values frugality, Ruby heard her tell Clement how incredibly awesome he is when he is prudent with their money as he scrimps and stretches it as far as he possibly can.

Ruby and I frequently notice that the Osterhagens don't have a lot of money, but they certainly do a lot with what they have. They are tight team members in moderation, turning it into a game. The village mice respect them because they don't waste a thing, especially money, time, or opportunities.

There was no snack for us tonight as I was under the weather. My good wife Ruby stayed near me and tucked the coverlet so snugly around me that I felt like I was a wrapped-up mouse. After that she sang me to sleep with a captivating song. Ruby said that she heard Aia singing it this afternoon while she was cleaning the kitchen cupboards. The song spoke about putting time into a bottle, a real wish to have more time in life. It also alluded to a box for wishes and dreams. We wondered if Clement and Aia have a bottle that they save time in or a box that holds their wishes and dreams. The next time we travel to the parsonage, we'll keep our eyes peeled to see if we can spot their time-bottle or wishes-and-dreams box.

– F.N.

The Baptism of Our Lord ~ Sunday, January 11

EVERYONE LOVES FINLEY, ESPECIALLY ME. UNTIL HE RECOVERS, I, RUBY, HIS WIFE, WILL record in his journal the current events at St. Pete's to the best of my ability. It is evident that he needs to rest because of his temp, sore throat, and severe cough. Even though he is indisposed, he still welcomes visitors from our village, noting that each one has encouraged him to get well soon. Their visits are informative and Finley has enjoyed being able to keep up on all the news that they pass on to him.

It was an uplifting morning at Historic St. Peter's as Lance and Holly Steinman brought their infant son, Andrew, for Holy Baptism, precisely on the day that the church observes the Baptism of Our Lord. Posey is our village collector of flower debris that she uses in creating her own fragrant potpourri appropriately named, "Posey's Petals." Posey was on duty hoping to gather up any petals that might fall from today's chancel floral arrangements. She said that when Pastor Osterhagen held baby Andrew, it might have led to his announcement about their baby arriving at the end of June or early July. After that, the parishioners clapped for them. That news, however, did not seem to surprise anyone sitting in the pews. Most parishioners told him that they had a hunch Aia was expecting, but they just didn't know what month the baby would arrive.

It's easy to see that Aia is feeling better and pregnancy sickness is disappearing. She constantly has a snack-sized food baggie or two ready in her pocket for cravings that come upon her. Ruby heard her tell Clement about her burning desire for particular foods. Going out of her comfort zone, Aia asked Clement to help relieve those urges by simply making a trip to Grocer Dan's. The strongest craving so far has been for cold shrimp, spicy cocktail sauce, and lemon wedges. Some of the mice have seen her in the breezeway eating a fresh cut up lemon without even puckering up. The shrimp craving is really, really hard to manage on a pastor's salary, so the last time that Clement went to the store he returned with several small packages of imitation crab meat instead of shrimp, hoping that her seafood craving will take a dive soon. He mentioned to Aia that he is optimistic that her next cravings might be for something more affordable like frozen strawberries or bran cereal. Aia's tummy is flat but Agnes, "The Blabber," stares at her which makes Aia self-conscious.

Dash, our mouse with the shortest tail, overheard Magnolia Brown when she cornered Aia at church today insisting upon an explanation as to why production of the church cookbook has been stalled for so many months. Aia told her that she really didn't have a clue about it, but referred her to Susan Hayes, the current editor of the project. Dash saw Magnolia hurry over to Susan and told her that she would like to take over the editorial responsibilities and produce a cookbook that Historic St. Peter's would be overjoyed with. (The mice community knows that Susan happens to be the third person that has attempted to be the cookbook editor.) After Magnolia's proposition, Susan quickly got rid of the job by instantly appointing Magnolia the next editor. After all, Susan conveyed to Magnolia that she has had this cookbook project spread across her twelve-seater dining room table for two full years. Her family has been uncomfortably eating all of their meals clustered around their small kitchen dinette. Dash heard Susan confide to Magnolia, by using a whisper voice, that she lost her spirit of enthusiasm to work on the cookbook when she got scolded for a few recipe names that had been submitted, like "Better than Sex Cake," "Garbage Hotdish," "Bloomer Droppers," "Lazy Butt Slow-Cooker Beef," "Fat Lady Squares," and "Irish Whiskey Cheddar Spread." Susan promised Magnolia that she will box up all the recipes that have been contributed so far and deliver them to her next Sunday morning.

Magnolia passionately revealed to Susan that under her direction St. Pete's will produce a cookbook worthy of county-wide attention. Dash mentioned to us that Magnolia's determination is in tack as she is an accomplishment-oriented, never-skip-anything, or take short cuts, type of overachiever. We notice that people don't seem to care for her because when she talks to them they get shaky and nervous. Magnolia's plans are to stand every Sunday morning adjacent to the ladies' washroom in order to catch every lady that passes by her. That way she can pressure each one for recipe submissions. Magnolia claimed that by handing them a few blank recipe cards and coercing them to fill them out with their favourite recipes, she will get plenty of recipes by the deadline which is in three weeks. Magnolia said that she will not buckle under if anyone finds fault with recipe names, as she herself is submitting one for "Gypsy's Arm." Dash said that Susan winced when she heard that. Magnolia told her to relax and unclench her teeth as "Gypsy's Arm" is only a sponge cake, similar to a jelly roll.

Magnolia's last words to Susan were about the title for the cookbook, which she has specifically chosen based on her own specialty recipe, Potato Pancakes. Envisioning the cookbook to be titled, "St. Pete's Potato Pancakes-A-Plenty," the cover design will feature a portrait of herself modelling an apron that is hand-embroidered with the saying, "When life gives you potatoes, make pancakes."

The mouse village has received word that they may have found a passageway to get under the loose and wiggly floor boards in the sanctuary. Lewis and Clark, our expert explorers, will venture out soon into the unknown attempting to discover the reason as to why the floorboards are loose.

At 11:30 p.m. I kept mouse vigil at home with my Finley and skipped travelling to the parsonage. Finley's sickness has had an unexpected positive effect on my waistline as I've lost a bit of weight, perhaps overall, but I notice that is it mostly apparent in my facial cheeks. I crawled under the coverlet tonight and expressed to Finley the thoughts and feelings that came from deep within my heart. I told him *"Mqvw plv xxat,"* ("I love you" in Mouse) and also "Ich liebe dich," (which means "I love you" in the German language). I am well acquainted with the German phrase because we have heard Clement and Aia proclaim those words to each other many, many times. Finley warmly and tenderly replied to me, *"wivqzpi,"* (in Mouse) which means "ditto" in the English language. Having just begun enjoying how it feels to be a liberated, bilingual, female mouse, I am open to learning many other languages. Plus, knowledge of other languages builds confidence in being adaptable to new situations that I might come across in the future. Who knows, someday I might benefit from having gained the knowledge of speaking Chinese, Portuguese, Italian, Nuer, New Englander (Maine-style, of course), Slovak, Dinka, Midwestern, Spanish, French, Swedish, Russian, Bostonian, German, Cherokee, Dutch, Pennsylvania Dutch, Southern, New Yorker, or even Estonian. I am certain there are many other languages in this whole big wide world, but those languages are just off the top of my head, until I have gained more knowledge about it.

We did spend a moment talking about Dash and the advantages he has of having a short tail. Concluding that there is a great safety advantage of possessing a short tail, we know that when danger arrives he is the first one of us to be completely hidden, far out of sight.

– Ruby Newcastle

Saturday, January 17

ROBIN BROOKS AND HER TWO SONS, INTELLIGENT AND GOOD-LOOKING BOYS, ARRIVED AT HSP early this morning to set up for a workshop that was sponsored by Our Lady of Lourdes Hospital. Twelve-year old Hunter and ten-year old Joel were eager to help their mother with the work needed to get ready for this community-wide event. Two mice in our village who are sisters, Amber and Ember, peeked out and watched the goings on done by Robin and her sons. Both Amber and Ember noticed that the boys are A-1 helpers, sensitive to what work needs to be done far before Robin even asks them. Hunter and Joel set up all of the tables and chairs in the Fireside Room. After that they ventured out into the freezing cold weather to make several trips back and forth from their van hauling in supplies for the event's mid-morning snack. They had their hands full transporting trays of fresh veggies and dip, fresh fruit, and muffins, along with a basket containing various flavoured tea bags. Amber and Ember commented to me later on in the day that watching the boys help their mother was nothing short of inspiring. They concluded that the boys are truly kind and caring, all the while emitting a sun-shiny attitude. Both Amber and Ember said that one day they will make outstanding husbands for their wives.

After Hunter and Joel finished helping their mother, Robin kissed and hugged them, and thanked them for helping her. She told them that the workshop will last three hours, finishing up at noon, adding that they were now free to be on their own to entertain themselves at the church. Amber and Ember noticed that the boys were very excited about being given free time at the church and that they had a happy glint in their eyes which forecasted that they were in for three hours of adventure and discovery time.

When the women arrived at HSP's Fireside Room this morning, Robin encouraged them to pour a cup of tea and relax for a few minutes by the fireplace, letting these precious moments be a mini-retreat or a breather from their regular rat race. (The attendance was quite low, but on a freezing cold day, that was to be expected.) After the workshop began, Robin introduced herself by telling the ladies that she is on staff as a registered nurse at Our Lady of Lourdes Hospital, adding that the Hospital Administrator had asked her to host this gathering for any ladies in Oswald County that are interested in improving their health and lifestyle. This morning's community workshop concentrated on providing practical information for women in order to work towards a healthier lifestyle by adding some creative tips to their current way of living. Robin is well-versed in this area, but she was cautious about overloading the women with way too much information. Robin added to her agenda a short presentation that included fun eating tips to elevate their emotions, mind, and body, which will in turn benefit their hair, skin, and nails. By using these excellent good-health suggestions, she reminded the women that they will gain more of the feel-good things that are helpful in life, like self-esteem, self-respect, self-regard, and increased confidence in their own self-worth.

Amber and Ember were on the lookout and followed Hunter and Joel during their adventure time. First of all, the boys played hide and seek in the nooks and crannies of St. Pete's. Following that, they did a fifteen minute jog around the circumference of Woolcox Hall. After that they ventured to the Youth Room, popped two bags of microwave popcorn and enjoyed eating their snack while they each drank a can of ginger ale found in the Youth Room refrigerator. While they ate their snack, they talked about how much they look forward to joining the High School Youth Group at church when they are old enough. Hunter mentioned that the most special part of being in Youth Group will be attending the exciting summer Youth Gatherings that are held in exciting cities like San Antonio, New Orleans, and Tomah, Wisconsin. Time was spent playing the keyboard and drum set, pretending that they were in a rock band which consisted of only two musicians. After that, they went on a walking mystery trip to peer in every single room of St. Peter's to see what was located where. It was at this point that they discovered the riding floor scrubber in the janitor's closet and could not resist wheeling it to Woolcox Hall and giving it a whirl. They plugged it in and completely scrubbed the entire floor of the parish hall twice. After they put the riding floor scrubber back in its place, they both went to the church kitchen and enjoyed a cookie and a glass of milk, making this their second snack of the morning.

Upon opening up the dishwasher door to deposit their soiled drinking glasses, Hunter and Joel found four decks of playing cards. This appeared to be completely puzzling to them as Amber and Ember observed the boys facial expressions. At that point, they proceeded to hand-wash and dry their own drinking glasses, surmising that the dishwasher was not intended for dirty dishes but for the storage of playing cards. After the drinking glasses were put away, they fetched a deck of cards and played many games of "War." After that, they got a ball of string out of the kitchen junk drawer and played cat's cradle. When Joel mentioned the words "cat's cradle," Amber and Ember were so full of twitchiness that they bolted as fast as they could to our home, arriving out of breath, so agitated and panicky that they were shaking all over. As they spoke, they revealed to us their knowledge about carnivorous cats: Cats pursue mice, cats capture mice, and the mice are never seen or heard from again. They added that the fluffy fur coat on a cat resembles white clouds in the sky, but not to let that buffalo you because cats are naturally flesh-eating beasts whose caviar of choice is mice. Even the mention of the word "cat" sends Amber and Ember into a state of panic and does not expose the best side of them.

As Amber and Ember were ready to return to their home they mentioned that they fully intended to stay there the remainder of the day or at least until their anxiety subsided. I felt the need to venture out to the church kitchen to see what was going on. After I got there, I saw Hunter return the deck of cards to the dishwasher. When their mother arrived after the community event was over, I followed Robin, Hunter, and Joel to the Fireside Room. They helped their mother with the cleanup, after which they enjoyed their third snack of the morning, leftover veggies and dip, fresh fruit, and muffins. The boys were thirsty, so, to quench their thirst, they must have gone back to the Youth Room and grabbed another ginger ale from the refrigerator. I concluded that three snacks in one morning seemed like a lot to me. If it is normal for growing boys to wolf down three snacks in a morning, followed by three snacks in the afternoon, three each evening, plus their regular three meals per day, that adds up to a total consumption of twelve meals per day. In all probability, this couldn't possibly be true. I wish I could just sit down and have a heart-to-heart conversation with Aia about this subject in order to obtain some answers. She is an expert in threes, being a true Trinitarian, a graduate of Trinity College, and I am certain she could provide answers for me.

At 7 p.m. I travelled to the Youth Room and enjoyed one drop of spilled ginger ale that had landed on the tile floor. I wondered if the ginger ale was American-made or Canadian-made, but by myself could not come up with an answer to my query. That treat was not sufficient enough of a snack, so I travelled to the church kitchen and found a crumb of an oatmeal cookie. At 7:30 p.m. I travelled to the Fireside Room and found a green grape that was just resting in one corner of the room. I felt alone as I had no one to visit with to process the day's activities. By that time I was so exhausted that it took every drop of energy that I could muster up just to travel back home and flop in bed. Finley and I slept until the sun came up, its brightness awakening us to yet another day. Writing down the details of Saturday, January 17, felt like a lot of work because I was suffering from severe fatigue. My writing ability today was at a less than desirable level, but at least I got it down on paper.

    – Ruby Newcastle

DARLA BUNGARD WAS STRIKINGLY DRESSED IN A CRISPLY-IRONED WHITE BLOUSE AND denim skirt today, along with a golden cowgirl hat that shimmered, cowgirl boots, and rhinestone jewellery. Most likely, all of it was purchased from the fancy, upscale Western store, LeRoy Edward's Western Wear. She was a show-stopper, impressively walking up front and positioning herself in Pastor's pulpit, adjusting the microphone to her level, ready and on fire to promote the upcoming chili competition. Her announcement lasted several minutes and during that time she got "microphone disease," the ailment that happens to some people when they hear their own voice projected in a microphone, fall in love with the sound of it, and enjoy being the centre of attention. Everyone seemed to know the details about the chili competition already because they read it in today's bulletin which contained the small handout Darla had designed. "Please," she said, "give this handout to a friend or family member, spread the word, and urge them to attend the chili competition with you." "Chili Eats Loud" came out of her mouth and she must have expected there to be giggles in church. However, when she said that, it flopped. Her husband, Will, was the only one who laughed because it might have crushed Darla if no one had laughed. If he hadn't laughed about chili eating loud, most likely he would have had to listen to her all afternoon talk about this.

Will wore Western wear also, which complimented Darla's. They must have rung up a Texas-sized bill at LeRoy Edward's when they purchased the ensembles. Both of them have changed the style in which they dress, a style that previously included mostly beige clothing. All of their beige clothing must have been donated to the "This 'n That Thrift Store" because they have adopted a Western-themed type of fashion. The village notices how wonderful it is that they both are going through their midlife crisis exactly at the same time. Together they have embraced and transitioned into a new look that is very Texan. Ruby and I think that it actually looks natural, as they say, "not makey-uppy."

During pleasant weather, the Bungard's never miss seeing a sunset. They have added a large porch to their home facing west so they can sit and enjoy the view. The house used to look plain, but due to a lot of work and money, it now has a ranch look. They often sit on the porch during cocktail hour, and because they are extroverts, they entertain friends and invite them for dinner, starting off with a glass of wine. But even their wine glasses have changed. They used to use their small crystal Irish wine glasses, but now they've put those away and have switched to Texas-sized wine goblets. The mice know all of this because Ruby has cousins that reside under the Bungard's new porch. When they visit us, they tell us details and happenings in Darla and Will's life.

At the microphone Darla asked for a show of hands from those who plan to attend the chili competition. Because the pressure was on, most people raised their hands, except for Penny Larson and Gwyneth Leszenski, both of whom carry a stylish cushion everywhere they go. The cushions are for evenly distributing their weight, helping to relieve any painful pressure. They claim that the cushions are crucial for helping both of them, especially in their condition, an ailment of some sort that they do not name out loud. With help, they both ordered the cushions from a catalog; Penny, with the help of her daughter Bethany Reed, and Gwyneth with her granddaughter Liza Jackson's assistance. Penny and Gwenyth haven't decided yet if they will attend the competition as they have to go home and check their food allowance chart. Consuming chili might be risky and might cause them some pain.

Darla ended her announcement with the best part. She said that there are many extraordinary chili contestants eager to provide a variety of distinctive chili flavours. Not one entry will taste anything like your mama's "bland" chili. After she spoke, Pastor thanked Darla for her hard work and dedication, mentioning that the fundraiser is already a success. Some people who cannot attend the event have already given a mission offering. Finally, Pastor was able to start the worship service. After all, that was the real reason why people attended church today.

Wilder was again in the church office hiding behind the trash can when the service began. The church treasurer burst in, Simon Thompson, who had slipped out of the sanctuary during the opening hymn. Simon hurriedly lifted up the lid on the copy machine and attempted to make copies, most likely for the brief council meeting that was to be held right after today's worship service. Most people must have thought he was off to the washroom. After noticing that the copier was not working, Simon saw that a light was on indicating that the toner needed to be replaced.

Wilder remembered that Sally Swanson had been the last person in the office who tried to make copies, saw that it needed toner, and ran away. She didn't want anything to do with replacing the toner because she knew how messy a job it can be, if you do it wrong. Her hands were adorned with a very fancy manicure. Her fingernails were painted with fuchsia nail polish. There were hand-painted yellow roses on each thumb. Her smooth, white, delicate hands reflect a youthful appearance, despite her being past middle age, he said.

All of the mice were impressed by Wilder's memory of the details of Sally's manicure. He is convinced Sally must fully follow beauty tips for keeping her hands smooth and ageless, not just by being cautious and putting into practice preventative measures, but by side-stepping and steering clear of any situation that involves a lot of work done with her hands. Sally's hands are not typical of those hands that perform oil changes, pickle beets, or are berry pickers, painters, or anyone who uses food colouring for icing cakes or colouring snowballs red, white, and blue and letting them hibernate in the deep freeze the remainder of the winter only to be pulled out for a good old patriotic and festive July snowball fight.

Wilder told us that Simon must have assumed it would take only a few moments of his time and that he'd be back in the sanctuary before the lessons were read. That was his first mistake. His second mistake was to put the toner in the machine upside down. The third and worst mistake of all was to yank off the plastic safety strap. Instantly, toner spread everywhere throughout the interior of the copy machine, completely shutting it down. Simon quickly left the office and headed back to the sanctuary and joined his wife, Liz, in the pew. Liz studied his face and stared at the black powder on his fingers, but said nothing during the worship service.

A telephone call at the parsonage tonight revealed that a dear member, Marie Schmidt, had died. Marie's daughter explained that her mother had finished supper, washed the dishes, rested in her easy chair, and simply died. She said she found her around eight o'clock tonight when she came over to play a game with her. After that conversation, Aia dialed up the church telephone number, hoping Clement would answer. He was in a stewardship meeting, but when it rang on a Sunday evening he knew it must be important.

When Clement returned home after the meeting, they talked about how Marie was a wonderful Christian woman who loved everyone regardless of how messed up their lives were. Perhaps that was because she had plenty of relatives with messed up lives. She respected Pastor and Aia even though a few of the parishioners seem to think that they are tender-footed greenhorns. Marie's Christmas present to the Osterhagens this year were five hand-knit cotton dishcloths along with a Christmas card that contained twenty-five dollars. Aia was touched by the gift, as she recently learned basic knitting skills and appreciates that each one takes time to make. The mice noticed that somehow a home-made dishcloth can communicate love. Aia herself has used her fragments of time to knit eighteen dishcloths, intending to give them away to relatives as Christmas presents, even though she hasn't made any for herself yet. That, too, sounds like love. To wash tomorrow's dishes, Aia opened up the towel drawer and pulled out a brand new green and blue dishcloth knitted by Marie.

At 11:30 p.m. I stayed home with my Finley and cuddled up to him. Finley is slowly getting better and he is noticing my weight loss. He said that it's okay, but that he has always liked my curves. At that point, I realized that men and mice are not that different when it comes to what they think qualifies as beauty in a female. Mice and men both like curves.

– Ruby Newcastle

MARIE SCHMIDT'S FUNERAL WAS AT HISTORIC ST. PETE'S TODAY AT 11 A.M. THERE WERE no bulletins to pass out, as the copier was still out of order. The funeral was followed by a committal service at Cedar Hill Cemetery, with a return to Woolcox Hall for a luncheon consisting of cold cuts, a bread and bun basket, potato chips, veggies, dip, pickles, desserts, and tea and coffee. Often referred to as the "Rosette Queen" of the county, Marie was a first place champion with her rosette entries at the Oswald County Fair. Marie had followers within the region that placed orders for specific designs of rosettes for special gatherings. Her rosettes simply propelled an occasion from being somewhat ordinary to something special. Once at church we saw her make rosettes, a delicate cookie made with a form that is dipped in batter and then fried in hot oil. Her culinary skills for making rosettes are not limited to the traditional rose form, but also include king-sized roses, butterflies, card suits (spades, hearts, diamonds, and clubs), Christmas trees, snowmen, angels, snowflakes, and bells. It was essential at this funeral luncheon that rosettes be present on the dessert table. Lillian Hansen was often a second place winner at the Oswald County Fair so it was natural that she was called upon to make rosettes for Marie's funeral luncheon. The family requested that Lillian make eight dozen butterfly rosettes. Being that the butterfly is a symbol of Christ's resurrection, it was just so liturgically appropriate for a funeral. Lillian considered it an honour to be asked to make the rosettes for Marie's funeral and triumphantly rose to do her very best.

At 11:30 p.m. I crawled into bed and told Finley that I am getting tuckered out from having to go out and about at church to do research for his journal. I only have enough stamina to do it a little while longer. He said he understood and added that tomorrow is a new day and we will figure something out. I told him that he is a wonderful Finley. Before falling asleep, I read everything out loud that was printed on an old empty matchbook, ate a whole potato chip from the funeral lunch, and then slept like a baby cuddled up to my Finley.

– Ruby Newcastle

PSALM 118:24 SAYS, "THIS IS THE DAY THAT THE LORD HAS MADE, LET US REJOICE AND be glad in it." Darla recited this verse from memory as she entered Woolcox Hall today. That's obviously her favourite Bible verse and everyone hears it when she's around. Each time she enters and exits Historic St. Peter's she quotes that verse. Darla is the Chairperson and Organizer for the Chili Competition. Today she greeted the volunteers by telling them that she is here to "git 'r dun" just right. Yesterday men from the church arrived to do the heavy work, which included setting up contestant booths, a portable stage for the banjo group performers, dinner tables and chairs for those attending, and a very special platform for Darla (who is also the emcee). From that position she will make announcements, sprinkled with a few jokes. It is also the spot from which the Bungard's will provide a special dance, one that she and Will have been rehearsing.

Ladies of all ages and several children were here today, including Aia and Gretchen, ready to decorate the hall for tonight's event. Darla has chosen decorations that are to achieve just the right "look" for the contest, a real spectacle. One of the mice heard Darla say that any old ho-hum and predictable decorations like red-checked tablecloths, poster board cut-outs of chili peppers suspended from the ceiling, or bandana-patterned paper napkins are unacceptable for this cook-off. Darla indicated that this event will have "Western Elegance" that is dusted with lots of shimmer and shine, with yellow and silver her chosen colours. There were several boxes of items that she has collected. Over the last year she has made weekly shopping trips to the local craft store, equipped with the weekly coupon from the ads. One of Ruby's cousins told her that Darla has walked into the craft store so many times these last eleven months that the manager and store clerks recognize her and have called her the "coupon lady," a title Darla does not appreciate.

Darla's "Western Elegance" theme began by transforming Woolcox Hall into the yellow rose of Texas. Rented yellow linen tablecloths and napkins began that transformation. Glass canning jars painted on the outside with silver glitter served as centerpieces. Each one contained a fresh yellow rose along with greenery and a fancy silver glitter decorator's pick. At each place setting was a clear plastic glass for lemonade containing a fancy gray-and-yellow-striped paper straw. The yellow rose of Texas theme was obvious to everyone which made Darla extra pleased with her creativity. She told a couple of people that she thought these table settings would stun and impress those who attend the chili competition. To Darla, this was not just about cooking.

There were twelve entries in this year's chili competition:

1. Paula Adamson, featuring "Prospector's Tasty Chili"
2. Effie Richardson, featuring "Chuck Wagon Chili"
3. Rita Grant, featuring "Rita's Quick Chili"
4. Tina Bailey, featuring "Michigan Avenue Chili"
5. Carmen DeVault, featuring "Suzie's Chili"
6. Auntie Patti Deibert, featuring "Crow's Nest Chili"
7. Dan Bradley, featuring "Thunderbolt Chili"
8. Joan Matthews, featuring "Take a Chance Chili"
9. Marti England, featuring "Classic Texas Chili"
10. Heidi Wisener, featuring "Zesty Chili"
11. Lynne Boettcher, featuring "Ring of Fire Chili"
12. Chester Dunn, featuring "Creole Chili"

Darla had to overcome one disappointment several weeks prior to the competition. Having studied the rules of several official chili organizations, she found out that "true" chili does not contain beans, macaroni, hominy, or any type of filler. Wanting Historic St. Peter's to feature authentically approved chili, Darla had hoped to follow the rules, thinking that the result would produce the most Christian type of chili. Having cornered all of the contestants and pleading with them to refrain from using fillers in their chili, people told her face-to-face that they wouldn't be interested in participating in that type of contest because their recipe always contains beans. By simply giving up and letting go of that restriction she rounded up twelve willing and excited contestants. She also gave up on the words of an American country music artist, Jerry Jeff Walker, who said "If you know beans about chili, you know chili has no beans." Darla told Will that after going from twelve "no" responses that catapulted into twelve "yes" responses, Jerry Jeff Walker and those official chili organizations don't know a hill of beans about church chili competitions. Darla told a couple of the members that Will reminded her, "Babe, remember, this ain't Texas."

Entertaining everyone with music were Granny Sullivan and her four banjo player sons, "The Nitpickers," who can out-pick any banjo performance group. Their music totally livened up Woolcox Hall. The group performs throughout

Oswald County and although Granny is elderly and the "boys" are all in their six-ties, they have not lost any of their appeal and retain as much popularity as ever. Darla, of course, requested that they play the traditional folk song, "The Yellow Rose of Texas," at the appropriate time, when she gave them the "go ahead."

At the opening of the competition, Darla stepped onto the stage and wel-comed everyone to the annual event. In her hand were a few index cards. Everyone was seated and the crowd was quiet, but they, most likely, were not listening to her words, but staring at her amazing fashion style. Darla resembled, if there was such, an actual "Yellow Rose of Texas." Having dressed in a mid-length white dress with long sleeves, Darla wore a bold, one-of-a-kind statement necklace. It consisted of shiny yellow and grey chunky beads that were interspersed with Czech crystals, drawing the eye to the single large yellow hand-carved rose placed in the centre. The totally unique necklace definitely was a cut above anything one could purchase at LeRoy Edward's Western Wear. On her feet were rhinestone studded silver cowgirl boots. It was not difficult to spot Will in the crowd, as he had on a silver metallic shirt with tight denim jeans, a rhinestone belt buckle, and his favourite well-worn cowboy boots. By looking at the two of them, attendees realized that their efforts brought sunshine to a gloomy winter's night. Darla kept it from being a boring event. Some churches have colourless, sleepy events, sim-ilar to a roll of wallpaper on a ninety-percent off sale in the paint shop that has little white flowers on a beige background. If someone were to attempt to hang up that wallpaper in a bedroom, just the look of it would have the power to put them to sleep long before the project was completed. A bedroom with that wall-paper could come in handy for some sleep-deprived people as it could function as a sleep aide, better than any sleeping pill available at the pharmacy. Not Historic St. Pete's. They know better ways that keep their members awake!

People ate as many samples of chili as they wanted, along with rolls and but-ter. Each attendee carefully and thoughtfully seemed to mark their ballots and then dropped them in the big yellow box. The results of this vote were to determine the People's Choice Award. Three judges, two from out of town and one local, delib-erated and chose who was to be awarded first, second, and third place. First place went to Dan Bradley for his "Thunderbolt Chili," second to Heidi Wiesmar for her "Zesty Chili," and third to Carmen De Vault for "Suzie's Chili." The people's choice award went to Joan Matthews for her "Take a Chance Chili," most likely due to the fact that she is an active member of the Ladies' Guild and the room was full of senior citizens who didn't want to try anything spicy. They all seemed to navigate naturally to Joan's very bland cooking style.

After "The Nitpickers" finished up one of their songs, Darla gave them the signal to play "The Yellow Rose of Texas." Will and Darla took their place on her emcee stand and the two danced, almost as though they were a bride and groom at their wedding reception. Because it was so adorable, many in the crowd took photographs of them, and also secretly wished that they could dance with their partners like that, could dress like that and could live their lives more colourfully by leaving behind the bland-beige patterns of their everyday lives. Many people talked about the Bungard's well-rehearsed Western dance, saying that it was so well done and so elegant that it could have been featured in a dance competition on television. Most agreed that viewing the dance between Darla and Will was worth the price of their ticket alone.

When all was done for the day, Darla ended, much as she began, by repeating the verse from the Psalms, "This is the day the Lord has made, let us rejoice and be glad in it." She mentioned that she was especially glad that it ended so well and also glad that it is over with for another year.

At 11:20 p.m. Finley sat up and told me that he is feeling better. He enjoyed a bite from the fresh roll that I brought back from the chili competition. He said that sometime next week he'll return to journaling. He thanked me again for helping him and said that I deserve some well-earned rest.

– Ruby Newcastle

SUBSEQUENT TO CONSUMING EACH OF THE TWELVE VARIETIES OF CHILI OFFERED AT THE chili competition last evening, Marvin Clarke was intent today to converse with several of HSP's members about his satisfying experience at the event. While discreetly hiding behind a bag of ice melt located in one corner of the church entryway, a village mouse by the name of Kipp overheard Marvin's puffed-up words claiming that, "God has given me an ironclad stomach," and after that he boasted, "I was the only one in attendance that consumed all twelve types." Snack, who happens to be Kipp's pal, was hiding behind a church pillar during worship this morning when he saw Marvin jolt up from his pew. The choir was in the middle of singing "I Need a Second Helping of Your Spirit, Lord, Today" when Marvin trotted out of the sanctuary sporting a peculiarly awkward stride. As he took mini baby steps, both of his shoes shuffled on the floor, and his legs were tightly held together. Marvin's pace was slow, deliberate, and cautious, but his facial expression showed signs of crisis, urgency, and discomfort. Snack, along with everyone else who was watching him, spotted these tell-tale signs and knew that he was headed to the washroom. Marvin's sudden digestive distress really put him in an embarrassing situation due to the side effects of chili gluttony. After Marvin returned to the sanctuary, he was able to walk normally, but it was noticeable that he transported along with him the scent of cinnamon spice air freshener.

After writing about Marvin Clarke's discomfort this morning due to his emergency bowel explosion, I had my fill of recording church work. To get refreshed, I spent the day with Finley. Together we decided that in a few days I could stay at home and be his recording secretary, writing down whatever he wants in his journal. He mentioned that he would like to record his ancestry, since it has never been written down.

At 11:30 p.m. Finley and I snacked on morsels of the day-old roll from yesterday's chili competition. Before we fell asleep we talked about the cause and effect of Marvin's chili gluttony by breaking the word gluttony into three parts— glut, ton, and knee. Finley thought that part one, a superabundance of food combined with part two, a measurement of vast weight, adds up to part three, health problems with human knees, mainly knee bursitis from obesity. After that he added that we had better look out for Pastor Osterhagen as he really enjoys his food and might be at risk of developing "vicar's knees" or "preacher's knees," common to clergy because of all the repetitive kneeling. After that discussion we fell asleep, happily keeping toasty in each other's paws on this cold winter's night.

– Ruby Newcastle

Thursday, January 29

TWO MICE, LEWIS AND CLARK, CAME TO SEE FINLEY THIS AFTERNOON. THEY ARE EXPERT explorers and are ready to tackle the mystery as to why there are loose, wiggly floor boards in the sanctuary. Discussing with Finley their plans to make their way underneath the floor boards in order to explore and map the territory, Finley reminded them that safety is the first priority. He expressed that if it appears to be too dangerous, just turn around and abandon the expedition. Lewis and Clark admire and respect Finley and listen to his advice. Finley, in turn, gave them his blessing, but told them to proceed cautiously.

Three of our mouse friends, Bentley, Harmony, and their brand new baby, Linwood, came over to visit us today. Bentley reported that he saw the copy machine repairman return to St. Peter's today to clean and repair the mess left by the toner explosion. He heard the repairman say that he couldn't believe his eyes at the damage, admitting that it is in such a mess it will take hours of work to clean and repair it. He began to wipe clean every little part, of which there were dozens. When finished, he explained to Pastor Osterhagen that whoever did this must not be very bright. He pleaded with Pastor to forbid that person from ever touching the copy machine again. Pastor told him that he could not do that because he doesn't know who was responsible for the mess. The repairman explicitly explained that if this happens once again the church will have to get a contract someplace else for copy machine repairs and maintenance.

After hearing about the copy machine dilemma, I spent the rest of the day visiting with Finley. His mind is coming clear as to how to approach dictating his ancestry to me. His energy is coming back as he feels a bit better.

At 11:30 p.m. we snacked on the remaining morsels of our stale roll from the chili competition.

– Ruby Newcastle

A CONCERT WAS HELD AT HISTORIC ST. PETER'S TONIGHT PRESENTED BY TWO SETS OF brothers from Eastern Tennessee, an Appalachian folk singing group called "The Cobblers and the Coopers." The quartet sang several traditional ballads that included "Barbara Allen" and "Sourwood Mountain," but many of the songs were original compositions created by a member of the quartet, Paulie Cooper. Paulie is a gifted song-writer with an intrinsic talent for creating appealing texts and singable tunes, some of which possess a hauntingly beautiful sound. The mice community joined along with the concert goers in the applause at the end of the concert. One of the mice, Little Lady Slipper, asked me if the people in heaven listened to the concert and applauded along with us from heaven above. I didn't know how to answer her question, but I told her that I hoped so. Everyone in attendance was enthralled with the quartet's story-telling ballads that were decorated with musical embellishments. Their ballads were stories of love, family, troubles, life, and faith.

Earl and Gwyn Wright, members of Historic St. Peter's, were present at tonight's concert. They pop up at all of the events, but have not attended a worship service, even once. Because Earl is quite rotund, he doesn't fit in a church pew and cannot sit on a regular folding chair as it might instantly collapse under that amount of pressure. For safety reasons, several years ago the Wrights purchased an oversized wing-back chair with cushy armrests from Gilbert's Furniture Store and had it delivered directly to St. Pete's. The "wing" is positioned against the back wall of the sanctuary just in case the Wrights ever decide to attend a worship service. However, when there is an event going on at the church, Earl's chair becomes mobile by travelling around the building to be of service to him. It was easily transported by his sturdy wife Gwyn from the sanctuary to Woolcox Hall this evening so that Earl would have a place to sit while he enjoyed the refreshments even more than the music.

Miss Sassafras, Ruby's close friend, kept out of sight by hiding behind an industrial-sized push broom in Woolcox Hall during the reception. She heard Pastor's voice and peeked out to see that he was sitting at a table with the Wrights. During their conversation, Miss Sassafras heard Pastor ask them a question that he must have wanted to ask for quite some time: "Is there a reason as to why you attend the events at the church, but do not attend worship services?" Miss

Sassafras was stupefied when she heard Earl tell Pastor that the reason they don't attend church is because neither of them enjoys peering at the backs of people's heads, really the only thing that there is to look at in church. After the Wrights gave Pastor that cheeky answer, they burst out in roaring laughter, followed by a changing of the subject. Miss Sassafras later heard Pastor thoughtfully ask the Wrights if they would like to receive Holy Communion at their home. After he offered that, both Earl and Gwyn mentioned that they have been missing out on receiving Holy Communion, something very meaningful and precious to them. They welcomed Pastor to come to their house and thanked him several times for being willing to give them communion in their home. Pastor asked them if Tuesday afternoon would be a good time, and they agreed to that.

After the reception was over, Clement walked back to the parsonage and sat down with Aia. Aia listened to him as he grumbled a bit about the Wrights lack of church attendance versus their perfect attendance at events. He added that they do not even count as "irregular" attendees, as they do not even show up at Christmastime or Easter.

After Aia listened to Clement, she advised him to come to terms with the fact that he won't get a straight answer out of the Wrights, evidenced by the manner in which they answered his question today. She suggested to Clement that he not bring about any inclement weather by asking them that question again, but instead be merciful with the Wrights. She said that for now the Wrights must think they have every right not to attend worship services. Aia suggested bestowing on them the eight blessings in the Beatitudes found in Matthew Chapter Five, as they might be "poor in spirit." Aia's words of encouragement to Clement were to give it some time, pray about the Wrights attending church, and wait to see what happens next.

At 10:30 p.m. Miss Sassafras knocked on our door and brought Finley and myself two chocolate sprinkles that had fallen off of a chocolate glazed doughnut from tonight's reception. She told us all of her observations from the big event tonight at HSP so I could write them down.

– Ruby Newcastle

FINLEY AND I PLAYED HOOKY FROM CHURCH TODAY AND WE UNASHAMEDLY ADMIT IT. When we skip church, it is usually because there will be a substitute organist. But that was not the case today; we were just too tired. Noticing when parishioners are absent from worship, St. Peter's head usher, Fitz Woolsey, unsoundly presumes that it must be because of sickness. Fitz's pattern and quest is to track down the person the following Sunday, quiz them about their health issues, and offer suggestions to improve their health. Each time he does this he advocates the health benefits of using diluted Oil of Oregano, specifically the wild Mediterranean type, to keep them in tip-top health, claiming that it cures everything from muscle pain to warts. The mice in our village are extra thankful that we don't have anyone breathing down our necks like that. What those people go through is nothing short of inner turmoil, exactly the same nervousness people face when they cross an international border and the guard interrogates them about where they are going, the reason why, and who exactly is the owner of the vehicle. Parishioners would not be troubled about an usher cross-examining them if they were accustomed to lying, though some Christians might feel they are breaking the Eighth Commandment. But if they could reveal the honest-to-goodness truth, it might sound like this: "We skipped church today because of a mountain of laundry that needed our time and attention. No one in the family even had a clean undie or a pair of socks to wear to church." But, one just can't say that sort of thing to an usher, especially Fitz Woolsey. Finley and I are convinced that it is far too blunt and too-too honest to divulge the cleanliness status of your personal undergarments to anyone, anywhere, especially at church.

Finley has the strength to dictate as much as he can about his family history today, mentioning that he has a gut feeling that we should get going on it right away.

Finley can trace his ancestry very far back because of older oral traditions. Many of his forefathers and mothers were on Viking ships that landed in Vinland, the Norse Viking settlement at L'Anse aux Meadows, on the northernmost tip of Newfoundland, which dates back to the year 1000. This accounting comes from the sagas, as mice, too, had their own sagas. At that point, the mice also were bilingual, speaking Mouse and Old Norse. When the Vikings gave up on their settlement three years later and sailed away on their Viking ships back home to

Greenland, the mice stayed behind, making a new life in a new land. Their descendants eventually migrated far and wide to other parts of North America. In 1982 many mice considered going back to their roots by boarding the Hjemkomst (meaning "homecoming") Viking Ship replica, when it planned to sail from Duluth, Minnesota to Oslo, Norway. At mice meetings the possibility was heavily weighed and discussed. All in attendance voted unanimously to let this opportunity pass by, just like their ancestors did when the Vikings returned to Greenland.

They did come up with a wonderful idea, though, about having a mouse family reunion. It would take place at L'Anse aux Meadows, a Natural Historic Site in Canada, a place of major significance and part of their roots. Additionally, it would be a learning and cultural experience for them to see the sod dwellings and workshops, hear how the Vikings lived, and see the artifacts. After all, this was home to their ancestors. All mice ended the meeting feeling excited about the upcoming plans.

Other relatives of Finley were part of the Roanoke Colony in Virginia. They were fortunate to witness the baptism of Virginia Dare on August 18, 1587, the first child of English parents baptized in the new world. Because the ill-fated Roanoke Colony became the Lost Colony, Finley's relatives were not captured or taken into any tribe, but instead quickly fled to all parts of the United States. They did not have time to carve anything into a post or tree like "Croatoan," or "Cro," as the English did.

A large portion of family members were from Oberndorf bei Salzburg, Austria. This is where it becomes a sticky, sensitive, and tender subject, definitely being the most uncomfortable part of their family history. It most likely is the reason why their ancestry has not been written down up to this point as it deals with shame and guilt. The year was 1818 and the St. Nicholas Parish organ was out of commission and totally unusable because some mice felt the need to sew their wild oats. Those mice were partying inside the organ, damaging organ parts, chewing holes in the leather of the bellows, and committing a lot of vandalism in there. The destruction was so great that the organ could not be used on Christmas Eve. Because of that, the world-acclaimed song, "Stille Nacht, Heilige Nacht," had to be sung with guitar instead of the organ. The mice were all to blame. They were so ashamed of themselves that the whole lot quickly fled to Denmark and caught a ship to the new world, hoping to forget their horrid past and find new opportunities and freedom in the United States from their sins and wrongdoings.

The UK is also home to many of Finley's kinsfolk, both living and dead, as there has been an ever-present village of Newcastle mice residing at a brewery there since its beginning. Finley considers the Newcastle side of his family heritage to be the most prestigious part, but he is far too tired to go into all of it right now. To keep it simple, the brewery's location in New Castle, Upon Tyne, UK, is only a short distance from the North Sea. At one point some of Finley's relatives kissed and waved goodbye to the relatives that wanted to remain living at the brewery, boarded a boat at the shipyard, and immigrated to the United States. Having said all of this, Finley is spent for the day and wants his rest. Just think, after all his dictation today, Finley has the least amount of words to say about the most important part of his ancestry, the Newcastle lineage. He closed by suggesting to you that you research it for yourself to obtain a general description of that brewery's history so that he doesn't have to tell you everything and it will save me the work of writing it all down.

Finley is emotionally exhausted from thinking about his descendants destroying an organ. He wept as he said, "How could they do that?" To Finley and myself, the inside of Historic St. Peter's organ is a holy place and we would never harm any part of it. We must chalk it up to the sins of our forefathers. Finley has decided that he is done dictating his family's ancestry. He had hoped to write down his genealogy also, but he does not want to take that project on any longer. Determined to look ahead, be a forward thinker, instead of being saddened by the past, is Finley's new resolution. I guess it is comparable to parishioners who prefer to be known as New Testament people instead of Old Testament people.

All last week Clement had been looking forward to today's Super Bowl. He was wearing his football jersey, sweat pants, and trusty slippers. We heard him tell Aia about his plans to respectfully and patriotically stand for the National Anthem (with his right hand on his heart), followed by parking himself permanently in his green leather recliner until the game was over. Right next to his recliner was a TV tray that contained a stash of his favourite snacks – hot cheese sticks from Wisconsin, a can of Cajun mixed nuts, teriyaki beef jerky, and two cold beers. Just as the soloist belted out the goosebump part of the song, "O'er the land of the free and the home of the brave," the Osterhagen telephone rang. Evidently that sound resulted in Clement feeling anything but free. Evelyn Deerfield was on the line needing his help. With many tears, she told him about her troubles. Andy, her husband, has cancer and had been keeping this news from her, but he could not keep it a secret any longer. Clement spent the next ninety minutes on the telephone missing out on the Super Bowl. He helped her to forgive Andy for not telling her about his cancer, trying to calm down her fears by ending the conversation with a prayer. All the mice felt empathetic for Evelyn and Andy, but more than that, they felt sorry for Clement as he doesn't get much time for leisure activities, even when he has done advance planning to carve out some time to be free and brave.

At 11:30 p.m. I travelled alone to the church youth room and found an abundance of deep dish pepperoni pizza morsels under the tables from the youth Super Bowl party. I quickly devoured a few gobbets and then gathered some and travelled back to Finley with my pizza gleanings. He so enjoyed what I brought him and it greatly improved his mood, up to a level of contentment. Finley is certain that pizza is a gourmet comfort food. He often mentions that he is jealous of human beings that can go to pizza buffet restaurants where there are so many different varieties of pizza available. While he was talking, I went deep into thought. I wondered if Finley might have some Italian blood in him, perhaps an overlooked or forgotten part of his ancestry. I pondered if some of his relatives might have boarded the exploration ship named *Matthew* that was navigated by the Italian hero Giovanni Caboto (John Cabot). My guess is that the sailors aboard Captain Cabot's ship probably enjoyed pizza on Friday nights, perhaps the way Aia makes it the Osterhagens's weekly "Happy Friday" main entrée. It would have been natural for the Italian sailors to have desired pizza. Without pizza they would have grown too homesick and heartsick for their fatherland. Lastly, I wondered if the *Matthew* might even have had on board a scaled-down version of an authentic brick oven for baking their pizzas.

– Ruby Newcastle

Monday, February 2 –
The Presentation of Our Lord
and the Purification of Mary

At noon today four women arrived at church to play cards and enjoy lunch together. Of course Agnes, "The Blabber," Toppler was present, along with Norma Lind and Milla Van Camp. A fourth lady was there, too, but the mice didn't recognize her, so they assumed that she must not be a church lady. After setting up a card table and four chairs in one small well-heated Sunday School room, they said grace together and ate their sandwiches. The mice who witnessed this gathering said that the card ladies must be environmentally conscious because the small paper lunch bags that held their sandwiches all looked alike. All were from the local pharmacy, the type of bags prescription medication containers come in. After lunch all four ladies folded up their paper prescription bags and tucked them into their handbags. In appearance they have a look about themselves that is somewhat unkempt as their hairdos are wickedly windblown plus they have decked themselves in their bummiest clothes. The afternoon conversation remained steady and lively as each one took on the role of a flibbertigibbet, telling tittle-tattle stories about people's lives. The mice fittingly dubbed the afternoon, "A three-hour wiggle-waggle of the tongues."

The afternoon continued on as the discussion focused on Pastor's wife's hairdo. Each one took a turn giving their opinion, and when combined it became one unanimous opinion. The three church ladies concluded that Aia needs to get a pixie haircut as it won't take very much time to fix it each morning. A pixie would look more like a "mommy" haircut, especially now that she is expecting another baby. Agnes said that one benefit of short hair is that it uses less shampoo and conditioner, which helps to stretch a dollar on a pastor's salary. Milla added that in a few months Aia's hair will be the length of Lady Godiva's and that she will practically be clothed in long hair. Adding to that, Norma said that Pastor must certainly be embarrassed of his wife's long hair. Their combined opinion was that Aia should get a Mia Farrow hairstyle, the one that Mia was recognizable for in the 1960's. Hashing around whether or not they should advise Aia of their opinion, they decided it was better to go directly to Pastor Osterhagen. But, for now, they decided to play a waiting game just in case Aia comes to her senses and gets a haircut, noting that hair only grows about one-half inch per month anyway.

Their remarks were viewed as unreasonable by the mice community. Dr. Theodore Simonson pointed out that the famous French artist Pierre-Auguste Renoir often featured women with very long hair in his paintings. His 1892 "Girls at the Piano" painting is evidence of Renoir favouring long hair on females. The mice concluded that, because Aia wears her hair in a crisp mid-length cut that she styles in a very attractive flip, she does not need to go to the beauty parlour to get a Mia Farrow pixie, an even better way to save money.

Milla recalled that when Pastor and Aia first arrived at Historic St. Peter's, one women in the washroom was overheard telling Aia that she doesn't look like a pastor's wife. Aia asked her, "What were you expecting?" The answer was, "Oh, someone very plain in appearance and dress, with short hair, and eyeglasses." The lady then proceeded to tell her, "Perhaps you and Pastor are not a good match for Historic St. Peter's. Most likely you will go to another parish within the year." When Aia heard this, it deeply hurt her feelings. After the not-so-kind lady left the washroom, one mouse heard Aia say under her breath, "as long as we live here I will not be listening to that woman."

At 11:30 p.m. Finley and I travelled to the small Sunday School room that was used for card club today and ate morsels of a bologna sandwich and some chocolate chip cookie crumbs. We guessed that all four card players brought exactly the same lunch from home. Finley has recovered and is now ready to be out and about. He will take over journaling from this point on.

– Ruby Newcastle

PASTOR DROVE AIA TO HER DOCTOR'S APPOINTMENT THIS AFTERNOON AND LEFT Gretchen at home with a babysitter. At this appointment they received more news than they expected. The doctor suspects that Aia is pregnant with twins, so he ordered an ultrasound to be taken to confirm this. After today's appointment, they headed to Clement's office so that they could talk quietly, without Gretchen interrupting them. They needed to process what they just heard.

Flaxseed, our village nutrition coach, overheard Aia tell Clement her thoughts on this news. Aia explained that because she is an only child, she is well aware of the disadvantages she experienced by not having a sibling. Aia said that she wanted one more baby so that Gretchen wouldn't be lonely or experience difficulty while socializing. Aia's childhood had some "only child" issues and she doesn't want that for their Gretchen. She wants Gretchen to have a sister or a brother, but now that plan has somehow turned into twins. Clement doesn't view this as a disappointment as he comes from a large family where he had three brothers and two sisters. He knows that twins run in his family as his great aunts are twins, and so are four of his first cousins. Aia took a big breath, looked at the twinkle in Clement's eyes, the loving smile on his face, and felt better, knowing everything will be what it is meant to be. She told Clement the only saying she has ever heard about twins is this: "Twins are twice as much to love, two blessings from above."

Ruby and I travelled to the church kitchen and snacked on morsels of spilled coffee grounds. That probably was not a wise idea. The caffeine is bound to interrupt our sleep tonight, sleep that is essential for our health so that we can live longer lives with abundant energy. Without deep sleep we'll miss out on our REM (rapid eye movement) sleep-cycle, therefore there will be no dreams tonight for Ruby and myself. We did overdo the caffeine. By the way, mice universally dream the same dream. The dream is all about cheese factories, cheese houses, and cheese chalets. Tonight we will lay awake and talk about the cheese facilities located in Wisconsin, Ohio, and Indiana, home to the abundant production of high caliber, distinctive cheeses. Just think, there are hundreds and hundreds of types of cheese made in just those three states, but cheese production is done in the other forty-seven states as well, which might mean that within the U.S. and Canada there are thousands and thousands of flavours of cheese.

    — F.N.

Saturday, February 7

A WHILE AGO CLEMENT HAPPENED UPON HIS TOY INDIAN TOM-TOM WHILE DIGGING through a box or two. The tom-tom was purchased at the reservation gift shop and is a souvenir from a boyhood trip. Long gone is the rubber tomahawk and the eagle feathers, but he kept the tom-tom with the silhouetted profile of a big chief emblazoned on the side of the drum. He brought it to the church a month ago to use in a children's talk about missions, sharing the Good News in word and in deed to other cultures, for example the Native Americans. The familiar song, "This Little Light of Mine," was sung to the beat of the tom-tom one Sunday last month. The distinct sound of the captivating drum beats attracted the attention of the mice village.

So, early last month, "The Ricochet Trampoline Club" was launched by a few members of our village. The club gathers in the nursery to sharpen their trampoline skills several times a week. Using Clement's childhood vintage drum (his "tom-tom") as their trampoline, they claim it is the best mid-winter entertainment available. Finding the drum to be anything but cheaply made, acutely durable, and wonderfully springy, the club members anxiously await their turns to practice their skills. Sessions on the trampoline have resulted in an anti-boredom movement that shakes away the winter blues from all of the club members. Individual members of the club talk about experiencing a gleeful euphoric high in their metabolism from all of the up and down jumping.

The entire mice village was invited to a high-flying trampoline show performed this evening by "The Ricochet Trampoline Club." We gathered together in the nursery where observers were hypnotized and wowed by the razzle-dazzle skyward performances. One female mouse in particular, Jilly Micklewhite, was the aerobatic superstar. Jilly has developed her skill so manifestly that her popularity is rocketing skyward. Tonight Jilly announced that she has adopted an appropriate stage name, Destiny Skye. It was a thrill to witness all of the performers, but especially to see Destiny's ability with her high flying twists and jumps. Her skyrocketing leaps almost appear as though she was born with wings.

After an evening of watching the tantalizing trampoline show, at 11:30 p.m. Ruby and I dashed to the parsonage and snacked on a tiny crumb of a snack cake. The *pièce de résistance* was patently the singular bite with the creamy filling.

– F.N.

VALENTINE'S DAY FALLS ON SATURDAY THIS YEAR. THIS MORNING PASTOR OSTERHAGEN and Gretchen passed out little Valentine cards that they prepared for the children who came up front to sit down and listen to Pastor's children's talk. Pastor captivated the children and Gretchen, too, with the true story of St. Valentine. They were all quiet and listened intently. Inside each Valentine card was a red foil-wrapped chocolate heart. Gretchen was so proud to share the Valentine cards with her friends that she helped make yesterday with her daddy.

At the end of the worship service, Pastor Osterhagen asked if there were any announcements. Darla Bungard left her pew, walked up to the chancel, and positioned herself at the pulpit microphone. She explained that a delightful idea came to her this morning while Pastor was speaking to the children. She enthusiastically talked about how it would be fabulously fun if St. Peter's adults would celebrate Valentine's Day together this year with a Sweetheart Dinner. She mentioned that since the holiday happens to fall on a Saturday night this year, most people can stay up late as they don't have to get up for work the next day. She mentioned that she would be happy to make arrangements for a private dining room at the Elkridge Mansion on Lake Harvey where the food is first-class. (Darla and Will, her husband, are close friends of the owners, having dined there dozens of times, always tasting excellent food.) Remarking that the ambience of Elkridge Mansion is absolutely resplendent during the winter season, Darla pointed out that the windows showcase the snow-capped pine trees that are illuminated with thousands of white lights. In the distance, one can see frozen Lake Harvey dotted with fishing houses.

Going on further, Darla remarked that Chef Axel O'Gara, who hails from the small Irish village of Tullywiggan, is the Mansion's Chef-in-Residence. She said that she is already privy to the Mansion's Valentine Dinner that will begin with a simple onion soup sweetened with apple cider, followed by a green salad dressed with the Elkridge Mansion's famous vinaigrette, which now happens to be sold in choice grocery stores throughout the state. Chef O'Gara will prepare his renowned crab-stuffed filet mignon with brandy peppercorn sauce, Irish Potato Drops which are a variation of the potato pancake, and spinach and mushroom squares drizzled with truffle oil. Noting that The Elkridge Mansion is renowned for their fancy dessert sampler plate, Darla described the contents of the sampler being a thin slice of Black Forest cake, a cream-stuffed fresh strawberry, along with a square of the delectable pink and white coconut ice, called Klapperys. Darla asked the members to speak with her on their way out of church or to call her before Tuesday, as she will need to make reservations early Wednesday morning. She touched on the fact that she will schedule the Sweetheart Dinner for 7 p.m. on Saturday, preceded by a cocktail hour at 6 p.m. After she finished promoting her ideas for the gathering, many people came up to her before they left church today and said that they wouldn't dream of missing the event. Not many parishioners shook hands with Pastor today because they were all so busy talking to Darla. Pastor just went to his office and hung up his robes.

Aia was one adult that did not approach Darla as she was having trouble with tears welling up in her eyes. After everyone left the building, Aia and Clement talked about what just happened and how unfortunate it is to sometimes have a member of the church who behaves like a cruise director. Aia told Clement that she had already made lots of plans for their Valentine's Day celebration, emphasizing, once again, how much she treasures holidays that are not plunked on the church calendar, like St. Patrick's Day, Halloween, Independence Day, and most especially Valentine's Day. She loves not having to share those days with the whole church. She has her heart set on their own little Valentine's party for just the three of them.

Clement shared with Aia the same feelings about going out to eat on Valentine's Day, but he knows the unwritten expectation, which is that the Pastor and his wife attend every event. He has a lot of trepidation about the cost of a fancy dinner at The Elkridge Mansion, which is not anywhere in the realm of their practical budget. Ruby and I have noticed that the Osterhagens rarely go to a restaurant, as Aia cooks abundant healthful meals at home. If they do happen to splurge and go out, it will likely be at a buffet restaurant. That way they can fill up and get their money's worth, especially if they go at lunchtime when the prices are lower than in the evening.

Aia told Clement that she has made plans to prepare their Valentine's dinner. She talked about making homemade pizza crust, chopping up a variety of veggies, and having plenty of meat lover's toppings and mozzarella on hand to prepare individual pizzas. She described how they would each form their own pizza crust in the shape of a heart by telling Clement that he could make his heart the largest, Aia's would be medium-sized, and Gretchen could make a baby-sized heart crust. Aia had already planned to prepare a simple green salad dressed with the Elkridge

Mansion's Vinaigrette, which she has already purchased at Grocer Dan's for this special occasion. Her plans were to end their meal with a heart-shaped chocolate cake with matching frosting, topped with strips of shaved chocolate. Clement understood that Aia has already put a lot of planning into a family-friendly Valentine's party and does not want to share this day with anyone but their family.

Because of her pregnancy, Aia is having a lot of wardrobe issues as many of her regular clothes are getting snug on her. She can't even imagine what she could wear to the Sweetheart Dinner, let alone putting effort into getting all dressed up to sit and visit for hours at a fancy restaurant. But that doesn't stop Aia from mentioning to Clement that Darla will once again be dressed to the nines, probably wearing a tight red leather blazer, black dress slacks, and red high heels. Clement and Aia decided together that they will not attend the Sweetheart Dinner, despite an upcoming telephone call that will come through this week from Darla. The "git-r-dun" girl will put pressure on them to attend Saturday's gathering.

At 11:30 p.m. Ruby and I travelled to the parsonage and snacked on a morsel of meatloaf and divided in half one kernel of corn.

− F.N.

AIA WAS EXPECTING TWO TELEPHONE CALLS TODAY, ONE FROM THE DOCTOR'S OFFICE, and the other one from Darla Bungard. When it rang after lunch today, her anxiety started up, hoping it wasn't Darla. It was the doctor's office saying that the test results came in and that she is definitely pregnant with twins. Instead of walking down the breezeway to Clement's office, it was faster to call him on the telephone to tell him the positive news. Aia told Clement that she felt like the most blessed woman in the world when she heard the news. She remembered hearing negative phrases about having twins, not from mothers of twins, but from other people, observers, who couldn't imagine what it would be like to have that responsibility. There are phrases about having twins like "double trouble," "you poor thing," and "you'll have your hands full." Those thoughts are not hers. All she felt was complete delight and thankfulness, and so does Clement.

Aia told Clement that she is doubly tired and hungry compared to when she was pregnant with Gretchen, but that's because there are two babies inside her instead of just one. Aia hung up the telephone with Clement, knelt down at the sofa, folded her hands and thanked God for these two babies, asking Him to bless their lives and to give her the strength to do all of the work she will need to do in the years ahead.

Not one mouse overheard anything about Darla pressuring the Osterhagens to attend the Sweetheart Dinner. Perhaps Darla just expects that Pastor and Aia will attend. It is still up in the air.

Ruby and I stayed home and snacked on a tiny part of a graham cracker we found on the sanctuary floor that must have fallen from a little one's snack container.

– F.N.

ONE PERTINACIOUS FEMALE IN OUR MOUSE VILLAGE HAS RECENTLY GONE TO THE DARK side, even though that place is the opposite of her beautiful name, Luminista. In the Romanian language, Luminista means, "Little Light." We all know that the dark side holds no light.

Luminista has set up shop in the church basement by creating a gypsy tent in which to hold readings with a crystal ball. This all came about after Cy Henderson, a parishioner who is an avid art glass marble collector, brought his green glow-in-the-dark marble to church last Sunday to show it off to several of his friends. Esko was quietly hiding near the basement stairs, peeked out from behind a door stopper and noticed Cy attempt to slip the marble back into his pocket, but missed. The marble dropped to the floor and rolled down the basement steps. Cy had no idea that his marble was not in his pocket, probably because it made no noise when it fell on the green carpet. Esko told me that he followed the marble downstairs and located it quickly because it was glowing bright green in the dark church basement. Being so enticed by the luminescence of the marble, he fetched his girlfriend, Luminista, to show it to her.

After seeing the unusual marble, Luminista put Esko to work helping her create an elaborate gypsy tent. Locating a square of psychedelic paisley fabric from the Ladies' Guild sewing area, Esko built and assembled a gypsy tent in the church basement, an area located behind a seldom used filing cabinet. Esko also crafted two signs for the tent. One was a business sign that said "Clairvoyant Madame Luminista" and another sign is a reversible open/closed sign. Being intensively creative, Luminista fashioned a pedestal base for her crystal ball, the art glass marble, out of cardboard. She placed that on top of a jute twine coaster. Underneath that was a red dish cloth that served as a rug for her customers to sit on while their fortune is to be read. Word has spread swiftly today throughout the village about "Clairvoyant Madame Luminista" and her new business establishment. Most mice are curious to find out from Madame her predictions about their future, especially about love and marriage, life, and babies. Many are hoping that crystal ball readings will fill holes in their hearts and minds so they don't feel so lost in life.

It is easy for all of us to see that Esko feels awfully sad inside. Luminista has basically ignored, or put on hold, their fun and romantic relationship because of her passionate and fiery interest in her new business establishment. She told Esko, without batting an eyelash, that she is "too busy to hang out right now and way too busy for love." Several of the mice who overheard Luminista say those words noticed that Esko's eyes were blinking wildly as he was attempting to hold back a bucketful of tears.

This might sound like progress to some, but many of the leaders in the mice village are skeptical about fortune telling and wonder if this practice might be condemned by the church or if it just creates a lot of unnecessary drama.

At 11:30 p.m. Ruby and I scampered over to the parsonage and found one bacon bit to split for our late night treat. Our conversation centered on the foods that fortune tellers might eat, wondering if the nutritionally right foods might increase the ability to see into the future. Ruby mentioned that a lifelong diet consisting of Andalusian Stew, Rabbit Pie, Gypsy Goulash, and Roasted Hedgehog might bring on crystal clear clairvoyant abilities.

– F.N.

St. Valentine's Day ~ Saturday, February 14

CLEMENT AND AIA ATTENDED THE SWEETHEART DINNER TONIGHT. THEY FINALLY buckled from the persistent pressure on Wednesday from Darla and said, "Yes," when they really wanted to say, "No." Together they had a conversation about why telling the truth doesn't seem to be allowed in some circumstances, and how that leads to a nagging feeling that somehow they had lied to Darla. They both wanted to say to the self-appointed church cruise director, "We won't attend the Sweetheart Dinner because we don't want to. We can't spend money at a fancy restaurant. We'd rather stay home. We don't want to hire a babysitter. We want to stay home with Gretchen and celebrate Valentine's Day with her." Sometimes the truth is just way too truthful. So tonight they wore their best clothing, arrived at the Elkridge Mansion prior to seven o'clock (skipping the Cocktail Hour to reduce costs), and arrived home around ten o'clock with too much rich food in their tummies. They were wired up and drained down by the evening's event, unable to calm down enough to go to sleep.

When they arrived home, Gretchen was sound asleep and so was Christine, the babysitter. The parsonage smelled like sugar cookies. Aia stepped into the kitchen and found that the counters were covered with dirty dishes and cookie sheets and that the floor was dusted with flour and red and pink Valentine sprinkles. When Christine awoke she apologized for the mess she left in the kitchen and said that she had intended to clean up after Gretchen was asleep, but that Gretchen needed her to stay with her until she fell asleep. Unfortunately, Christine fell sound asleep, too. Aia and Clement told Christine not to worry about the mess as they would deal with the cleanup in the morning.

At 11:30 p.m. Ruby and I travelled to the parsonage and snacked on morsels of heart sugar cookies and Valentine sprinkles. Our snack was so festive and special that I got over-excited and told Ruby right then and there in a very quiet voice in the parsonage kitchen, *"Mqvv plv xxat, Uupz,"* which, once again, means, "I love you, Ruby." She told me that I am her Valentine. We usually don't speak when we are at the parsonage, as we don't want the Osterhagens to hear us. But this time, the words just came spilling out of me. I think that the three Osterhagens were too tired tonight to hear us anyway.

– F.N.

PASTOR MADE AN ANNOUNCEMENT IN CHURCH THIS MORNING THAT SPARKED THE interest of the members. As a result, there was a great deal of enthusiasm for an upcoming event. Many weeks ago he had contacted the Von Engelberger Singers in New Jersey and invited them to sing at Historic St. Peter's, whatever Sunday would fit into their schedule. Clement received a response on Saturday to his invitation which said that they would be delighted to sing at Historic St. Peter's on Sunday morning, May 3. (This news was so hot-off-the-press that a committee has not even been formed yet to take care of all the details.) Darla Bungard approached Pastor after church today and told him not to worry about anything, as she will make all of the arrangements for a spectacular dinner following the worship service, mentioning that it will have a German-Bavarian flare to it. She assured him that everyone, including the Von Engelberger Singers, will enjoy this festive day here at St. Pete's. Pastor thanked her for her enthusiasm at volunteering to make the event extra-special. He told her that food service is not one of his strengths. He also told her that he is thankful for her gifts, especially the gift of hospitality, adding that his worries about church functions that include a meal virtually disappear when she is at the helm. Darla thanked him for his kind words and gave Pastor a hug.

In writing my journal, I have purposefully decided not to write down anything about the subject of money. Money appears to be an all-time favourite topic at St. Pete's board meetings, especially when it comes to counting and measuring nickels, dimes, and even the wee pennies. At first the mice tried to have an interest in money discussions, but soon realized that there are advantages and disadvantages to listening to or even learning from these conversations. One group will want to raise money, but only squirrel it away in the bank for years to come. Another group will want to spend every bit they have. Some groups are right in the middle, where they will spend some and save some. During observations at HSP, the mice have concluded that the formulating of budgets must be lacking the benefits of blessings and joys. They just appear to be an albatross, a millstone around the parishioner's necks, a woe leading to misery, another one of the crosses that they need to bear. The mice are agreed that church budgets end up being extremely distressing and unpleasant, something that everyone wants to keep their distance from. Skat, one of our younger mice, said that because of all of the talk at church about the "budget" he has made a connection to something in the English language that is referred to as the "B" word. Skat said that he is certain that the "B" word means "Budget." Many of the faces of the mice took on an appearance as though the weight of an actual moose was standing on top of their noses because their eyes were opened so widely after hearing Skat's very, very perceptive deduction explained. From now on the "B" word is no longer a baffling mystery in our village, thanks to Skat. We now have the skinny on that one. Today we learned that we need to listen to the younger ones because sometimes they are more insightful than those of us who have been around a long time. Some of us have become crusty and cantankerous due to being so staunchly set in our ways.

Squirreling away money leads to discussions about how the church cannot afford anything. The thought is that if they spend the money they have, the church will lose their feeling of safety and independence. Keeping the money in the bank is thought to eliminate future worries, making them feel that they have some power over it and are still in control. Spending the church's money can have a positive effect, as the church won't be missing out on pastoral opportunities and social interactions. Having money to spend alters the ideas of what work really needs to be done. Jonathan Swift, who became the Dean of St. Patrick's Cathedral in Dublin, said it best when he is quoted as saying, "A wise man should have money in his head, but not in his heart." FYI, there is a lot of talk about money at church, but I won't be mentioning it ever again. It doesn't matter if there is too much, too little, or just the right amount of it, most people just love to talk and thrash about the numbers. Some people are just non-stop number-oriented. We mice feel very sorry for them in so many ways. (So much for my resolve to write nothing about money.)

At 10:45 p.m. Ruby and I travelled to the parsonage and snacked on a tiny morsel of crispy chicken that missed hitting the waste basket after the Osterhagen's supper. God provides.

– F.N.

IMMEDIATELY AFTER EATING A HEALTHY, EXTREMELY LOW-CALORIE "BREAKING-OF-THE-fast" breakfast, consisting of plain yogurt, sliced fresh strawberries imported from Mexico, and strong black coffee, Clement put on his coat and hurriedly said goodbye to Aia and Gretchen. We watched him head out the door, sporting a gait very much like a man on an accomplishment-minded mission.

Today is not a regular old Tuesday, but Shrove Tuesday, a day of feasting and celebration before the lengthy season of Lent begins. After arriving at his destination, Zuzanna's Polish Bakery, Clement later told Aia that he was eager to purchase three paczki (pronounced "poonch-key"): one for himself, one for Aia, and one for Gretchen. He stood patiently in the cold, dreary weather in a line that had formed outside the bakery door. He was extra-determined that he would return home with the traditional Shrove Tuesday paczki. During this unusual free time, we suspect that Clement must have had the opportunity to think some things over by reminding himself of what they talked about at breakfast, that his mission was to purchase three paczki; one rosehip paczki for Aia, one chocolate-filled one for Gretchen, and one Bavarian Cream paczki for himself. As he looked at the display in the bakery window, it didn't take very long for him to change his mind from a small purchase of only three paczki, to a full baker's dozen of thirteen paczki. After reading the bakery marquee advertising Shrove Tuesday's special, "PURCHASE ONE DOZEN PACZKI, GET ONE DOZEN FREE," he walked out of Zuzanna's Polish Bakery the proud owner of way more than three paczki.

Clement later told Aia that he overcame his doubt about his large purchase by communicating to her that this is what every single Osterhagen would have done if found in this particular situation on Shrove Tuesday. Each year the Osterhagens observe the proper time, the day before Ash Wednesday, to delight in this very special, sweet, and traditional part of Polish cuisine and culture, even though they are not of Polish descent. The rich, calorie-laden dough is deep-formed into a sphere, after being filled with delicious fruit or custard, and then enters the depths of a deep fryer, lastly being sprinkled with sugar. A paczki is similar to a doughnut, but far, far more flavourful and better tasting because it is usually made from a centuries-old recipe, which often includes a dash of spirits. This year Zuzanna's Polish Bakery had a wide variety of paczki fillings to choose from. Clement made decisions from the following flavours: plum, spiced apple, raspberry, Bavarian Cream, rosehip, strawberry, custard, prune, lemon, apricot, blueberry, cherry, chocolate, strawberry, cream cheese, or ricotta. A new and flashy flavour this year at Zuzanna's Polish Bakery was mango, but Clement told Aia that particular flavour will most likely be a big flop in loyal paczki customer circles.

For the first fifty customers at Zuzanna's Polish Bakery this morning, customers received a baker's dozen of thirteen paczki, instead of the regular twelve, along with another thirteen, if they so desired. Pastor spent a few minutes visiting with Zuzanna, but told Aia it was so busy inside the bakery, or piekarnia, as Zuzanna calls it, he decided to cut the conversation short by telling her that he would see her at church tomorrow for Ash Wednesday's worship service.

Aia questioned Clement as to what they will ever do with twenty-six paczki. Because they come in at roughly five hundred calories each, Aia told Clement that she will not consume more than one paczki this year because she is already so terribly worried about her figure and what she will look like after the twins are born. She even took the conversation so far to as to ask Clement if he was going to have his own paczki-eating contest today. If so, she told him he could have headed downtown to Jakub's Pub where an official contest is being held. Most champions consume around eighteen to twenty paczkis, alongside pints of beer, all within the one hour allotted time period. Clement expressed to Aia that his intentions were to wrap them up individually in plastic sandwich bags and freeze them. He will take one along with him every time he goes on a shut-in visit. It will be kind to take them something besides the weekly bulletin, the monthly calendar, a daily devotional booklet, and most importantly, Holy Communion. Aia realized that Clement's heart and tummy are in exactly the right place, and told him that she admires what he is doing.

After that, Aia steeped a pot of Irish tea, on the strong side, and told Clement, because it is Shrove Tuesday, she would enjoy two paczki this year, one for each of the twins. She chose one rosehip paczki and one plum paczki, her favourite-forever flavours. As they enjoyed their Shrove Tuesday delicacy, Aia told Clement that next year they must attend the town's Mardi Gras parade. After all, they live right by the official parade route. If they miss out on it again next year, it could easily be compared to arriving at the Grand Canyon and refusing to exit the tour bus to see an overwhelmingly immense hole. Clement told Aia that his Granny Selena, due to lack of interest, grouchiness, and over-all fatigue, actually did that exact same thing when she went along with his parents and siblings to see to the Grand Canyon. She remained in the van the entire time while the family felt guilty spending time being inspired and amazed as they viewed the giant spectacle without her. Clement revealed that it is still overwhelming to him, and his family, too, when looking back at his granny's behaviour. It most likely can all be explained, Clement said, by the fact that she was always an unusual sort of woman. He asked Aia who else would serve pickled herring with Passover matzos, along with elderberry wine, to her guests any season of the year, summer, fall, winter or spring, and she wasn't even Jewish.

Clement asked Aia if elderberry wine, herring, and matzos even came close to constituting a good wine and food pairing. Aia shrugged her shoulders, ignored his question as she looked deeply at Clement's eyes and facial features, noticing how very handsome he is. She felt steamy today, probably due to some aphrodisiac ingredient in the paczki. Aia said that perhaps they should both enter the paczki eating contest next year because she likes the feeling she has after eating that delicacy. Aia knew quite a bit about the competitive eating rules of the contest from what was printed in "The Oswald County Gazette." She explained that it requires a fifteen dollar entrance fee and lasts exactly one hour, with no getting up from your spot, for any reason. The winner's photograph each year is hung on the Pub's "Paczki Hall of Fame." Aia told Clement that it is actually a really big honour in Oswald County to have your winning photograph hung up at Jakub's Pub.

Clement said that people have enjoyed Paczki Day since the Middle Ages, reminding her of the fine art book they own which includes the painting by Pieter Brueghel the Elder in 1559, "The Fight Between Carnival and Lent," of a community depicted in the Southern part of the Netherlands. Both of them discussed the struggle between enjoyment and the religious observances of Lent. Aia told Clement she intends to give up complaining for Lent, and Clement told Aia that he intends to give up so many evening meetings. They encouraged each other on their Lenten journey, saying that, after all, it is only forty days and forty nights, and Sundays don't count.

At 11:30 p.m. Ruby and I travelled to the parsonage and snacked on morsels of rosehip, plum, Bavarian Cream, and spiced apple paczki which must have dripped a bit on the floor while Clement and Aia were packaging up the extras for the freezer. Ruby and I agreed that we are totally spoiled living next to the Osterhagens, who have exquisite culinary palates. Tonight's morsels made us feel like being close and intimate. We also wondered what the Grand Canyon must look like. When we have time, we will ask Dr. Theodore Simonsen to research that. It must be a popular sight, but we think it is basically appealing to people who are not elderly grandmothers that are very tired.

    – F.N.

AFTER OPENING UP THE PARSONAGE DOOR TO THE BREEZEWAY THIS MORNING, CLEMENT'S troubles increased as he saw that the breezeway floor had been sprinkled with a profusion of New Year's Eve paper confetti. He took a walk throughout the church and discovered most surfaces and floors were scattered with the stuff. The Osterhagens had slept well last night and did not hear a sound. Once again, the church gremlin, "Griffin," played a trick on the church by making it messy, even on Ash Wednesday. Griffin obviously has a master key to the church. Clement telephoned Property Director, Will Anderly, and reported the problem to him. Will told him that he'll get a locksmith out here today in order to stop this type of devilry.

We heard Clement tell Aia that if she would be so kind to get the church vacuum out and get busy hoovering up as much of the confetti that she can, he'll take them to North Carolina for their next vacation to The Andy Griffith Museum in Mt. Airy, North Carolina. Another stop will be at a historical pickle factory that is located in another small town on the corner of Sweet Pickle Street and Dill Pickle Avenue. It was no problem for Aia to dive into the clean-up project with Gretchen by her side. Gretchen helped, too, by going over and over the carpet using her toy vacuum cleaner.

Ash Wednesday worship this evening was well attended. Everyone who was present at the worship service received ashes in the sign of the cross on their foreheads, marking the beginning of the liturgical forty day season of Lent. Ashes remind them of their mortality and that they are dust. Josie, the organist, seemed to be sick with a severe cold, as she covered her mouth with a tissue each time she wasn't playing the organ. She kept a tea tumbler next to her to quench her sore throat.

Most in attendance were parishioners, but one woman showed up, whom Pastor Osterhagen recognized as Yolanda, an employee of the City Utilities Department. Each month Clement walks to the Utility Department to pay his bill and Yolanda waits on him. Clement noticed when they shook hands after worship tonight that her appearance looked quite different than it usually does at the Utility Department. Tonight she wore a very fashionable, trendsetting, green winter coat, carrying along an over-sized shiny black designer purse. Yolanda complimented Pastor on his excellent sermon and then asked him if she could have a few minutes of his time to receive private confession and absolution. He agreed to that and told her to come to his office in a few minutes. Yolanda found his office and waited in there for him. Clement arrived and was ready to hear her private confession. As he was speaking, she unbuttoned her green winter coat and removed it, exposing a very low-cut dress which showed him a thing or two that any man would have to be completely blind not to notice. She placed her large open purse on his desk and took out a video box. Clement looked it over and recognized Yolanda's picture and name as one of the "stars." She asked Pastor Osterhagen if it was wrong to be a part of this smutty movie, since she was only acting and didn't actually do this in real life. While answering her question, Clement quickly stood up and opened the door. He used a phrase about "the flesh and the spirit," reminded her about the meaning of the ashes, and quickly gave her the card of a female pastor in town that does counselling.

After Yolanda left, Pastor came home and told Aia about the incident. Together they decided that from then on it would be worth the price of a stamp to simply mail their utility bill, even though the Utility Department is only three blocks from the church.

Ruby and I travelled to the parsonage at 11:30 p.m. and snacked on a minuscule morsel of a fish stick that fell on the floor from the Osterhagen's supper. While we ate, Ruby and I spoke softly about the word "smutty" and concluded that, to our knowledge, the word only applies to jokes, not to movies. We decided that "Smutty" must be the title of the film, or the name of the main character, possibly the Yankton Sioux chief Smutty Bear.

    – F.N.

OUR EXPERT MICE EXPLORERS, LEWIS AND CLARK, HAVE BEEN STEADILY AND methodically getting a bit closer to figuring out why HSP's sanctuary floor boards are loose and wiggly in one particular area. As a follow-up to the Annual Mice Meeting held in January where they were commissioned to begin an exploration, Lewis and Clark needed to seek out Finley today to discuss their conclusions. Having gone partway underneath the floor boards, they found their first discovery or clue, perhaps something that might be of vital importance. It was a handwritten note. They don't quite understand the contents of the note, which might not be important at all, perhaps something that fell out of someone's pocket. However, we know that the information on the note contained words that were used by the Underground Railroad during the years surrounding the Civil War in the United States, the effort that brought escaped slaves northward to freedom. The note contained specific words like "North Star," "Safe house," "Station," "Stop," and "Midnight." Some parts of the note were written in a secret code or language hinting that St. Peter's members might have helped the slaves that came their way. Lewis and Clark knew better than to touch the note. Perhaps it is an artifact from the actual time when slaves followed the North Star to find freedom in Canada. They memorized the contents of the note, left it in its place, and told Finley what was written on it.

The second discovery during their expedition was the size of the space directly underneath the sanctuary floor boards. The capacity in there was large enough to hide several people if they were to lie flat and rest on their backs. Against one edge of the wall was a small, old-fashioned hymnbook. The hymnal was open to the song, "Shall We Gather at the River." Finley, Lewis, and Clark put their heads together and talked through these discoveries all afternoon and evening. At the end of the day, they logically made a decision that slaves came to the "Station" for safety, and that Historic St. Peter's was used by these slaves as their secret "Station." Finley remembered hearing that during that time period bounty hunters would come to the church looking for escaped slaves. Ushers were constantly on duty peering out the church windows to see if any bounty hunters were heading toward the church. When they were spotted, someone would interrupt whatever was going on and say, "Sing." The congregational insider code was only one word, "sing." At that point, they would loudly break out singing the spiritual, "Shall We Gather at the River." After floor boards were hurriedly lifted up, the runaways crawled beneath the floor boards to quietly hide, positioning themselves flat on their backs on the sub-floor, and were covered over by the top floor boards. They remained there until the bounty hunters left, disappointed again at coming up empty-handed.

The third find did not come from the hiding place underneath the sanctuary floor boards, but was found in an old wooden box in the church basement. Among the piles of dusty, old, spider-web encrusted boxes they found a wooden box that contained very old, out-dated HSP documentation. It had the word "Station" painted on it. Lewis and Clark found a small hole in one side of the box and discovered that it contained records about the runaways that Historic St. Peter's had assisted on their way to seeking freedom. The three of them decided this find should be made known and preserved, as the contents are a pivotal component of the history of the United States.

I told them how grateful I was for their efforts. I asked them to help with the effort to get the news of this discovery to Pastor Osterhagen who will know just how to proceed. After much discussion, we decided that they need to come up with a blank piece of paper, write a note on it, and slip it under Pastor Osterhagen's office door. I will carefully and thoughtfully ponder over the exact words to write on the note. For now, Lewis and Clark need to go as soon as possible to the church office in an attempt to bring back a plain sheet of paper.

At 11:30 p.m. Ruby and I travelled to the parsonage and snacked on a morsel of broiled brown-sugared grapefruit.

– F.N.

Friday, February 20

WHEN PAULETTE PAULSON, THE ONE-DAY-A-WEEK CHURCH SECRETARY ARRIVED FOR work this morning, Lewis and Clark quietly waited for their chance to enter the church office for the purpose of obtaining an 8 ½ x 11 inch sheet of plain white paper. The first thing Paulette consistently does after she arrives at the church office is to check the telephone messages to see if there is anything important, newsy, or gossipy that has come in. After that Paulette's pattern is to turn on the computer, the copier, and the coffee pot. She refers to this routine as "The Three C's."

Her Friday arrival sequence at HSP is to proceed to the ladies' washroom with a comb, hand-held mirror, and a can of hairspray. She has arrived at work on time, but she has not finished primping for the day. She usually spends fifteen minutes in there, as her hairdo is an important project. After weeks of the mice observing Paulette's morning routine, Lewis and Clark are familiar with her timing. After she exits the washroom, her hairdo looks vastly improved from the moment she entered the washroom. Walking down the hallway she emits the fragrance of hairspray.

While Paulette was preoccupied with fixing her hairdo, Lewis and Clark took this as a prime opportunity to obtain one sheet of paper. Luckily, Paulette left the office supply cupboard door open when she headed to the washroom. Placed on the bottom shelf of the cupboard was a stack of copy machine paper. Lewis and Clark worked quietly and carefully, but after obtaining a sheet of paper they launched into breakneck speed. As they hurried from the church office they looked similar to an airplane building up speed on an airport runway. Practically in flight, they ran as fast as they could while gripping tightly on to two of the corners of the sheet of paper with their mouths. Behind them the sheet of paper also took flight because of their whirlwind speed. That paper flew nearly two inches above the ceramic tile floor. All the while that they were running, they were careful not to crumple the paper. Both of them were determined that this sheet of paper would be delivered to me in perfect shape, in flawless condition without wrinkles.

I hope I will not disappoint the mice community with the words that I write on this consequential note to Pastor Osterhagen. The mice seem to have so much confidence in me that I will know just the right words to write. Their expectation of me makes me jumpy. My tummy is clenched in a labyrinthine knot, a triple fisherman's knot. I keep telling myself something that my mum used to say to me about just trying to do my best. It meant a lot to me that Lewis and Clark told me that I had a brilliant idea about writing this note. I was thankful to receive a compliment from them and appreciate their support. I wouldn't have been able to accomplish this undertaking without their help. I dictated the note while Lewis and Clark took turns writing the words on the note with very large, clearly written letters. It read:

CONFIDENTIAL DETAILS FOR PASTOR OSTERHAGEN: Critical historical information has been revealed at Historic St. Peter's. This information could very well connect the church's history to the Underground Railroad Movement where slaves of African descent, in life and death situations, ran with all their might to seek freedom. It appears that Historic St. Peter's was a vital part of that movement as the church helped slaves on their way to find freedom in Canada. The church might have been a "safe house," a part of a detailed network, a portion of the movement's secret escape route.

Hopefully, you will understand this news better by simply lifting up a few of the squeaky, loose floor boards in the sanctuary, near the pulpit, to look at what is found underneath. There is a space under the floor, a place where runaway slaves could hide quietly in a horizontal position from bounty hunters on the search for them. In that space is a handwritten note, written in the code language used by the Underground Railroad. The note is fragile and discoloured, aged as an actual artifact of that time period. An antique hymnal is resting in one of the corners, which might have been left there whilst someone scurried to the hiding place. The hymnal is open to the hymn, "Shall We Gather at the River." That hymn might have been a secret "code" song that everyone at Historic St. Peter's sang when bounty hunters were spotted coming near the church. The very second that the parishioners broke into this "code" song, the runaway slaves scurried into their hiding place, while others hurriedly covered them up with the floor boards.

Another historical find is that of a wooden box located in the church basement, marked on one side only with the word "Station" written in black paint. This box contains some paperwork of this time era at Historic St. Peter's, the contents of which seem to be connected to the Underground Railroad.

Please quickly notify the State Historical Society of this find, an undiscovered part of the history of the United States. At that point, an official investigation could begin. Thank you, Pastor Osterhagen, for taking over with this information. We feel this discovery is now placed in good hands.

Sincerely,

Anonymice

With that work accomplished, Lewis and Clark promised me that they would deliver the note by slipping it under Pastor's office door as soon as the coast is clear.

At 11:30 p.m. My good wife Ruby and I travelled to the parsonage and snacked on a dropped morsel of a salmon cake. It helps me to spend time with her as she doesn't expect me to be perfectly brilliant and full of answers at all moments. When I get all knotted up about something in life, she listens to me and helps me to unravel knots that no one else would even attempt to untangle.

– F.N.

TWO MONTHS AGO A MAN BY THE NAME OF FAKEER SINGH TELEPHONED PASTOR Osterhagen and in his thick Punjabi accent inquired if Historic St. Peter's had a parish hall that was available for rent. Pastor informed him that Woolcox Hall is often rented out for community events and accommodates up to 250 people. After Fakeer heard this good news, he asked for an appointment to meet with Pastor. Mr. Singh mentioned that he would bring along his brother, Ramneek, in order to decide whether or not the accommodations at Historic St. Peter's would work well for their group.

Fakeer and Ramneek, wearing their turbans, arrived at church for their appointment two days after the telephone call. Pastor met and welcomed them to St. Peter's. The very first thing they did was to remove their shoes, even though Pastor said it was not necessary. After that, the three men walked together to Woolcox Hall to take a look at it. Ramneek asked if they could also see the church kitchen. Fakeer and Ramneek were very impressed and pleased with the facility so they began making further inquiries about renting Woolcox Hall along with permission to use the church kitchen. Pastor Osterhagen told them to take a seat at one of the tables and that he would be right back with the church calendar and the parish hall rental agreement.

When Pastor asked Fakeer and Ramneek what type of an event they were planning to host in Woolcox Hall, it led to a very interesting answer. Fakeer explained that the Sikh Community in Oswald County is in the process of building a place of worship, a Gurdwara. Their temple is very detailed and will take several years before completion, but an extremely simple and temporary Gurdwara is already being built on their property and should be completed within the next two months. Until then, the Sikhs are in need of a place to worship and a kitchen to prepare one meal each Saturday. Ramneek mentioned that they are currently worshipping in one of the smaller buildings at the Oswald County Fairgrounds, but that they need more room now because several other Sikh families have moved to Oswald County to join their community. He explained that this is the reason that they are inquiring about Woolcox Hall, finding it to be just the right size. Ramneek told Pastor that they want to rent the hall for six Saturdays in a row, beginning on February 21. After Pastor checked the church schedule, he found those Saturdays were available, so the paperwork was completed and the three signed their signatures at the bottom of the rental form.

After signing the contract and putting down a large deposit, Fakeer and Ramneek were very appreciative that the Sikh Community would be able to rent Woolcox Hall for their worship service and that a meal could be prepared on the premises. Three of the female mice from our community, Twiggy, Dandelion, and Clover, heard the men's entire discussion and told everyone at our village meeting tonight that the only time that Pastor looked a bit confused was when he talked about the tables and chairs that they could set up and take down each week. Fakeer told Pastor that they don't use tables or chairs as they sit on the floor during their worship and also sit on the floor when they share their meal.

The Sikhs met at St. Pete's yesterday and left Woolcox Hall and the church kitchen spotlessly clean. Even the floors were pristinely clean as each Sikh removed their shoes as they entered the building. The only evidence of their presence at St. Pete's yesterday was the lingering smell of curry and exotic Indian spices. When Daphne Archer walked into the building this morning she loudly complained about the church smelling like an English Curry House. She, of course, would be an expert at that because she refers to herself as being the only "Limey" at St. Pete's. Most of the members think it smells wonderful, but Daphne decided to carry on about it. After church some of the mice heard Daphne tell Pastor that the Sikhs need to cut down on their spices as we all have to be good sports and share the air around here. To the mice that saw this, Pastor Osterhagen looked like he didn't have the first idea how to respond to Daphne.

Clement told Aia that after church today Fakeer called and asked him if they left everything in good enough order at the church yesterday. He replied that the building was left in excellent condition. Fakeer told him that his fellow Sikhs are so thankful that they can use Woolcox Hall during this time as they appreciate the larger floor space. Fakeer said that the Sikh Community wants to thank all of the members of Historic St. Peter's for letting them use the building during these weeks by putting on a communal meal on Sunday, March 8, after St. Peter's worship service. He said it will be a time for oneness and sharing. Fakeer said that the whole church is invited and the meal is free. The Sikh men plan to set up tables and chairs for the members of St. Pete's to sit down at as he knows that they are not accustomed to eating a meal while sitting on the floor like the Sikhs. After those kind and welcoming words, Pastor did not have the heart to say a peep about Daphne's complaints of the current Sunday morning air quality, so he gave Daphne's grievances a sturdy set of wings and let them fly out the nearest window. Pastor told Fakeer that it was very kind of him and the Sikh community to invite St. Peter's members to a complimentary Sunday dinner. He said that he will invite everyone by putting it in the Sunday bulletin and also will announce it in church.

At 8:30 p.m. Ruby and I travelled to the choir room and spotted a lemon drop on the floor. Occasionally we find lemon drops in that room as they appear to be a "choir thing," trumpeted as the "no-joke-it-works" solution to help the amateur singer clear out one's throat. I told Ruby that I heard there was a new member of our mice village who just moved in, and her name happens to be Lemon Drop. Hopefully she will be pleasant, not sour like Daphne today when she arrived at church and complained about the curry aroma. However, I do enjoy listening to Daphne speak, whether the words are pleasant or unpleasant, as I adore the sound of her heavy British accent. I pretend that I am taking a quaint mini-tour of England, a trip plum full of anything and everything British.

– F.N.

AFTER PASTOR OSTERHAGEN SPOKE WITH FINN LARSSEN AT THE STATE HISTORICAL Society yesterday, Finn travelled the eighty miles from the State Capital out to Historic St. Peter's. Finn arrived, took off his coat and toque, made himself at home in Clement's office and listened intently, once again, to Clement's words. Clement showed him the note from "Anonymice" and later escorted him to the sanctuary where he gently lifted up the floorboards so that Finn could have a look. Finn saw the hiding place, the antique yellowed piece of paper, and the old open hymnal. Because of this finding, Finn told Clement that the sanctuary will need to be cordoned off and will be temporarily taken over by the State Historical Society. As of today the Society will proceed with an investigation into this discovery.

Clement attempted to explain to Finn that the Lenten Season has begun. His words fell on deaf ears when he told Finn that St. Peter's needs to use the sanctuary twice a week for worship services throughout the Lenten Season. Finn told Clement that would not be possible. Finn highlighted his words by reminding Clement that this discovery is part of United States history and it can't be tampered with. Finn suggested they have their worship services in another room until the State Historical Society has finished their work. Clement said that he understood that, but also mentioned how much extra work it will be to hold worship services in Woolcox Hall for an undetermined amount of time. He said the real brunt of the work will be setting up and taking down folding chairs twice a week in Woolcox Hall. Finn thanked Pastor and told him that Historic St. Peter's is a historical treasure and that he knows the church will cooperate in every way while the Historical Society performs their investigation. Clement affirmed his words and both men shook hands on it. Clement handed Finn a key to the sanctuary doors which Finn immediately used to lock up the old wooden doors. Finn applied official notices to the outside of the sanctuary doors stating that this is a State Historical Society investigation area and is temporarily closed to the public.

At 11:30 p.m. Ruby and I travelled to the church kitchen to brew a pot of tea. This notion came about after we stumbled upon a children's tea set in the nursery. The white porcelain set is stunningly hand-painted with two grinning mice enjoying a tea-for-two party. Inasmuch as we daily hear Aia mention the word tea, or sweet tea, we wanted to try tea, too. I am embarrassed to write in my journal that Ruby and I really slipped-up when it came to logically thinking through this tea party idea. First of all, we could not even boil water. Secondly, we did not have any tea leaves, and thirdly, the sugar cubes reside in the tip-top kitchen cupboard, in a completely unreachable spot. We abandoned the tea party idea and moved forward by making several trips back and forth from the church kitchen to the nursery to return all borrowed items.

On our way back home, Ruby came across a two and one-half inch long white paper package with writing on both sides. We took it home in order to study the writing and the artwork that was printed on the paper. We had barrels of fun scrutinizing the red and black printing. On one side it was written in black lettering, "Chu Shi Restaurant," and on the other side there were beautiful red symbols, the sight of which we have never come across before. Ruby calculatingly opened the package with such dainty paw motions that she looked like she was doing surgery on the ear of a ladybug. We were elated to find a toothpick inside the package that smelled like peppermint. We split the toothpick and enjoyed the mint flavouring for our snack. As we sucked on our treat, we discussed what we should do with the fancy paper package that the toothpick was housed in. Ruby had an excellent idea that we immediately put into action. We hung the paper on the wall in our dwelling with the red symbols facing out. We deliberated over what the puzzling symbols meant and came up with not a thing. So, together we contrived a meaning for the decorative art, saying that the symbols denote, "Happy Marriage." The "Happy Marriage" wall hanging adds atmosphere to our home and is now a prized possession of ours that really should be on display in a fine museum of art.

– F.N.

Thursday, February 26

CLEMENT WAS ALL EARS AS HE LISTENED TO AIA EXPLAIN THEIR SHOPPING TRIP TO THE Last Chance Second-Hand Shop near Trout Lake. Thrilled that she found several pieces of new-to-her maternity clothing, Aia enjoyed telling about two gents that they met, a father-son duo, that obviously spend most afternoons at this new thrift store. Noticing that the pair cruise the aisles at a snail's pace, she commented to Clement that they must be keenly seeking to find flawless, artistic, showy collectibles, not for their own home, but to sell for a monetary profit. Today they were delighted to find a fine crystal miniature pig with a label that said, "Made in West Germany."

After the men spotted the crystal pig, Gretchen told them how cute the little pig was. Because she already considered them her brand new friends, ones to chit-chat with, she suggested that they place the pig on their kitchen window ledge where the sun will shine right through it and make it sparkle.

Because of Gretchen's friendliness, the men introduced themselves as Lester and Lloyd Labreque. After that, Gretchen introduced herself and her mother, followed by instantly inviting them to attend church on Sunday at Historic St. Peter's. She was certain to tell the men that they could sit with them, adding that she would spot them because they both look and dress alike. Gretchen guessed that their favourite colour is beige, adding that she has two favourite colours, pink and green.

The last that Aia and Gretchen saw of Lester (whom Lloyd refers to as Pop) and Lloyd, they were relaxing on two rickety chairs in the furniture section of the thrift store. The chairs looked as though they were likely to collapse, but the men seemed contented to sit and read two of the thrift store's books. Lester was scanning *Fondue for Beginners* while Lloyd was altogether captivated by *Leprosy All Through the Ages*. Aia explained to Clement that the comical part about the scenario was that they were perched directly across from two undressed mannequin women's body forms that must have been donated by a department store that had gone belly-up. She said that it resembled something from a thirty-minute British television comedy show.

Clement said that their experience this afternoon made him think of First Timothy 6:8, "But godliness with contentment is great gain. For we brought nothing into the world, and we can take nothing out of it. But if we have food and clothing, we will be content with that."

At 10 p.m. Ruby and I stayed away from the parsonage. We travelled instead to the church kitchen where we found an individual butter packet that must have dropped on the floor when someone put the other little butters back into the refrigerator. We assumed that there were no crumbs at the Osterhagens tonight. They might be running out of food as it is the last day of the month. Thank goodness for the Osterhagens (and us) that payday is coming up soon.

– F.N.

The Second Sunday in Lent ~ March 1

AFTER DECIDING THE BEST TIMING, CLEMENT AND AIA SETTLED ON MAKING AN announcement in church today about expecting twins. Clement was honoured to broadcast the news as he revealed that the due date is during the last week in June. Aia told Clement after church today that she is so relieved that the news is out. She says that his announcement should put an end to the constant tummy checks she sees parishioners giving her. Now that everyone has heard the news about the twins they should stop gazing at her tummy and forget about judging how much weight she has gained. Most parishioners knew that Aia is pregnant, but did not know until today that the Osterhagens are expecting twins.

Early each morning one of our mice, Flip, does a thirty-minute workout in Woolcox Hall before anyone enters the building. His real name is Percy, but long ago he was nicknamed Flip by the mouse village because of his jaw-dropping abilities in gymnastics. Flip was more than content to put his plain old name of Percy aside, finding that he much prefers his cool new name instead. His gymnastic movements are not your usual round-offs or cartwheels. He has crafted three unfamiliar flips never done before: the flick, the whick, and the jolly-over.

After Flip finished his daily workout, he saw Clement walk down the breezeway with his sermon in hand hoping to have a few quiet moments to himself in his office. That is his pattern early on Sunday mornings, as he finds great benefit in this undisturbed time. Everything goes better for him if he can organize his thoughts and kneel in prayer before anyone arrives at HSP for worship. He needed only one photo copy because the original printing was too small for him to see easily. Standing at the copy machine, he removed his eyeglasses and placed them on the office counter in order to see if he could read the small print without them. He couldn't see it well enough, so he made an enlarged copy. After that, he walked back to his office carrying the copy with him and sat down at his desk.

In just a moment he heard the familiar sound of the church door opening up. He must have expected that he would have to forfeit his quiet time today because someone would need his full attention. But no one interrupted him and he must have had a strange feeling about that. Within seconds, the church door closed. Pastor got up from his desk and returned to the church office to fetch his eyeglasses and to see if anyone was in the building, but he discovered that his eyeglasses were gone, and no one was there. Two of the mice, Butter and Tart, were peeking from behind the children's book rack in the entryway when they saw a very strange look come over Pastor's face. After a moment, he must have realized that someone had entered the building and outright stolen his glasses. Clement was not only upset, but it threw him into a panic. To solve the problem temporarily, he hurried back to the parsonage and retrieved his old eyeglasses, outdated ones from his seminary days. All of the mice know that Clement only wears those old spectacles when he is doing messy jobs like painting projects or cleaning the garage. He explained to Aia what had just happened to him. Aia right away mentioned that it must be another clever prank done by the church gremlin, Griffin. Clement told her that the ugly antique frames would just have to do for right now. She told him that he should put on his polyester red shorts and his favourite Jesus Christ Superstar t-shirt, along with his old brown sandals to perfectly match his out-of-style eyeglasses. He didn't have time to chat or laugh with Aia, so he headed out to the breezeway, obviously thinking about Griffin, trying to figure out just who it is that is responsible for periodically doing mischievous escapades at the church. Clement knew this is the day that the Lord has made, but also knew it was not off to a very good start.

At 11:30 p.m. Ruby and I travelled to the parsonage and snacked on morsels that dropped off of a hot dog: a sliver of sauerkraut and a bit of dill pickle relish. Ruby and I decided that we favour the taste of sweet pickle relish far more than that of dill pickle relish.

– F.N.

Monday, March 2

AFTER THE OSTERHAGEN'S FINISHED LUNCH TODAY, AIA AND GRETCHEN STATIONED themselves at the dining room table and began rolling out homemade pretzels. Clement sat at the far end of the table and reviewed his Lenten preparations, especially his upcoming sermon notes. Ruby and I kept a close watch on the pretzel production from the crack in the dining room wall as we were riveted to the skilled knotting technique used to hand-form each pretzel. We heard Aia remark that this is the first time Gretchen has helped make the Lenten pretzels, but after just three tries she has the knotting technique down, adding that Gretchen is already a Trinitarian, just like herself. Aia told Clement that most of the pretzels will be put into their chest freezer to be pulled out whenever they want a treat during this "it-gets-longer-every-single-year" Lenten Season. The plan was revealed by Aia that they would enjoy an all you can eat pretzel feast for supper tonight, along with several yummy dipping sauces.

While Ruby and I were observing the smoothly-flowing pretzel production line in full operation, there was a firm knock on our bungalow's door. I answered it and found Wistful and Wisteria asking if they could come in. After they sat down they asked me a question anticipating I would answer it. Wistful and Wisteria are best friends, mostly because they share the same ambition, that of being life-long learners. Both of the girls take classes from Dr. Theodore Simonsen, our mice village librarian, as it is their goal to obtain a liberal arts education. Wistful told me that this type of education builds up one's thinking skills so that one can rationally think for themselves. One can expose oneself to differing world views with the result that the more you learn the more you want to learn. Wisteria added that a liberal arts education helps a person to be well-rounded and creative. Together they said that they don't want to bother Dr. Simonsen with their question because he appears to be swamped writing his dissertation on "Aztec Mice of the Fourteenth Century." They have heard that it contains notes on human sacrifice, especially noting the devastating effects that Aztec human sacrifice had on the mice who witnessed this brutality back then. During that time a lasting shock-wave travelled through the mice community and the fear all these years later has been passed down from one generation to another. The effects of the shock-wave are still felt by some of the mice in one particular remote region of Mexico. Finley agreed with Wistful and Wisteria that Dr. Simonsen is truly overwhelmed and weighed down with his research and that the Mice Village Council is currently looking into hiring an assistant librarian to help with all of the work at the village library. Until that happens, Finley told Wistful and Wisteria that he will try to answer their questions.

After Wistful and Wisteria relaxed a bit, they asked the question that they were seeking an answer to: "What is Lent?" I asked them to explain why they were curious about this. They mentioned it was because they have come across this word so many times lately at St. Pete's and they are without any knowledge as to what it actually is. Wistful said it is so bewildering because there are many words similar to Lent in the English language like spent or bent. After that Wisteria added the words dent and gent. My head went back and forth from Wistful to Wisteria as I watched a verbal ping pong match between the two of them using words that rhyme with Lent. They volleyed these words: tent . . . rent . . . pent . . . meant . . . went . . . vent . . . sent . . . scent . . . and maybe even, if you want to stretch it, president. Finley praised them for coming to talk to him about their query, because none of us at this time needs to bother Dr. Simonsen when he is deeply into writing his thesis.

I did my best to explain to Wistful and Wisteria what the word Lent means. They listened attentively as I explained that it is a forty day long season observed by Christians that begins with Ash Wednesday and ends with Easter Sunday. Lent is finished on Easter Sunday because that is the day that Jesus Christ rose from the dead after suffering for the sins of the entire world on Good Friday. The reason that it is called "good" is that God gave his Son to die on the cross so that it would wipe away people's sins and provide a home for them in heaven when they die. Wistful and Wisteria nodded their heads after I explained what Lent means and were very appreciative and satisfied with the answer. But I could tell from the look on their faces that they were going to do some extra research on this topic, intending to add this knowledge to their liberal arts education.

After they left, Ruby and I continued watching the pretzel production and whispered back and forth about Gretchen's well-skilled ability to tie pretzel knots. I wondered if her expertise in this area would lead to a successful career as a ship's assistant tying nautical knots, or maybe on a cattle ranch actually roping cattle, or tying ropes for mountain climbers on a search and rescue team. Ruby looked at me and shook her head back and forth and told me that I was completely off base, emphasizing that Gretchen will one day be an opera singer and that's that, adding that the opera world is a knotty enough career as it is.

At 11:30 p.m. Ruby and I travelled to the parsonage and snacked on two crystals of kosher salt, the only thing that we could find. It was a good thing that there were two drops of lemonade on the floor as the salt made us terribly thirsty. After we returned home I revealed to Ruby that I am upset that Dr. Simonsen is writing a thesis. I feel he is copying me because he knows I am writing a journal. Ruby comforted me by saying that of course Dr. Simonsen is copying me by becoming an author, and to remember the level-headed truism, "Imitation is the sincerest form of flattery."

– F.N.

DUE TO THE CHANGE OF VENUE, JOSIE PLAYS THE PORTABLE KEYBOARD FOR WORSHIP IN Woolcox Hall because of the regulations issued by Finn and the State Historical Society. Today she appeared to have a heavy duty cold. As she spoke with people, she kept a tissue firmly planted over her mouth. Josie does an excellent job musically of leading the worship services, but she has not done as well lately, perhaps due to a health issue. She seems to get head colds and it affects the quality of her playing. Hopefully she will be better by Wednesday's Lenten service.

Everyone at church today was visibly excited about attending today's Sikh meal to be held right after worship. Round tables and chairs had been set up in Woolcox Hall for both the worship service and the meal afterwards. Floating in the air were the tantalizing aromas of mysterious spices. The Sikh Community had prepared three long tables of generous foods. They kindly labeled each dish with a white index card that told the name of each dish along with a short description of it. They also marked on each card the pungency zing by using little chili pepper stickers. Most of the cards had only one chili pepper, as the cooks were kind to keep the heat down in the mild zone. Foods presented were Dal, Chapati, Sabzi, Tandori chicken, Kebabs, pickles, chai tea, and a tasty dessert prepared with coconut milk called Kheer which tasted similar to a perfect rice pudding. Pastor Osterhagen was certain that Daphne Archer, "The Limey," would complain about the church smelling like an English Curry House again, but she was the one who seemed to enjoy the meal more than anyone. Pastor asked her if she was keen on Indian food to which she replied that there is no better food in the whole world. He then asked her about the smell of the spices, referring to the other Sunday when she was upset. Daphne told him that it bothered her that day because she was going on a blind date with a new acquaintance that afternoon and she did not want her hairdo to pick up the smell of curry. She mentioned that it was their first date and she only had few seconds to make a good first impression. After that she told Pastor that it really was nothing to be concerned with because, as it turned out, the man she went with didn't make a very good first impression on her. We perceived a look on Pastor's face projecting some confusion when it comes to understanding women. He does get a lot of practice at it, though, because St. Peter's is full of them.

At 5:30 p.m. the entire mice village arrived in Woolcox Hall ready to sample Indian food simply because we are curious to know what it tastes like, having noted that the aroma is incredibly enticing and mysterious. But we were out of luck tonight because the Sikh Community spotlessly cleaned everything up in Woolcox Hall and the church kitchen. We simply could not find even a speck of anything. We all went home with reverberating empty tummies and mentioned that we hope tomorrow will be a better day.

    – F.N.

Wednesday, March 11

THE MIDWEEK LENTEN SERVICE WAS HELD TONIGHT AT SEVEN THIRTY WITH ORGANIST Josie appearing ill as she continued to cover her mouth with a tissue when she spoke to people hoping to prevent them from catching her cold. Clement told Aia that he suspects Josie is covering her mouth with tissues so that people won't smell alcohol on her breath, but admitted that he doesn't know where to go with that information. Pastor Osterhagen was spiritually on fire tonight and it was evident that he is excited about his sermon series, "Keeping Lent Holy." Tonight it was about the sacredness of Lent.

After everyone had gone, Clement headed home to a tuckered out Aia who was sitting on the reclining sofa with her feet up. She told Clement that Gretchen had fallen asleep during church tonight. She somehow carried her home and tucked her into bed, not bothering to change her into her sleeper. Even though Gretchen went to bed with her teeth unbrushed, it was better than waking her up. If she had done that, Gretchen would have had trouble going back to sleep.

Aia grumbled to Clement that she does not like it that every single time they go to church Mylo Kalb is waiting there with his pockets full of suckers ready to give them to all of the children that arrive. When he sees Gretchen, he bends down and asks her what colour sucker she would like. He gives her one, usually a purple sucker that stains her mouth and clothing. By the time church is over, Gretchen has a sticky mouth, face, hands, and clothing. Aia doesn't want Gretchen to have junk food that will promote tooth decay as she is very careful about restricting sweets. Aia said that Mylo should pay for Gretchen's dental bill if she ends up with a cavity. She enforced her point by adding that Mylo is Johnny-on-the-spot when it comes to passing out suckers to all of the children. He gives himself credit for performing some Christian act of service to the church. Mylo disappears when it is time to clean up all of the wrappers and sucker sticks that are deposited on the pews, in the hymnal racks, and on the floor, showing no responsibility for the cleanup. Aia talked about how she felt tonight when Mylo gave Gretchen a sucker. After he did that he gave Aia a sucker too, like she was a child, and asked for a hug from both of them. Aia told Clement that she has had enough of this, and notices that other people have, too. She explained that every time he does this she gets a queasy, squeamish feeling. She told Clement that she just wants to go to church and she doesn't appreciate being part of the sucker handout.

Clement agreed with everything she said, but doesn't know how to stop Mylo. He says that when the time comes that Mylo can no longer attend church, there is already another church member waiting in line to take Mylo's spot. Clement has seen so-called "candy men" in church his entire life and it just doesn't stop. He thinks that the practice started up after World War II. Throughout his dad's ministry, and now his own ministry, they both have looked out during the worship services and seen children of all ages licking suckers. He says that they might as well get used to it and try to overlook it.

Because Aia is extra-exhausted tonight, she became extra talkative and negative. At first her words seemed positive, but later slid toward the negative. She began by telling Clement about the seasons of the year by describing what is beautiful and fun about each one of them. Aia told Clement that she delights in the springtime because there are pussy willows, warmer temperatures, Easter arrives, and there are tulips, crocuses, and rainy days when she and Gretchen can put on their matching yellow and white daisy wellies and take a walk with their umbrellas. Summer is wonderful because there are lots of picnics, swimming, vacations, no need to wear a jacket or coat, and lots of sweet tea and homemade lemonade. She is especially fond of summer because the programs at church shut down until September and they are able to take a well-deserved break from planning, preparing, and attending all of those events. Fall is sensational due to the cooler temperatures, the colourful leaves, walks on the trail, and everything that is pumpkin related: Jack-o-lanterns, pie, squares, muffins, bars, donuts, soup, candy, spiced tea, *"It's the Great Pumpkin, Charlie Brown,"* and outdoor welcome mats with pumpkins ink-stamped on them. Winter is fantastic as well because there is Christmas, hot cocoa, shorter days and longer nights with more time for sleeping, occasional hoarfrost on the trees, limitless varieties of homemade hot soup, and a chance to wear her ivory-coloured faux-fur mitts.

Clement wondered why she was talking about the seasons, and then Aia confessed that the only season that she doesn't like is the Lenten Season. She said that she understands how important it is in the life of a Christian to prepare for the Resurrection, but for her it is difficult to go to two worship services a week, instead of just one. It takes double the time, energy, and church outfits. The parishioners socialize forever after church and expect her to stick around and talk to them. Clement said he understood that Gretchen's bedtime is exactly when the Lenten Services are scheduled and that he can't change the worship times without a lot of people complaining and saying, "We always do it this way." Many of the parishioners who attend on Wednesday evenings are older and do not have little ones at home. They can spend their time socializing after church and then go out "pie-ing" at a restaurant, which is to share a piece of pie with another person. They also order a glass of water and tea or coffee, so they are completely coffeed-up and watered-down. He told Aia not to worry about it and to cut back by attending the Lenten Services every other Wednesday instead of every week.

Clement is a pro at listening to how Aia feels, even though she often has many subjects going all at once in a conversation. Aia told Clement that she is scared and has so many fears about being the mother of twins and is nervous that she won't be able to handle it. She explained that her distress is about becoming a mother of three, instead of just one. Clement told her that she is experiencing a bit of something called, "The Dark Night of the Soul," when she is sad about a few things and doesn't think that the sadness will ever lift. It is not depression, but an awareness of what's meaningful and what isn't in her life. He said her emotions might be tender because of the pregnancy, but that is temporary, and that there are many changes ahead for her. He told her that he has confidence in her and that she has the ability to be a mother of three, and that after awhile she will feel much better. He added the most important thing he can say to Aia is to tell her that he loves her just the way she is. Clement reassured her that he is there to help her, too. Aia told him that she felt much, much better, saying that he helped calm down her worries. Together they crawled in bed, snuggled, and visited about other things until they both fell deep asleep.

At 10:50 p.m. Ruby and I travelled to the parsonage and snacked on morsels of corn chips and dill pickle dip. Aia seems to have hunger pangs for salty foods now, especially classic potato chips that are the old-fashioned thinly cut style, not the rippled ones. The Osterhagens were out of potato chips tonight so corn chips had to fill in for potato chips.

– F.N.

Monday, March 16

TODAY WAS ST. URHO'S DAY, A DAY TO HONOUR THE MYTHICAL AND LEGENDARY Patron Saint of Finland, the mighty purple and green-clad man who chased all of the grasshoppers out of the country, saving entire vineyards. Clement's side of the family has celebrated this holiday for many years, marking it with a special meal, home-made entertainment, and dancing.

Yesterday Clement asked Aia if she would prepare a kettle of Finnish split-pea soup, called Hernekeitto, for their supper on St. Urho's Day. Aia did just that. Ruby heard Clement tell Aia that he would provide the St. Urho entertainment, to play a recording of tango music and to teach her the beginning steps of the tango. In preparation for the dancing, Clement pushed all of the furniture in the living room against the walls which somewhat transformed the room into a dance studio. Aia was lickety-split at learning the basic tango moves but became exhausted and short of breath when it came to the Boleo move. When Clement twirled her around, the very fast whipping action made her weak in the knees. Ruby and I concluded that some of the tango moves were far too extreme for Aia to perform during pregnancy. She isn't limber enough now to bend, swirl, and dip low in the shape that her tummy is in.

Clement learned how to dance the tango as a young boy. Ruby and I heard him tell Aia that his folks enjoyed the tango at their lake cottage after it got dark outside. They had some fun while getting in their fitness workout at the same time. He was excited for Aia to learn the basics of the complicated dance. Clement mentioned to Aia that someday they will travel to Finland to be a part of the *Tangomarkkinat*, the annual summer Finnish Tango Festival. We saw a twinkle shine in Aia's eyes. We witnessed Clement's words, "Travel to Finland," swell enthusiasm within Aia, after which she tried extra hard to learn the moves. Aia told him that she would love to travel to Finland and be part of the *Tangomarkkinat*, even if she never becomes silver-footed at the tango.

A village mice meeting was held tonight in a small room of HSP's basement where the main conversation centered on information Ruby and I learned about St. Urho. The mice have heard Pastor Osterhagen talking about it for several days. Everyone agreed that it is important that all Saints have their place in the yearly calendar.

Everyone also talked about St. Patrick being credited with banishing snakes from Ireland. The mice agreed that they have missed the boat when it comes to honouring a mouse as their patron saint with a day named specifically for the golden one. They made a decision that it was their job to appoint a Patron Saint of All Micedom. The first mouse and only mouse that came to mind was Philycis (pronounced Fill-a-sis), a mouse from Malta known worldwide who is credited with perhaps performing a miracle. After discussing his promotion to sainthood, the mice declared his birthday as a day to honour Philycis, now named the Patron Saint of All Micedom.

St. Philycis lived on the Isle of Malta around the time of the invention of the home computer. He is accredited with driving out excess cats on the island as they were doing so much harm to the environment in one of the small villages. Not only were the cats a threat to the mice that lived in the village, they were an even bigger threat to the bird population. Residents would often let their cats run loose around the village for fresh air and exercise. The owners were completely unaware that the cats were killing local birds. Because cats are natural hunters and predators, Malta's national bird, The Blue Rock Thrush, was on the verge of becoming extinct. Many cats were capturing and feeding on this bird so that they were almost disappearing, as well as endangering and wiping out other native birds in the area. Villagers were no longer hearing the "birds sing sweetly in the trees," like the phrase in the cherished hymn, "How Great Thou Art."

Under St. Philycis's organized and effective leadership, the cats were hastily driven out of the village, crazed by a terrifying sound. The cats fled the short distance to the Mediterranean Sea and catapulted into the water. It was similar to what is recorded in the fifth chapter of the Gospel of Mark where a whole load of possessed pigs rushed down a steep bank and drowned in the sea. But these cats did not drown, for they were devoured in a feeding frenzy by sharks.

The modern computer mouse also needs much credit for chasing the cats into the sea. You see, most cats are frightened of the clicking noise that the computer mouse makes and act very oddly when they hear the *click, click, click*. When a cat is stressed by that sound, they will run round and round in furious circles, bump into things, have fits of hysteria, and then run wildly, as fast as they can, to get far away from the source of the sound.

St. Philycis organized an entire mouse crusade to get rid of the cats. At a pre-arranged date and time, each mouse hopped onto a home computer mouse and clicked as many times as was in their power to do. The sound drove every cat berserk, spun them out of control, exposing their wild nature. This happened on a Friday in May during the mid-1980's. The events of this time were not written down, but were communicated via the grapevine to most mouse communities, which spread throughout the world. Five o'clock was chosen as the perfect time for this mission, as it signaled the time for cocktail hour when everyone in that small village went outside to relax on their decks and porches, a time for visiting with their neighbours over cocktails. It is part of the legend that the humans did not notice the clicking, but were happily talking and sipping Maltese Slippers (cocktails of orange and melon liqueur, lime-flavoured vodka, sweet and sour mix, and grenadine) from martini glasses.

At that moment in history every mouse in that village incessantly clicked a computer mouse repeatedly, driving the household cats into a tizzy. When the cats were still panicked about the incessant clicking sound, they dashed through the open sliding glass doors, running the short distance to the sea. When they entered the sea, before they could even get the hang of the swimming technique, let alone the dogpaddle, many sharks devoured them in a feeding frenzy.

Amazingly, the cat owners did not seem to mind that Cuddles, Boots, Jasper, Boo, Midnight, Miss Kitty, Harley, Lolo, Jazz, Bandit, Misty, Socks, and Tinky, were never coming back home again. The citizens of that small village seemed to value the Blue Rock Thrush more than their cats. They thought it was a lot of work lately to own a cat and were sick and tired of being blamed for their cat making deposits in neighbourhood vegetable and flower gardens instead of their own litter boxes. The homeowners did not miss having to walk around their small homes in a tiptoe fashion so as to avoid making any little noise that would give their cat stress and anxiety. Neither did the tourists mind there being fewer stray cats in Malta. The mice, of course, were the most jubilant.

St. Philycis accomplished a brilliant feat, a miracle of sorts, by removing cats from that village. It was a safety issue for the mice but also stopped the great wave of extinction that the cat population was causing, namely to the Blue Rock Thrush. In his honour, our village chose to call Philycis's birthday St. Philycis, Patron of All Micedom. The mice at HSP from now on will refer to September 4 as St. Phil's Day. This was serious business, affecting future generations, and there was no pussyfooting around about the decision we made tonight to honour St. Phil.

At 11:30 p.m. Ruby and I travelled to the parsonage and snacked on a morsel of an odd looking chip of some sort. Earlier tonight we peeked out of the crack in the dining room wall and saw Gretchen sitting at the dining room table wearing ten cone-shaped snack chips, one on each finger and nibbling at her pinky fingernail. The fake nails look like Halloween fingernails but are golden in colour instead of green. She very slowly ate one at a time, stretching out this time. Gretchen earlier told her parents that she wanted to stay up late and watch a film. They let her do that until she fell asleep on the sofa with her blanket and her teddy bear, Horace.

Ruby and I really want to try a Maltese Slipper Cocktail. When it was described at the meeting tonight, our taste buds spoke to us, sort of like watching a person eat a fresh lemon. Our taste was whetted for something new, something sweet and sour. The only thing we could find tonight was a tiny morsel of a cone-shaped chip, so we shared that and went home.

We wore our new slippers tonight. Ruby knitted us each a pair using two wooden toothpicks she found on the floor in the church kitchen and some colourful yarn that the ladies dropped in Woolcox Hall after their quilting session last week. It felt comforting to have warm paws and to crawl into bed wearing our new trendy coloured Juniper green slippers. Maybe sometime we'll get to taste a drop of a Maltese Slipper Cocktail.

– F.N.

St. Patrick's Day ~ Tuesday, March 17

THIS WAS AN EXCITING DAY AT THE OSTERHAGEN HOME, FILLED WITH MERRIMENT AND celebration of anything and everything Irish. One would think that either Clement or Aia are of Irish descent, but neither one has a drop of Irish blood in them. Aia has made many preparations for this day, a holiday she treasures because they can have it all to themselves. Clement followed her leading and went along with the plans she made for the day.

The first item of the day was to select an Irish first name, a name that they would own for the day. Putting aside their given names today, they will pick them up again tomorrow. Clement decided to go by Aidan, Aia was Meara, and together they decided Gretchen would be called Bridget, also changing their last name of Osterhagen to the Irish last name Brannigan. Dressing in something green today, Aidan wore his dark green vest, and both Bridget and Meara dressed in their matching green mountain Vermont sweatshirts. After a full Irish Breakfast, including Irish tea, they put on their winter coats and stood outside to watch the Knights of Columbus St. Patrick's Day Parade travel down the street right in front of them, as Historic St. Peter's is in the centre of town, located on the parade route. The mice in the village posted themselves on the basement window ledges so that we would not miss out on watching the parade. The mice community also honours St. Patrick because he got rid of all of the snakes in Ireland, as snakes are a deadly threat to mice. This afternoon the Brannigans watched an Irish movie. It was a true holiday for them.

Last evening Meara began preparations for tonight's Irish supper. She prepared Beef and Mushroom Stew with fresh rosemary, ladled on top of roughly mashed potatoes. There was a lovely green gelatin salad, rainbow-coloured freshly baked bread with honey butter, and a pickle and olive tray. Vanilla ice cream with Irish oatmeal cookies finished the feast. After the meal, the three Brannigans went for a long walk all around the church interior with Bridget safely tied in the church's wheelchair. Aidan and Meara's conversation centred on the twins and how they will rely on God's help to strengthen them in the years to come. Meara mentioned several times how much fun she had today. Ruby and I noticed that Aiden smiled at her, as though he thought no one in the world is as lovely as his Meara.

At 11:30 p.m. Ruby and I travelled to the parsonage and snacked on morsels of tonight's Irish feast. We agreed that the Brannigans, actually the Osterhagens, are nothing short of spellbinding, all the while being absolutely charming.

– F.N

Oodles of enthusiasm and excitement were present within the mice village tonight. For several days the buzz within the community has centered on details of an upcoming social event. Gathering together in the church basement, the mice were presented with a beginner line dancing class, taught by our instructor, the beautiful Bryndle. Bryndle is mostly known for collecting infant-sized hair bows, until now. Occasionally a hair bow will fall to the floor when loving parents bundle up their baby daughters in their hooded winter rompers. Bryndle waits until everyone has left the building and then travels out to see if she can find a hair bow to add to her colourful collection. Tonight Bryndle is wearing a maize-coloured newborn hair bow which happens to flatter her cornflower blue eyes.

Bryndle recently gained access to a line dancing instructional video accidentally left behind by Mona Wigstrom, one of the seniors at St. Pete's who intends to teach the technique to the Seniors Group. Bryndle has burned a lot of midnight oil by repetitively watching Mona's left behind tape on the church tape player. Tonight she was elated that within just a few attempts, the mice gained confidence by conquering the repeated sequenced line dance steps, assuming that they are now prepared for a line dancing jamboree. Music was provided by "The A Capella Cowboys," a quartet of male mice consisting of Flint, Bart, Logan, and Ash. They wore their felt cowboy hats that were hand-made by the female mice who attend Wednesday's sewing circle. They sing in harmony with paw-claps, tail thumps, and beat boxing. Providing excellent country music, "The A Capella Cowboys" sang music all evening that truly kept everyone's steps in sync.

After the line dancing finished for the night, the mice recharged their batteries by resting and talking about the benefits of line dancing. To propel the idea of line dancing to the members of Historic St. Pete's, Bronson suggested that he would take it upon himself to write a note and drop it in the suggestion box so that they might be encouraged to try line dancing. After all, roughly one-third of the members of HSP appear to be in the adult overweight and obese range. Line dancing would help to get them to move while having fun. Bronson offered to add an additional recommendation in the suggestion box, that of belly dancing, as he stressed that type of dancing promotes a terrific cardio workout.

A refreshing beverage was served at the line dancing jamboree tonight. Two of our mice came across a bottle of yellow soft drink that was left behind in the youth room. It took fourteen of our strongest mice just to remove the cap. After that, it took another nine mice to help pour the 16 oz. contents of the bottle into plastic mini shot glasses. Montana, a newer member of our community, used to reside at the local Sportsmen's Club. Upon hearing about the line dancing jamboree, Montana travelled back to the Sportsmen's Club along with a few helpers and loaded up a plastic grocery bag with plastic shot glasses. While travelling home tonight, Ruby and I discussed the thievery, and decided that this stealing needs to be addressed at the next village meeting.

Ruby was far more interested in telling me about the winking game going on between Bryndle and Bronson than any shot glass shenanigans. She mentioned that a fiery infatuation between B & B developed tonight. We surmised Bryndle and Bronson will be certain that tonight's line dancing jamboree is just the first of many jamborees yet to come.

    – F.N.

VANDALISM TOOK PLACE IN THE CHURCH KITCHEN DURING THE NIGHT. ALL OF THE cupboard doors were left wide open. Hot dogs from the refrigerator were heated on the stove. Pop cans were littered here and there. Cigarette ashes were dropped all over the kitchen counters and the tile floor. When Clement discovered it he called the police immediately. One unit gathered up pop cans and cigarette butts so they could be tested at the police station. The police cordoned off the kitchen until further notice. All mice were sound asleep, so none of us knew about the vandalism occurring, an extremely quiet form of mischievous destruction. Perhaps it is another bit of trickery done by the church gremlin, Griffin.

As if vandalism wasn't enough of a troubling way to greet the day, Josie Johnson was having an absolute hissy fit after she arrived at St. Peter's to practice today. Her precious pencil collection, which she has gathered from far and wide during well-deserved vacations with her husband Eldon, has vanished. She has always kept them under lock and key at the organ as she uses those particular pencils to mark up her music. This relocation, due to the State Historical Society, has turned everything upside down for Josie because she now plays the keyboard in Woolcox Hall and is not able to lock anything up. Someone must have thought that her pencils were there for the grabbing. She assumed the theft must have been done by Griffin the Gremlin. Being so upset, she told Pastor about it, and added that he should change the name of his entire Lenten emphasis to, "Thou Shalt Not Steal" instead of "Keeping Lent Holy." As she spoke to him, her lower lip began to quiver. Close to tears, she obviously needed sympathy about the loss of her pencil collection. As Pastor listened, Josie explained the many pencils that were precious to her, each one imprinted with the name of the place they were from. There were pencils from the Eastman School of Music, Wartburg College, Sechler's Pickle Factory, the Spam Museum, Concordia College, the Abraham Lincoln Museum, Waverly College, Pelee Island Winery, Hershey's Chocolate Factory, Oswald County Humane Society, Cape Cod Chips, Fort Ticonderoga, the Jell-O Museum, Hy-Vee, Old Financial Insurance Company, Home of Good Living, The Little Brown Church in the Vale, High Spot Liquors, Porky's Sausage Shop, Schultz's Meat Market, The Friar's Clinic for Invalids, Patti's Peanut House, Hiram Walker's, Bronner's in Frankenmuth, the Gateway Arch, Central

Home of Hardware, Mike's & Mac's Meats, Oberlin College and Conservatory, Sterling Bakery, Oddie's Trout Farm, Piggly-Wiggly, Laura Ingalls Wilder Historic Home and Museum and the Amish General Store, just to name a few off the top of her head. She added that there were many, many more in her collection. The only pencil that was not stolen was the one printed with the words Oswald County Sheriff's Department on it, and that one she doesn't even count as being a collectible.

Pastor Osterhagen noticed that Josie seemed to find some comfort in her tea tumbler, which he suspects does not contain tea or coffee, but a much stronger concoction. He told Aia that he will watch for signs of this in the upcoming weeks, but for now, he'll leave the subject alone because he has way too much on his plate.

At 11:30 pm. Ruby and I travelled to the church kitchen, crawled under the locked door, and snacked on morsels of hot dogs, buns, and spilled pop. We nibbled on cigarette ashes but spit them out due to their nasty, noxious taste.

– F.N.

PASTOR OSTERHAGEN HASN'T BEEN FEELING WELL FOR A COUPLE OF DAYS BUT WE NOTICE that he has continued to do his work. Being at his office early this morning for some quiet time before worship, he ended up going back to the parsonage to rest for a few minutes in his bed. One of the ushers spotted him walking down the breeze-way holding on to his side. At that time, Aia and Gretchen were sitting in folding chairs in Woolcox Hall listening to the prelude. Josie kept repeating the same music over and over again as the worship service did not start on time. After ten minutes of listening to a rendition of "Immortal, Invisible," an usher suddenly appeared in front of Woolcox Hall having arrived from the side door. He motioned for Josie to stop playing the keyboard. With a booming voice he announced, "We've called an ambulance for Pastor." After hearing his words, Aia picked up Gretchen, left Woolcox Hall and hurried down the breezeway only to arrive at the parsonage where she found at least twenty parishioners roaming around their living quarters. A few people were in their bedroom watching Clement sprawled on their bed in a lot of pain. Four people were moving the dining room table against the wall so that there was a clear pathway for a stretcher to get through. Some of the people were not helping at all, but were there simply being observers. They relaxed and made themselves comfy by sitting in the living room chairs and were quietly chatting with each other as they watched the parade of paramedics taking their pastor to an ambulance headed for Our Lady of Lourdes Hospital.

The three Osterhagens rode together in the ambulance to the hospital where Clement had emergency surgery to remove his appendix. Thank goodness Aia had the forethought to pack some food and juice boxes in Gretchen's activity bag to keep her from being hungry while they were at the hospital. Following surgery, Clement rested safely in his hospital room. Later on Aia must have realized that she and Gretchen had no way to get back home. Several mice saw Aia's good friend, Annette, bring them home from the hospital, even though Annette was not properly dressed. Wearing a yellow housecoat and black and white slippers that resembled Holstein cows with big glassy eyes and pink shiny noses, Annette was a sight not to miss. After arriving home, Aia tucked Gretchen in bed and did the same herself. Awakening a few hours later, she found that her pillowcase was soaking wet from her many tears. Feeling like she was under too much pressure to handle everything, she cried again. Being pregnant with twins, taking care of Gretchen all by herself, and Clement being hospitalized was too overwhelming. Ruby and I are certain that Aia will not be so bleak in a day or two when she will have her Clement back home. Ruby and I heard Aia say a prayer out loud. We so wanted to express to Aia hopeful and reassuring words. We wanted to tell her not to worry so much, but we are debilitated when it comes to communicating with humans. We so wish that Aia's woes would be gone.

Aia must have remembered that she hadn't eaten anything since breakfast as she got up from bed, went to the kitchen, and searched in the refrigerator. Pulling out blue cheese, she cut off a chunk and placed it on top of flatbread. We have heard Aia speak of the health food benefits of consuming blue cheese. She has mentioned that blue cheese helps to improve memory, has a low fat content, is anti-inflammatory, prevents cellulite, is full of milk protein, a real fighter against arthritis, plus helps prevent osteoporosis. Aia soon took seconds of blue cheese and flatbread. After that she returned to bed and rested on her dear Clement's side, where his pillowcase was dry and smelled just like him.

At 11:30 p.m. Ruby and I travelled to the parsonage and snacked on a morsel of shredded wheat. It doesn't appear that the Osterhagen family ate anything at home today except for shredded wheat, blue cheese, and crisp flatbread from Sweden.

— F.N.

I HAD NO TIME TO WRITE ANY NEWS IN MY JOURNAL TODAY. THERE WAS AN IMMEDIATE issue in the village and I spent all of my time today hearing both sides of the story and offering solutions to remedy the issue. Finally, I threw up my paws and told them that I was out of ideas on how to solve their problems, let alone come up with an instant cure for them. There is a limit to how much volunteer help one can give.

At 11:30 p.m. Ruby and I travelled to the church kitchen and snacked on a morsel of a dropped oatmeal cookie. It wasn't the best, but we ate it anyway. We decided that Aia's oatmeal cookies are far better quality because of the high calibre of the oatmeal that she purchases in the health food section at Grocer Dan's. Aia uses steel-cut Scotch oats instead of the standard over-processed, rolled oatmeal that is so commonly used. We decided that Alexander Graham Bell, the famous Scottish inventor, must have been nourished each morning by consuming a brimming bowl of Scotch oats porridge which gave him the strength and "stick-to-it-tive-ness" to invent the telephone.

– F.N.

Saturday, March 28

EARLY THIS MORNING CLEMENT WALKED THROUGH THE BREEZEWAY HEADED TOWARDS his office, still a bit sore, but oh so glad to be out of the hospital. After he unlocked his office door he became absolutely astonished by what he saw. Placed on his quaint, old-fashioned, but highly glossy solid walnut desk was one object, one familiar and personal item of his which was stationed in the exact middle of the black desk pad. Right before his eyes were his missing eyeglasses that were snatched by Griffin the Gremlin on Sunday, March 1. Clement returned home right away with his eyeglasses and told Aia that he was stumped as to how Griffin was able to obtain access to his office as he must have opened the door with a key. He told Aia that he mistakenly assumed that he was the only person at church with a key that fits his office door, mentioning that even Chuck Brownton, the janitor, does not have a key for his office. Twenty-eight days of wearing his old eyeglasses from his seminary days were instantly drawn to a close today, due to Griffin returning the pair he had swiped.

After Clement regained his composure, he mentioned to Aia that he had experienced an upside to wearing his old eyeglasses. Many parishioners complimented him on the style of those eyeglasses and wondered if they were brand new, having an avant-garde look about them. Ruby and I heard Clement tell Aia that perhaps he will keep wearing his old eyeglasses for a while longer, even though he thinks they are not at all cool but painfully passé. Later on today we saw him pick up the lost, but now found, eyeglasses from the dining room table as he said out loud, with no one but us listening, "Who in the world is Griffin the Gremlin? I need to sort out who is responsible for all the pranks and capers that go on at HSP!"

At 11:30 p.m. Ruby and I travelled to the parsonage and snacked on a crumb of a rusk and a nubbin of smoked baby Swiss cheese, a premium variety that we crave continuously. We are aware that there is a jar of capers in the Osterhagen refrigerator, but we have no access to them. It is dispiriting, because just one tiny but truly mighty caper would have truly elevated and accentuated the hint of pungency contained in the smokey baby Swiss.

— F.N.

THESE LAST WEEKS MANY ANTSY PARISHIONERS HAVE PRESENTED OBJECTIONS TO PASTOR about worshipping week after week in Woolcox Hall. The apparent slow-motion of the State Historical Society makes it feel as though St. Pete's is being held under captivity. Members want to know the exact date when the Society will finish up their investigation. Most say it will not feel like God's house if they have to worship in Woolcox Hall on Maundy Thursday, Good Friday, and Easter Sunday. An added complaint is that the rickety and wobbly old wooden chairs in Woolcox Hall are damaged and should be discarded by donating them to Margot's Miscellany, the newest thrift store in Oswald County.

Aubrie Willington pointed out to Pastor that the wooden seats on the chairs are so abrasive that they are similar to a square of extra coarse sandpaper with a grit size of 40. She emphasized her point by stating that three pairs of her panty hose have already rubbed against the prickly wood and have numerous runs and snags, so they had to be tossed into the waste basket. While she had Pastor's attention, Aubrie delivered a speech containing her gripes about the hazardous chairs by including a personal experience. She said that one Sunday she stood up for the Apostles' Creed to profess her faith. As she did that, her pantyhose got hooked on the wooden rough spots. After she pulled them free there were two to three inch wide runs on the back of each leg. Aubrie continued by asking Pastor if he had any clue how distressing it is to have runs in her support pantyhose while walking up to receive Holy Communion. Not only are the runs fully visible to the others attending worship, but she could not settle down and take her mind off of the disaster in order to be prepared for Holy Communion. Not being fully composed with her heart, mind, and soul was a new experience for her and not one she wants to repeat. Lastly, Aubrie added that the ramshackle chairs are hazardous; very shortly someone is bound to get a colossal splinter in one of their bum cheeks. Adding to that, she asked Pastor what the church's policy is on handling a splinter that gets deeply embedded in someone's caboose, and secondly, whether the church's insurance will cover the medical costs of splinter removal from a person's wazoo. We noticed that Pastor seemed tongue-tied at this point.

Worshippers are also muttering about missing out on the sound produced by HSP's dearly loved pipe organ, those moments of "heaven itself touching the earth," as we heard one person word it. Many people clearly do not appreciate the sound of the cheap, sub-standard keyboard in Woolcox Hall. They claim that the instrument is far too ineffectual to lead the singing of the liturgy and hymns, especially the hymns that are triumphant or majestic like "Lift High the Cross" or "Jesus Christ is Risen Today."

Having invited out-of-town relatives for the Easter weekend, parishioners have openly spoken about their fear of having to worship in Woolcox Hall on the most holy day of the year. They were asking Pastor for assurance that Historic St. Peter's elegant and well-ornamented sanctuary will be opened up and regained for this weekend and beyond. Pastor, too, admitted to some that he also is tired of this sluggishness by the State Historical Society. After church we heard Clement tell Aia that he will make a telephone call to the Historical Society to inquire if their investigation is nearing the end so that they can return to their beloved, historical, and beautiful sanctuary.

At the end of this morning's worship service, Pastor Osterhagen delivered this announcement: "Palma Evenson, Historic St. Peter's oldest member, is one-hundred years old today, which falls exactly on Palm Sunday. Her birthday is another reason to shout our loud hosannas! The name Palma means Palm Tree, so along with all the palm branches we have in church today, it is fitting that this is her special day, too. A few weeks ago, Palma was asked if she would enjoy having a birthday party at church and she responded to that invitation with delight. These last few weeks the church bulletin has been announcing and inviting everyone to her birthday party, so I hope you will all stay today to celebrate her birthday with her."

After Pastor Osterhagen made his announcement, he invited the whole church to sing the traditional Happy Birthday song to Palma. Also, Palma's first cousin who was visiting from Sweden, Jennie Ekstrom, only eighty-six years old, sang a short solo in the microphone, a Swedish birthday song that actually mentioned turning one hundred years old in the text. At first Jennie sang it in Swedish, then in English. Part of the text went like this: "Yes, may she live for a hundred years; O sure, she will live for a hundred years!" Palma, for sure, has done just that.

Following that, it was time for Palma's birthday party. Hand-decorated cupcakes from the new bakery in town, The Sweet Indulgence Bake Shop, were on the table along with tea sandwiches, mixed nuts, and coffee and tea. Most important to Palma were all the hugs and good wishes that she received. Pastor presented with her with a huge birthday card that was made out of a piece of white poster board folded in half. Everyone had signed the inside of it and on the outside was written "Happy 100th Birthday, Palma," decorated with one-hundred colourful butterfly stickers. We mice have observed that all the members seem to think that she is an incredible lady, and a classy one, at that!

During the party Palma was perched in a regal-looking armchair, which her daughter, Debra Brinkman, brought into St. Pete's from Palma's living room just for this affair. Debra seemed amused to mention during conversations that her mother insisted on wearing a new dress for this occasion, as nothing in her closet was suitable for her one and only 100th birthday celebration. Palma dressed in a hue of powder blue, and adorned her ensemble with her oldest ornamental brooch, an oval-shaped white-on-blue cameo which she received on the day of her confirmation, eighty-seven years ago. It is a possession that is very treasured by Palma and also would be highly appraised by any knowledgeable antique jewellery dealer.

Palma was honoured that a letter was on display in Woolcox Hall that was written on White House stationary and signed by the President of the United States. It contained warm congratulations on her one-hundredth birthday. Many people sought Palma's advice about achieving longevity. She did not have an answer to that question but she did repeat several times that it is best to live your life depending on God and His promises, and to be a ray of sunshine, not wasting days and years worrying about anything, but praying about everything. She added that God's love has kept her safe and free of fear.

It wasn't until eight years ago that Palma stopped walking the two blocks distance to church due to arthritic pain in both of her knees. That led her to becoming acquainted with Stan, the taxi driver, who not only drives her to and from church every Sunday, but guides her up and down the church aisle. They sit side by side, and Stan helps her during worship by finding the pages in the hymnal. After church each Sunday, Stan drives to The Farmer's Harvest Restaurant and picks up Palma's standing order of an old-fashioned chicken dinner. Then he drives Palma home and helps her to get safely inside. Today Stan's wife, Patsy, was in church, too, and not only is she a pleasure to look at, but she sings really well. Bonbon, the newest mouse in the village, announced at the village meeting tonight that she thinks Patsy might start attending church and even join the choir because she seemed to like it at St. Pete's today. Bonbon told us that she is so glad to be a new resident in our village and prefers to live here rather than at The Sweet Indulgence Bake Shop. When the opportunity arose yesterday, she made haste to run up the ramp and propel herself into the bakery's delivery van, hiding inside there until the cupcake delivery was made at St. Pete's. Because Bonbon had heard such good things about Historic St. Peter's from a casual conversation she had with one of Percy's (Flip's) relatives, she made it a goal to join our community, even putting herself in danger to accomplish that. We all clapped for Bonbon, proud of the courage it took for her to arrive at St. Pete's in order to join us. The last thing that Bonbon talked about was her lack of a sweet tooth and how unsuitable it was for her to reside at a bakery, never experiencing a craving or an urge to indulge in something sweet.

John Overby was acting a bit peculiar in church today. He thought he was invisible, but he was mistaken. Two of our sweetest mice, Candy and Cane, were secretly observing him. John simply hung out in Woolcox Hall for awhile and waited for his chance to enter the church kitchen. When he saw that the coast was clear, he took his chance. Mabry Montgomery happened to walk into the kitchen to refill the mixed nut bowl when she spotted him loading up a tray with about fifteen or sixteen fancy birthday cupcakes. John never saw Mabry because she quickly backed out of the kitchen with silent footsteps. Candy and Cane reported to the village that John skedaddled out the kitchen door that leads directly to the church parking lot, most likely to reach his car. After witnessing the theft, Mabry appeared to not know exactly who to tell about this. So she procrastinated until the birthday party was completely over and then approached Pastor Osterhagen, explaining to him all that she had seen.

At the end of the day today, Clement and Aia discussed whether or not Palma Evenson might have gotten weary from all the attention given to her by being adored, cherished, glorified, and marvelled at, but they said it is far better than not being cared about at all. At least Palma doesn't need to be afraid that the only day people will care about her will be at her funeral, when she is gone and not around to hear anything that they say about her.

At 11:30 p.m. Ruby and I travelled to Woolcox Hall and snacked on crumbs of a variety of gourmet bakery cupcakes.

– F.N.

Monday, March 30

It took Pastor Osterhagen nothing but a brief telephone call to Finn Larssen, State Historical Society Representative, to inquire about unlocking the sanctuary doors so that they could return to using the sanctuary for worship, especially since Holy Week and Easter are upon us. Finn responded positively to Clement and gave him the go-ahead, as their investigation is now completed. He said the sanctuary can be put back to use and he was just about to call him with the news this morning. Finn also told Clement that when October arrives, he wants Historic St. Peter's to welcome historical tours on all four of the Saturdays from 10 a.m. to 4 p.m. Finn told Pastor that he will be there every Saturday along with another Historical Society tour guide. History buffs of the Underground Railroad are enthralled about the discovery at Historic St. Peter's. Therefore, bus tours from all over the state will be coming to the church to view the role Historic St. Peter's has played in the history of the United States.

After that, Finn Larssen explained to Pastor that he is a church-goer himself, and that his wife is president of the ladies' guild at their church. He suggested to Clement an idea given to him by his wife, Peggy. She mentioned that Historic St. Peter's Ladies' Guild could serve lunch on the four Saturdays in October to the tourists that arrive. They could make a bundle of money for their group in just one month. Kicking off Underground Railroad Month on October 4, Finn told Clement that he will formally mark and dedicate Historic St. Peter's as a national treasure, a valuable "Station" in the movement of the Underground Railroad. Clement was happy to hear the news, thanked Finn, and told him that he will present the lunch idea to HSP's Ladies' Guild. He laughed and said that the ladies will jump at the chance to serve in this way, as they are always eager to make a buck or two so that they can squirrel it away for later.

At 11:30 p.m. Ruby and I travelled to the parsonage and snacked on a dropped shaving of a pork tenderloin sandwich and a tiny portion of a homemade Dutch fry. We dipped the fry in a droplet of mayo and also in a driblet of some orange-red spicy curry ketchup.

– F.N.

Holy (Maundy) Thursday ~ April 2

PAULETTE PAULSON, THE ONE-DAY-A-WEEK CHURCH SECRETARY, ARRIVED AT CHURCH this morning ready to buckle down and produce the Easter Sunday bulletin, today's goal that needed to be accomplished no matter what. She was in a hurry because she had big plans that were to begin at three o'clock in the afternoon.

It is obvious that Pastor Osterhagen is concerned with the quality of the Sunday bulletins, making certain that they are free of typos before they make their passage through the copy machine. Paulette makes dozens of small typing errors, like "Diving Service - Setting I" instead of "Divine Service - Setting I" and "Historic Satan Peter's Church" instead of "Historic Saint Peter's Church." They are small mistakes, but somehow terrifying.

Enjoying newsy tidbits is what Paulette fancies about her job as she delights in putting a spin on them. Confidentiality is not one of her strengths. Parishioners often call up Aia at the parsonage and ask her if the bulletin announcements are actually correct, or if there is misinformation, because they can't believe what they have read. One time she typed that the church picnic food would be "grilled children" instead of "grilled chicken." Now that's a clear example of a really, really big boo-boo of a typo.

Today she wore something distinctively "Paulette:" a lightweight faux fur coat, a clingy mauve-coloured sweater, fashion boots and shiny polyester leather-look slacks. She explained to the Barber Shop (four retired men that hang out at the church office every Thursday while their wives are cleaning the house, but hang out mostly because they like to watch Paulette) that she had big plans following work today, plans that she is not going to share with them. That flirty line of hers sparked their imaginations and they all had a look on their faces like they needed to re-read the Sixth Commandment and "What does this mean?"

Today HSP's Barber Shop brought take-out coffees along with them to Paulette's office. They came with four black unleaded (decaf) coffees, one for each of them, and one special double cream leaded coffee for Paulette. Together they sat in the church office and jabbered about the church, how it's going, and about Pastor Osterhagen. Paulette continually delighted them with some new gossip that they can take to their Friday evening card party to share with the other card players while the hands are being dealt.

After the Barber Shop left church to return home to their wives at lunch-time, Paulette quickly finished her typing, skipped proofreading the contents, loaded the bulletin covers in the copy machine, and pushed the print button. When they were done, she placed them in a box on the counter in the office, leaving them for volunteer Hella Summerfield to dutifully fold in half and stuff with special inserts.

Maundy Thursday worship was this evening and all in attendance received Holy Communion. Organist Josie again covered her mouth with a couple of tissues every time she spoke to people.

At 11:30 p.m. Ruby and I travelled to the Osterhagens and sampled part of a homemade herbed crouton.

– F.N.

ORGANIST JOSIE MUST HAVE BEEN ILL, AS SHE CALLED PASTOR THIS AFTERNOON AND TOLD him she couldn't play the organ tonight. She assured him that she would definitely be there on Easter Sunday, ready to play at the Sunrise Service and also at the late service, which she calls the "sleep-in service." Aia stepped in to replace Josie at the organ for the Service of Darkness.

During this service the church noise level dropped to zero. It was so quiet that the mice had to be especially still, for fear they would easily be heard. The only sound was Pastor Osterhagen's voice. He was telling a story from the Bible that most of us mice find remarkable. It was about how God our maker sent his Son to become a human being, and to give up his life, being nailed onto a cross to pay for the sins of the whole world. We mice thought how lovely it must be for humans to have God become one of them and rescue them personally from all the terrible things humans do. After the sermon the church got very dark, and we all jumped at the sound of a loud noise. Ruby said is was Pastor Clement striking a hammer blow on a piece of wood, but it sounded like it would scare the devil himself.

Gretchen sat next to her mama at the organ bench keeping busy dressing and undressing her fashion doll. The doll clothes are a hodgepodge of clothing, but Gretchen thinks they are all beautiful. After worship tonight, Gretchen got a ride back to the parsonage in the wheelchair.

At 11:30 p.m. Ruby and I travelled to the parsonage and discovered mouse gold, feeling like we were a part of the gold rush. It was a tidbit of Old English Cheddar.

– F.N.

Holy Saturday ~ April 4

Heath and Heather Hill and their two children, Hawk and Hayley, arrived at St. Peter's this morning bringing along two hundred and eighty-eight jumbo free-range organic eggs. These eggs are to be scrambled and enjoyed at tomorrow's Easter Breakfast. The Hill Family raises Golden Cornet chickens on their farm, Hillsborough Haven. Two other church families who volunteered to host the Easter Breakfast this year arrived at HSP early this morning to make preparations for tomorrow's meal. The group worked efficiently and quickly and are prepared to host the Easter Breakfast at 7 a.m. tomorrow.

Late in the evening, Geraldine Greenmeyer arrived at church and unlocked the door, having borrowed a key from one of her friends who serves on the Altar Guild. Last Sunday she asked Pastor Osterhagen if she could display her abundant collection of Easter porcelain figurines at church. He agreed that a table could be set up for her display. Tonight she made four trips from the trunk of her car to the sanctuary carrying boxes that contained her carefully wrapped porcelain Easter figurines. One of the mice reported that Geraldine looked around for a table, but did not find one, so she displayed her collection throughout the chancel. Geraldine placed porcelain figurines here and there amongst the Easter lilies and on the altar. Standing back and observing her handiwork, she appeared to be very proud of her Easter figurine collection, all thirty-eight of them, in various sizes. She seemed confident that Pastor Osterhagen and the entire parish would recognize how much beauty this display added to the sanctuary on Easter Sunday morning. She took her four empty boxes with her and exited the church. After the mice talked about it, we all knew for certain that she would be back tomorrow morning to attend the Sunrise Service to see the people's reactions.

At 11:30 p.m. Ruby and I travelled to Woolcox Hall and snacked on a pink jelly bean that was accidently dropped on the floor. The host families made festive table centrepieces of Easter grass and jelly beans for the Easter Sunday breakfast.

– F.N.

PASTOR OSTERHAGEN VESTED IN HIS CLERGY ROBE AND WHITE STOLE THIS MORNING readying himself for the Easter Sunrise Service. Shortly before it began, he entered the narthex and lined up behind the Senior Choir. The sanctuary was dark in anticipation of sunrise. As the organ introduced the opening hymn, "Welcome, Happy Morning," the lights came on, parishioners opened their hymnals and stood to sing and watch the procession. The crucifer was the first one to march down the aisle holding high the processional cross, followed by choir members walking in side by side, with Pastor Osterhagen at the end of the procession. All went well until Pastor's eyes scanned the chancel. At that point he stopped singing because what he saw took his breath away. There were dozens of porcelain Easter bunnies tucked here and there, everywhere. Proceeding to count the number of figurines, he came up with thirty-eight. Realizing that the figurines were placed in the chancel by Geraldine Greenmeyer, several mice thought Pastor must have wondered what Jesus would do in this situation. Later on he told Aia his thoughts. He concluded that if they were still worshipping in Woolcox Hall, somehow this wouldn't seem as bad as it did in the formal sanctuary. But, in the sanctuary of Historic St. Peter's, the figurines depicting the secular Easter Bunny did not come anywhere close to matching or showing reverence for the holiness of this very day, let alone fitting for the dignified old-English architecture. He told Aia that he did not understand how Geraldine Greenmeyer could even imagine that her Easter bunny figurines were appropriate in the sanctuary, or was it because she does not understand the true meaning of Easter. The mice noticed that Pastor tried extra hard to deliver his sermon today so that everyone would understand that Easter Sunday is about Our Lord's Resurrection, Christ's rising from the dead by which He saved all believers by conquering sin and evil, preparing a home in heaven for them. Pastor felt compelled to add that Easter is not a bit about the Easter Bunny. The mice agreed with Pastor, but the bunnies that live in our neighbourhood are our good friends. In the summer we often share space together in the church gardens.

Dacus Brown, A.K.A. the church alligator, attended the 6:00 a.m. Easter sunrise service. At one point he was in an immense hurry to get upstairs to the choir loft, taking two steps at a time. Approaching Josie during the reading of the Easter Gospel, he had just moments to berate and put her down before she needed to introduce the sermon hymn. In a hard-nosed, steely, whispering voice he told Josie that she is the "worst organist this church has ever had." Immediately Josie was crushed, but gathered enough strength to whisper back at him, "Dacus, if you can do a better job than I'm doing, I'll get off the organ bench right now and you can finish playing for the worship service." He turned around, looking stunned that his bullying didn't work very well, so he went downstairs and returned to his pew.

At today's Easter breakfast, Josie was determined to find Lynda Galway, St. Pete's former organist, to tell her about the criticism that she had just received. Lynda told Josie that Dacus had done the exact same thing to her, in just the same way, also on an Easter Sunday. Lynda revealed that she was so traumatized that she immediately wrote her resignation letter on a sticky note, the only paper that she had handy at the organ. After church she gave it to the former Pastor and told him that she did not want to talk about it. The mice thought it was very unfortunate that both organists were recipients of harsh words from Dacus. Josie tried to finish today's service by playing a festive rendition of "Jesus Christ is Risen Today," but was unsuccessful because of hurt feelings and flowing tears. She could not see the notes through her tears, so today's postlude sounded more like "O Sacred Head Now Wounded" instead of the Easter fanfare she had planned and was prepared to play.

Dacus continued his persistent bellyaching throughout the Easter breakfast, annoyed and grousing about how every single year at Easter with all the Easter lilies the church looks and smells just like a funeral parlour. He also added that every single Christmas, with all the poinsettias and way too many lights on the Christmas tree, the church looks just like Las Vegas.

Ruby and I were in the tummy of the organ today, heard everything, and cried when Dacus spoke in such a roughshod way to Josie without any respect for her feelings. What cold-hearted Dacus said was worse than mean, it was wicked. Because of this, Josie might increase her habit of sipping from her tea tumbler and speaking with a tissue held over her mouth.

At 8:30 p.m. Ruby and I travelled to Woolcox Hall and snacked on morsels of scrambled eggs, sausages, blueberry muffins, fresh fruit, and streuselkuchen that had fallen to the floor from the Easter breakfast.

– F.N.

THERE WAS A FUNERAL TODAY AT HISTORIC ST. PETER'S FOR A LIFELONG MEMBER WHO was the founding organizer of St. Peter's Ladies' Guild. Throughout all the years of her leadership, she gave many, many ladies consternation. Now that she's gone, a few of the ladies have opened up and have started to quietly speak about her oddities. Emma Woolcox passed away a week ago, but because of Holy Week and Easter Sunday, the Woolcox family decided to wait until today to hold her funeral. Emma was the matriarch of the Woolcox clan, which resulted in her family spending whatever amount of money it took to make her funeral extra special, just the way Emma would have wanted it to be, if she could have been there to attend it – alive, that is.

The church had more flowers in the sanctuary surrounding Emma's casket than the contents of most floral shops, plus there were the Easter lilies left over from church yesterday. The floral aroma was so overwhelming that it overpowered one of the pallbearers, Kyle Woolcox, triggering a dangerous asthma attack. During the funeral, he had to leave the church and be taken to the emergency room at Our Lady of Lourdes Hospital.

Several old hymns were sung at the funeral, ones that were special to Emma, but her favourite song was a jazzy Christmas song called, "Carry Me to Bethlehem." The Woolcox family asked for special permission from the publisher so that the song could be used at the funeral. They told Pastor Osterhagen that they were aware that it is a Christmas song, not really appropriate for a funeral, but asked if he would make an exception just for them, just this once. Pastor said that they could use the song. The Woolcox family soon found out that no one in town could even sing this song, along with the fact that it was far too difficult for Josie to play, which made them realize they were out of luck with having live musicians. They asked Pastor if they could play a tape recording of it, which lasts, incidentally, only three minutes and twelve seconds. Pastor agreed and they played the song at the funeral today. This really puzzled St. Pete's Ladies' Guild members which led them to discuss why Emma would have ever enjoyed that song. Not one of them cared for the sound of it.

Throughout the funeral service Josie was stationed at the organ keeping a box of tissues handy. She needed a supply of them as she was crying, not at all about the loss of Emma Woolcox, but about what the church bully, Dacus Brown, had said to her on Easter Sunday morning. She had her tea tumbler along with her today which contained something to help her make it through the funeral service, as she was simply falling to pieces. Ruby and I sat in the tummy of the organ and listened to the entire funeral and mentioned that Pastor Osterhagen is a great preacher as he gives people hope about life everlasting. We're so proud of him.

At 11:30 p.m. Ruby and I travelled to Woolcox Hall and snacked on morsels that fell on the floor from the funeral lunch, especially the wide variety of squares, cakes, various desserts, and fruit platters.

– F.N.

Wednesday, April 8

THE APRIL DAYS HAVE BEEN FILLED WITH RAIN, ONE SHOWER AFTER THE NEXT. BRADY IS a mouse in our village that has been utterly enjoying these rainy days. Performing acts of kindness is usually his favourite thing to do, especially when any mouse in our village gets lost in HSP's gigantic building. When that happens, he not only helps them find their way, but usually says, "Follow me and we'll be there in no time!" He has not been doing much of that this month as the rain and the puddles it produces are uppermost on his mind.

Last Sunday Brady overheard a conversation between two parishioners when one of them mentioned these words, "April showers bring May flowers." Brady was confused as to what these words meant and I was baffled, too. I forwarded this befuddlement to our Head Librarian, Dr. Theodore Simonsen, requesting him to research it. After his investigation, Dr. Simonsen responded by saying that this is an extremely old English phrase that dates from the 1600's. However, since that time the original phraseology has changed a bit. The historical wording was "Sweet April showers do spring May flowers." Brady and I still did not grasp the meaning so I asked Dr. Simonsen to translate it into plain Mouse, and he replied, *"Ooz busnop virs lliounpoin wec."* Brady and I were thankful to hear those words as it lead to our complete understanding. I will convert the phrase into English so you will grasp the meaning. The phrase translated from Mouse is, "By tolerably experiencing a meager amount of various miserable circumstances, at the current time, each one of us will therefore encounter some magnificent things in the future."

As I mentioned, Brady is known widely throughout the village for his acts of kindness. Just lately he has become even more well known for enjoying wading in the numerous puddles (which he refers to as small lakes) on St. Peter's property that have resulted from the abundance of April showers. In fact, he spends so much time wading from puddle to puddle the village officially decided to change his name from Brady to Wade, a much more distinctive and fitting name for him.

Ruby and I have learned a new song simply by listening to songstress Aia. For several days Aia has been singing the song, "Wade in the Water," as she strums along on her Kentucky guitar. We are keen on the melody as well as the text. Due to that, the song has become a new addition to our repertoire. If called upon, we are prepared to gladly perform it in public. We thought it best to share this song with the entire village so that they can enjoy it, too. After a quick invitation to our home, the villagers arrived this afternoon to listen to Aia sing her song. The mice heard the words and melody and learned it straight away. We also heard Clement tell Aia that he is absolutely enthralled as he listens to her God-given mezzo-soprano voice that is abundantly full of artistry, grace, and virtuosity. Clement then invited Aia to sing "Wade in the Water" during the worship service this coming Sunday. Aia questioned Clement about the song being appropriate for church, doubting that the parishioners would enjoy this soulful song. She said that she notices they prefer churchy songs like "Just a Closer Walk with Thee," "Just as I Am," or that old Southern hymn composed by Eliza E. Hewitt, "Just a Little Sunshine." (We all picked up on Aia speaking Trinitarian once again, making her point in threes.) Clement admitted that he was unfamiliar with that hymn, so Aia proceeded to sing a small part of the refrain that ends with these words: "Telling love's sweet story, everywhere we go." Clement immediately recalled the song as it is a favourite of Blanche Browne who moved up here from Eufaula, Alabama, decades ago. (Last year, Blanche made a special request to Pastor to include her favourite hymn in one of the worship services.) Clement assured Aia that "Wade in the Water" would provide new exposure to a spiritual that has been so vital in North American history, and is entirely appropriate to be sung at a worship service. He said he liked its allusion to Holy Baptism which is an important part of Easter's message. Clement also added that it is far superior of a song than "Just a Little Sunshine." He further went on to explain that "Wade in the Water" happens to be an Underground Railroad Song that was sung by slaves as they found the route to freedom, as the song contained directions of where and how to travel to Canada in a secret code found in the lyrics. Those directions included telling the slaves to wade in the water so that the bloodhounds were unable to track the escaped slaves because when they enter the water their scent was lost. After that Clement and Aia talked a lot about Harriet Tubman. We noticed that Aia was inspired by Clement's words along with the vast expanse of historical knowledge he has on the tip of his tongue. She asked him to call her Harriet for the remainder of the week, just until after she has sung "Wade in the Water" during the worship service this coming Sunday.

Since the entire village has mastered memorizing "Wade in the Water," we have come up with big plans to surprise Wade while he is wading in one of the little lakes. We plan to circle around the puddle and sing our song, followed by disappearing in a flash. In a way, it would be an act of kindness done by the villagers in appreciation for Wade's many acts of kindness. Thankfully, the forecast is for rain all day tomorrow, so the surprise has been scheduled for early in the morning. Wade does not know one iota about it. He has actually been logging in over twelve thousand steps per day wading in the water. Yesterday I asked him if he was tuckered out from all of those steps. He replied that his paws feel fine, but admitted that it is very stressful to count in his head to twelve thousand every single day.

Several of the mice thought it would be historic if we created our own spiritual, hoping to devise something as stirring and bewitchingly impassioned as "Wade in the Water." Right then and there we formed a committee, set up upcoming meeting times, giving instructions to each committee member to compose lyrics for a spiritual, followed by asking them to be prepared to present them at the next meeting. The remainder of the day I spent thinking about some lyrics. So far all I have come up with is, "There ain't no sunshine, but sunny days are ahead." Perhaps I will completely ditch that idea and start over as it sounds a bit too similar to "April showers bring May flowers."

At 11:30 p.m. Ruby and I travelled to the parsonage and interestingly enough found an orange slice, a little bit of liquid sunshine under the dining room table on this day that has been anything but sun-drenched. The weather here currently feels like the United Kingdom. We can count our blessings that we do not have to put up with one hundred plus days of precipitation per year like the U.K. After we got under our coverlet, Ruby mentioned to me that we sang "Wade in the Water" far too many times today. She suggested that we sing Johnny Nash's song, "I Can See Clearly Now" before we fall asleep tonight. Hopefully when May arrives we will have bright, sunshiny days.

– F.N.

Friday, April 10

CLEMENT RECEIVED A DISTRICT REGISTRATION FORM IN THE MAIL TODAY FOR THE upcoming three-day pastors' conference to be held next month at "The River Swan Lodge." He was in a hurry to complete and return the registration form, as promptness will increase their chances of obtaining a hotel room that overlooks the breathtaking River Swan, so named because it is home to a large number of beautiful white swans, a sight not to be missed. This is a required conference for clergy, but many spouses attend it, too, as they delight in a time away from the daily grind, a non-stop lifestyle, always on duty in case there is an emergency.

Because the conference is ninety miles away from the parsonage, Clement and Aia will sleep two nights at "The River Swan Lodge," the cost being paid for by Historic St. Peter's, taken out of the clergy education line item in the annual budget. Aia is especially excited to attend this gathering with Clement because they will be able to squeeze in couple time. She told Clement that she is dreaming of being lazy by sleeping in both mornings. Clement spoils Aia at these conferences by awakening her with coffee and breakfast in bed. He delivers a tray containing a warm plate of the hotel complimentary breakfast knowing just what she wants on her tray. It's the only time of the year that Aia eats biscuits and gravy, a real splurge of Southern food that is calorie-laden. The other meals, during the conference, are at restaurants. Thankfully, for her, the only meal they have to share with the entire group is the closing banquet.

Aia is looking forward to having time to browse and shop at the unique stores in the area. She told Clement that shopping is exactly the woman's equivalent of men going hunting for deer or fishing for walleye. After she told Clement how excited she is to attend the conference, he realized how important it is for his wife to have some freedom, a time without so many responsibilities. When the conference rolls around again next year, it will be nearly impossible for Aia to attend. They both know they won't be able to find anyone with enough strength, patience, and endurance to watch Gretchen and the baby twins.

In the past they hired Flora Vickstrom to stay with Gretchen while they were away. Flora temporarily moved into the parsonage and lived with Gretchen. But the Vickstroms moved away to sunny Florida in January because Vic, her husband, took advantage of early retirement and ceased to work at his job at the end of December. Flora was wonderful at bonding with Gretchen. A couple of times she took Gretchen to the public library, returning home with a stack of various children's books to read to her at bedtime. They played games together, both inside and outside, so that Gretchen got lots of fresh air and they both got plenty of Vitamin D. Together their four hands made crafts and special treats, and their four ears listened to each other's stories. Each evening when supper was ready, Flora would dial up Vic and then put Gretchen on the line. Gretchen would invite him to come over and eat supper with them. Gretchen really liked him because after the first supper that they ate together, there was fun time. Gretchen even changed Vic's name from "Mr. Vic" to "Mr. Napkin Noggin." Mr. Napkin Noggin got his name after he placed an extra large white unfolded cloth napkin over his head, topped it with his eyeglasses, and tucked a bit of the napkin into his mouth. If that wasn't enough of a hoot to watch, Mr. Napkin Noggin would speak, move his head, gesture with his arms, and say many funny things. The laughter would flow from Gretchen and Flora. The laughter wasn't just regular laughter, but the real kind that is from your gut, the fall-off-your-chair variety involving shrieks and roars. Aia has been on a hunt all day to find a replacement for the Vickstroms, but has been unsuccessful so far.

While Aia spoke to Clement about the situation, an old hurt of hers surfaced and she shared it with him. Aia explained the time her parents, Arni and Juliette, left home to attend a teachers conference for three nights, leaving her in the care of Mrs. Moldenhauer, an older lady from the neighbourhood. Aia told Clement her memories of Mrs. Moldenhauer were of a grumpy, sour, mean-spirited, contentious, ill-tempered, cross, and down-right crabby widow, who never had any children, didn't even like children, and had ugly black bushy eyebrows, spindly legs, and coarse horse-hair on her head done up in an unbecoming hairdo that was anything but her crowning glory. During day two that Mrs. Moldenhauer was watching five-year old Aia, she sensed some human wickedness in the old devilish woman. Being so full of fear, Aia thought about running away, but didn't know where to run to, or even how to hide from her. She was certain that Mrs. Moldenhauer was a real witch, just like the one she saw once on television that really scared her. So, Aia asked Mrs. Moldenhauer if she was a witch. After Aia's witch question, Mrs. Moldenhauer became angry, seemed insulted, annoyed, and put-down by a measly five-year old. She told Aia that she would receive punishment for what she had said to her. Mrs. Moldenhauer did punish Aia, like she promised, by making her sit on the bottom step of the stairway which led to the second level of the house, located in the entryway. Aia was within two feet of the front door, at the base of the tall grandfather clock that painfully played Westminster Chimes on each hour, quarter hour, and half hour. Aia was told to sit there from 12:30 p.m. until 5 p.m. and if she disobeyed, Mrs. Moldenhauer warned her that there would be no supper for her. Mrs. Moldenhauer's scratchy voice and long, skinny finger threatened her to not leave that spot except when she had permission from her to use the washroom.

A lot happened between those four and one-half hours to little Aia. Aia learned how very long a minute is and how slow the hands on the grandfather clock move when you are being punished. Mrs. Moldenhauer would check on her every few minutes to see that she was still stationed on the bottom step. Aia told Clement that to this very day she cannot stand the melody or sound of Westminster Chimes or the look of any grandfather clock because of the punishment she received that day so long ago.

At two-thirty in the afternoon, Mrs. Moldenhauer stopped what she was doing and ceased paying attention to Aia because she was riveted to her two favourite soap operas. For one solid hour she did not pay any attention to Aia. It was during that time that relief arrived for Aia in the form of her friend from across the street, Jeffie Donaldson. Because the weather was warm, the front door of the house was left open so that the breeze could come through the screen door. Jeffie arrived at the open front door and saw her sitting on the step doing nothing and asked her what was happening. Little Aia immediately started crying, and, when she stopped, she explained everything to him. He said that he would help her because they were friends. Jeffie sat outside the front door and kept her entertained by describing every car that drove up and down Prospect Boulevard. He explained in detail his hopes and dreams of someday owning a convertible, a blue one. After awhile he told her that he was going home and would be back in a few minutes, before the grandfather clock would chime again. When he returned, he had two paper plates containing saltine crackers that were topped with easy cheese spread from an aerosol can. Jeffie even had a joke to add to their afternoon treat conversation in which he said, "What do you call a cheese that is sad?" Aia didn't know the answer to the joke, so Jeffie revealed that the answer was "Blue Cheese." They laughed quietly together many times, but Mrs. Moldenhauer didn't hear them because she was so wrapped up in her two soap operas.

Jeffie went home a couple more times. Each time he returned with supplies to entertain her, like alphabetical and numerical flash cards, a children's joke book, a menu from the restaurant that his folks owned, and a cardboard cigar box that contained his marble collection. He held one marble up at a time for her to see as he announced the name of each type of marble. She remembered that his cat's eye marble and the Bennington marble were his favourites. She thought the Bennington marble was just beautiful at the time, which is why Clement and Aia now own a couple of pieces of Bennington Pottery, hoping to add several more pieces to their collection. (As a side line to her story, she mentioned to Clement that she would like it if they could take another Vermont vacation one of these years and bring home a couple more pieces of Bennington Pottery.) When she heard Mrs. Moldenhauer coming to check on her, she wildly motioned for Jeffie to get away from the front door and get into hiding. He scooted to the corner of the front porch, not visible to the Wicked Witch, and stayed there until she went away.

Shortly before five o'clock Jeffie said goodbye to Aia and told her a couple of things, good and hopeful news. He said he wanted to help her so he told his mother about her punishment given by the Wicked Witch. His mother said that she will speak to Mrs. Moldenhauer and ask if Aia could come over and have supper with them. His mother also said that she will call Mrs. Moldenhauer after supper and ask if Aia could stay overnight with them. In the morning, she will call Mrs. Moldenhauer once again and ask if Aia can stay all day and play with Jeffie. Then she will keep repeating this until Aia's folks return home from the teachers conference. Aia told Jeffie that he was a real gentleman, even though he was only six years old, and thanked him for finding a way to get her away from the Wicked Witch. Jeffie told her that when they grow up he is going to marry her, purchase a blue convertible, work in a grocery store, and that they will have lots and lots of children together, probably thirteen in all.

After telling Clement how Jeffie saved her life so long ago, Aia said that she is going to quit looking for someone to watch Gretchen while they are away at the pastors' conference. She has decided to take her with them as Gretchen will have a blast. She'll take her to the hotel swimming pool, shopping, and the playground. Aia reminded Clement to be certain to take along their two camping chairs, and Gretchen's little camping chair, so at four o'clock they can sit next to the river and watch the swans while enjoying a cup of coffee. Aia said that she will bring along a tape that has Tchaikovsky's "Swan Lake" on it and they can quietly listen to it while they watch the swans. Complimentary coffee can come from the hotel lobby and she'll bring a juice box for Gretchen. The view of the swans on the river will be a little glimpse of heaven itself, a memory maker for the Osterhagens that they can capture and add to their lives well-lived.

Aia confessed to Clement that when she was five years old she also wanted to marry Jeffie Donaldson and has often wondered just what happened to him. She heard from her mother a while ago, who ran into Jeffie's mother while grocery shopping, that Jeffie is still an available and handsome bachelor who has never found the "right girl." Her mother also said that it was just too unfortunate that he didn't get together with Aia. Mrs. Donaldson told her mother that Jeffie has an established career as a professor of mathematics at an Oklahoma university, having taught there a long time. Aia told Clement that she has wondered if they would have been right for each other, had the timing been different. Clement looked a bit hurt when she said that, but after Aia told him that she loved him and that he was the right one, all quickly became peachy again between them.

Aia said that Mrs. Moldenhauer was never hired again by her folks. After Ruby and I heard the gut-wrenching story from Aia's own mouth, we wondered why people are so afraid of mice. Mice wouldn't do anything like that, and we don't have anyone in our village resembling the witchy Mrs. Moldenhauer. It seems to us that people are the most afraid of one another.

At 11:30 p.m. Ruby and I travelled to the parsonage and snacked on a morsel of one chow mein crunchy noodle we found under the dining room table. That wasn't very filling, so we both went to bed with grumbling tummies. Maybe tomorrow's gleanings will be better.

– F.N.

MANY WEEKS AGO, PASTOR OSTERHAGEN WAS ON A SEARCH TO COME UP WITH A substitute organist to fill in for Josie after she requested to have Sunday, April 12th, as an off-duty day from her job as organist. Josie and her husband are now away on a weekend getaway to an Ohio bed and breakfast, spending the daytime hours of their weekend hunting for quality antiques and the evening hours dining and attending a two night live drama of the Passion Story.

Ruby heard Clement tell Aia several weeks ago that there is a false saying out there that claims people with organ skills are so common that there is an actual abundance of them, and that they are "a dime a dozen." Clement said that saying is utterly false. Telling Aia how difficult it is to find an organist, he decided to simplify his search. His new emphasis for finding a musician for today was to place less prominence on the quality of their performance, but place it on the dependability and reliability of the fill-in musician. He is looking for a substitute musician to arrive early at church and be prepared to play the music. Josie repeatedly arrives at the last minute in a sauced-up tipsy condition clasping tightly to a tea tumbler containing something far stronger than steeped tea with double cream and double sugar.

After calling up nearly everyone on his list, Clement resorted to calling the last person on his list, Willard Blankley. Willard is an elderly bachelor who plays the hymns far too slowly and softly, exhibiting not much musical leadership. When he played for HSP in the past, he brought along his brother-in-law, Milton Braxton. Milton is his personal page-turner who cannot read music, but has the ability to fully follow facial signals from Willard as to just when a page needs turning. Willard is not an organist, but he is able to accompany the hymns and provide any incidental or background music on the console piano that is located near the pulpit.

Willard has social anxiety and constantly is certain that everyone is staring at him, resulting in getting an uneasy feeling from it. His feelings are overwhelming, making him even more nervous and anxious, and any staring at all simply ends up creeping him out. In order to move out of the eyeshot of the parishioners, Willard came up with a solution that he brought along with him the last time he played the pianoforte at St. Peter's.

Last night our village botanist, Phylum, spotted Willard arriving at church with his brother-in-law helper, Milton. Phylum became interested in the wide variety of large houseplants that they were unloading from the back of Willard's old pickup truck. The plants were a combination of actual live plants along with some high quality artificial plants. Some plants were five feet tall. Milton placed a small clear plastic tablecloth on top of the piano in order to protect the varnished wood from any water leakage. After that, Willard and Milton arranged plants snugly on top of the piano. By strategically placing the tallest plants on the floor, an entire thick greenhouse surrounded the piano. At that point Willard sat at the piano while Milton rotated from pew to pew, from angle to angle, checking to see if anyone would be able to see him while he was stationed at the piano. After the plants were situated in just the right position, the men left the sanctuary sporting full smiles. On their way out, they talked about what beverage they would order at their favourite watering hole, the Green Valley Pub. Phylum reported that they told each other they deserved to enjoy a couple of refreshments after all of the work they had just done to get ready for the worship service.

After Willard and Milton left the building early Saturday evening, Phylum urged all of the mice to come out to see the breathtaking plants. There was just enough light in the sanctuary from the eternal light to view the many varieties of plants. Phylum pointed out to everyone a philodendron, a Swiss leaf monster, a small canary palm, a dracaena warneckii, a Boston fern, a Ficus tree, and something called a ZZ, among others.

With Willard on the piano bench this morning and Milton posted on a small side chair, the prelude began with the song, "In the Garden." "In the Garden" was played several times, not just for the prelude, but also when the offering was collected, during communion distribution, and finally as a postlude. The mice on patrol noticed that most of the parishioners seemed very tired of listening to it and wanted Willard to play something else. Ozzie Strong muttered to his wife, Beverly, that even Billy Graham himself would have gotten tired of that song if he attended Historic St. Peter's today.

One cheery moment this morning was the arrival of two visitors, the university-aged daughters, Crystal and Claudia, of Stan, the taxi driver, and his wife Patsy. All of the mice cheered that HSP had two young visitors, but that delight was curtailed when one mouse from our village, Patchwork, overheard the girl's discussion that took place in the ladies' washroom before worship. Crystal and Claudia were deeply discussing something disturbing. Patchwork shared that they were unsure as to why their parents suddenly have a desire to attend church, as this has never happened before. In fact, Crystal and Claudia have never entered a church before. Today is the third Sunday in a row that Stan and Patsy have attended St. Peter's. Not only that, Claudia added that their parents speak so lovingly of Historic St. Peter's that she wonders if they are being lured into a cult. If it is a cult, this church will soon capture all their money, time, and energy, as they will be taken advantage of by the cult leader and followers. Both worriedly confessed that this cult might even separate them from their parents because they will get hooked and so engrained that they will never be able to leave. Both agreed that if this happens they will need to capture them, take them home, and find some professional to deprogram them. Crystal urged Claudia to join her in keeping her eyes and ears open this morning to see if their parents are new recruits that are being brainwashed.

At 7:30 p.m. Ruby and I travelled to one of the Sunday School rooms and snacked on a morsel of a gummy worm. We talked while we ate about how green the church was today with the addition of the personal plant collection Willard brought to church from his home.

A few of the mice overheard some of the ladies in the back of the church talk about Willard and his attachment to the colour green. They said that all of his upholstered furniture in his home is green, along with the carpets and drapes. He even has a large collection of green Depression glass dishes in his dining room china cabinet. They are bewildered as to why a bachelor would even care to collect antique dishes.

Ruby and I concluded that it might be just very natural for Willard to favour the colour green. Perhaps sometimes he gets green with envy, or is happy when he gets a green light, or is somewhat of a greenhorn at something, or he might be looking for greener pastures, or gets shyness on the green (the fear of not performing well in a golf game). Willard's favourite watering hole is even called The Green Valley Pub. We think he should come back to HSP and play the piano in church on any of the Sundays after Pentecost, because the liturgical colour is green. Ruby remembered that bit of information because she read it on the church liturgical calendar that is currently hanging in the church office.

– F.N.

Monday, April 13

FIRST THING THIS MORNING, A VILLAGE MEETING WAS CONVENED DUE TO A CLOSE SHAVE involving a member of our community during yesterday's worship service. This heart stopper of a situation required prompt attention with vigilant and wide-awake thinking on everyone's part.

Yesterday's crisis concerned one of our older members in the village, Napoleon, who prefers to be called Nap. Unfortunately, Nap suffers from chronic narcolepsy. He can fall asleep anywhere, anytime without warning. After admitting to me yesterday that his condition has escalated to new heights, Nap said that his ailment has joined the realm of being out of control. He pleaded with me to help him overcome the rigid grip narcolepsy has on him. Pointing out that his shut-eye dilemma places the entire mice village at risk, Ruby and I agreed with him that safety needs to be our first priority, as well as helping Nap. Nap had questions about whether or not comprehensive holistic or naturopathic treatments would help him, or if he should go straight away to an acupuncture clinic. He even asked us if we know of a twelve step program for recovery. Nap described that his days and nights are spent taking siestas as he seems to require way more than forty winks. He never knows when or where he will suddenly start snoozing. It is a life of feeling exasperated and drained out round-the-clock, day after day. I told him that I did not know the answers, but that a special meeting would be called and everyone will think about the issue logically in order to come up with a solution for him. After that, Nap calmed down by taking a nap at our dwelling. Ruby covered him up with a crocheted, groovy-patterned afghan blanket that she handmade from a variety of colourful yarns that she noticed in the quilting supply cupboard at St. Pete's. As Nap slept, Ruby said that he is fully living out the words of Psalm 4:8. She told me that she has them memorized because they are so comforting. They go like this: "In peace I will lie down and sleep, for you alone, LORD, make me dwell in safety." I concurred with her about that verse.

Nap enjoys a Saturday night ritual each week by travelling to the sanctuary and spending the night sleeping on the floor in the pulpit. So far this has worked out well, until now. He rises early enough on Sunday mornings and gets a move on before anyone arrives at church. Nap must have been really pooped out yesterday because he overslept and was injured by Pastor Osterhagen. Telling the villagers about his trauma, Nap relayed that while Pastor was standing in the pulpit preaching an awe-inspiring sermon, he moved his foot just slightly and stepped on the end of Nap's tail, crushing it with the tip of his size-twelve black wingtips. It was a cliff-hanger of a moment for Nap, who was having a dream about running blindly and being chased by a farmer's wife with a carving knife. Somehow he kept quiet while suffering through excruciating pain. He managed to get behind the square electric box that controls the pulpit microphone that is positioned on the rear floor of the pulpit. Nap said that he hid behind the box waiting quietly in that spot for the worship hour to be over.

The pros and cons of Nap's narcolepsy were thoroughly discussed at this morning's meeting. The villagers unanimously agreed that we need to eliminate the close calls, those scary, spine-chiller moments when your knuckles turn ghostly white and you are scared to death that our village will be discovered. Many pros were mentioned by Morning Glory as she announced her recent move to Loving Arms Nursing Home, wondering if Nap would like to reside there also. Morning Glory said that it is a place where they mostly spend their time chilling out by napping. She also mentioned that every Sunday they serve a Napoleon pastry for dessert that has seven layers of puff pastry filled with custard and whipped cream, quite a bit of which ends up on the floor. When Nap heard the description of the irresistible Napoleon desserts, he was downright intent on relocating to Loving Arms Nursing Home.

At 11:30 p.m. Ruby and I travelled to the parsonage and snacked on two poppy seeds that Aia must have dropped on the kitchen floor when she was making Lemon Poppy Seed Bread this morning.

– F.N.

Friday, April 17

THE LAST SEVERAL MORNINGS AFTER GRETCHEN AWAKENS, SHE SPRINGS OUT OF BED AND straightaway puts her bunny slippers on her bare feet. The overstuffed slippers are of a classic design, have whiskers and a cotton ball tail, along with her favourite part of all, adjustable bunny ears. Gretchen used her fast-walking technique to arrive at the window in her parent's bedroom that overlooks St. Peter's backyard. She was there to observe one particular wild rabbit that sits in the same spot every day soaking up the sunshine. The rabbit, which Gretchen appropriately named Slippers, looks and acts like a garden statue, similar to a gargoyle, angel, Buddha, or gnome crafted out of resin. Frequently Gretchen runs to and from the window checking to see if Slippers is still in her spot.

The hubble-bubble this morning occurred when Gretchen discovered that Slippers was not in her usual spot. Throughout the next couple of hours she frequently hurried to the bedroom window hoping to find Slippers sitting in her spot.

Gretchen has been told about putting safety first and being wary of danger. Ruby and I overheard her ask her mother if a mean stranger might have snatched Slippers. Aia reassured Gretchen by suggesting that Slippers might have gone on vacation or perhaps found a new home that is probably near some crocuses that will soon be blooming. Gretchen proceeded to ask her mommy, "Where do bunnies hang out for fun?" Before Aia got a chance to reply, Gretchen answered her own question with, "The Hare Salon." Asking Gretchen where she heard that riddle, she replied that her friend Alaina Carter told her that joke on Easter Sunday. Gretchen mentioned that at first she did not understand the answer, so Alaina, whose mother, Giada, owns the "Ooh-La-La Beauty Salon," explained it to her.

The remainder of the morning Gretchen shifted her attention to the contents of a little red suitcase which contains Aia's childhood paper dolls. Over and over Gretchen changed outfits on Shirley Temple, the "Little House on the Prairie" characters, the many children in The Old Lady in the Shoe, and the Lennon Sisters. We noticed that the majority of her time, however, was spent playing with her favourite paper dolls, the Bridal Party Wedding Collection.

At 11:30 p.m. Ruby and I travelled to the parsonage and split one pumpkin seed, a phenomenal nutrient-rich health food. Together we visited about what happened to Slippers. On Sunday evening I will bring the disappearance of

Slippers up at the village meeting and perhaps we can form a search committee to find out her whereabouts. Then again, there just might be a simple answer to this. Perhaps Slippers has taken refuge in a gloriously colourful barberry bush.

– F.N.

AT TEN O'CLOCK THIS MORNING, JOEY CABOT AND JOCELYN MURRAY ARRIVED FOR THEIR appointment with Pastor Osterhagen. They are newly engaged and wanted to speak with Pastor about arrangements for their wedding. Pastor asked them how they met. Both of them were delighted to explain to him how they met at church, right here at Historic St. Peter's.

Jocelyn mentioned that one bitterly cold Sunday last January she arrived at church with Ian, her son, and Maisie, her daughter, to attend church and Sunday school. Jocelyn helped her children remove their snow garb, the boots, hooded winter jackets, mitts, and toques, the whole lot. As she took a step backward while reaching for a hanger, she accidently ploughed into a man who wasn't standing in that spot just a minute prior to that. Jocelyn mentioned that if she had been driving a vehicle, she, of course, would have turned around and looked, but in this case she didn't even bother to turn around and look before she backed up into the stranger, assuming that no one would be standing there. After making an embarrassingly skittish, timid, and nervous apology, she introduced herself to someone new, a strikingly handsome man with blue-green eyes. He introduced himself to her as Joey Cabot. Joey mentioned to Pastor that because he is a fairly new member of Historic St. Peter's, he and Jocelyn had never met before. Most everyone in his family belongs to the little country church with the big cemetery. Joey said that he transferred to Historic St. Peter's in order to meet some new people. The church out in the county is so small that he knows all of the parishioners because they are mostly his relatives.

Jocelyn explained to Pastor that six years ago she met and married a man from Ireland by the name of Basil Murray, having become close to each other while they were students at university. After they graduated, they got married in her home town. Two years ago Basil flew back to Ireland by himself for a family reunion. While in Ireland, Basil was involved in a horrific car crash after which he lived only a few hours. At that time Ian was only three years old, with Maisie just ten months old. Jocelyn revealed that she was heartbroken, but that God has helped her to heal.

Joey mentioned that after a couple of Sundays, they got to know each other and started dating, mentioning how quickly they had become close to each other.

When Jocelyn arrives at church with her children each Sunday, Ian and Maisie hurry over to Joey and give him big hugs by wrapping their arms around his legs to squeeze him. The four of them sit together in church and are already becoming a family.

Pastor knows that Cabot's Lumber Company, Inc. is a family-owned operation that draws business from all over Oswald County. Joey works for the company while Jocelyn works as a grade three teacher. Even though Jocelyn has had abundant sad and lonely times since Basil died, she doesn't seem to be sad or lonely now. She has done all that she can do to be a wonderful mother, but now she is not alone, as Joey is helping with the parenting. Joey admitted that being a bachelor has had a lot of sad and lonely times, too, but the mice are certain that this couple's sad and lonely days are now over.

Pastor Osterhagen thought they would plan the wedding date for Saturday, November 14, at Historic St. Peter's with him officiating. Even though that date was available, Joey and Jocelyn actually suggested a new, but very old-fashioned idea, of having their wedding on Sunday morning, November 15. Pastor Osterhagen replied that he and his wife were married on a Sunday morning, too, and they were so glad they did it that way. Jocelyn and Joey became very curious about the idea and wondered if that would work for them, inquiring if they could instead be married on Sunday morning, November 15. Pastor checked the church calendar, answered any questions they had, and it was settled. Pastor talked briefly about a pre-marital course that they will need to take, but told them that there is no rush just yet to begin the course.

At 10:50 p.m. Ruby and I travelled to the Osterhagens and snacked on a dropped morsel of a veggie pizza.

– F.N.

FOLLOWING THE WORSHIP SERVICE TODAY, OUR GOOD FRIEND ECHO JOINED US FOR lunch. Prior to eating lunch, we showed Echo the small hole in the parsonage dining room where we peek into the parsonage. The three of us listened carefully to the Osterhagen's conversation. It began with Aia bursting forth words of regret as she told Clement about hurt feelings that she had been suppressing since yesterday. Admitting to Clement that she tried to hold it all in, she told him that she needed pastoral counseling from him. Playing the organ for yesterday's wedding of Joleen Webb and Spencer Radcliffe at Word of Hope Christian Church ended up in being a big money-drainer for Aia. Because Word of Hope is located in neighbouring Franklin County, a thirty-minute drive away, Aia mentioned that she had plenty of time while driving back home to logically think things over. She said that she plans to make concrete boundaries when it comes to taking on the role of a guest organist so that she never gets taken advantage of again.

The bride and groom had contacted Aia several months ago about playing the organ at their wedding. They had heard first-hand from a friend that Aia Osterhagen was the most accomplished organist in the area. Even though Aia was flattered to receive the compliment, all the kudos dissipated during her drive back home following the wedding ceremony. Letting off a bit of steam after church today, she told Clement how it felt to be swindled and taken advantage of. We noticed that Aia is careful when it comes to money, but the expense involved was exorbitant. She spent money on gas to travel back and forth on Friday night and Saturday afternoon. Joleen even requested a specific song to be played at their wedding that Aia did not have in her organ collection. In order to fulfill Joleen's request, Aia had to purchase an organ book that contained that one particular song. Unfortunately, that song was not in sheet music form but was only to be found in a wedding book along with twenty-nine other wedding songs that already were in Aia's wedding music collection. She explained to Clement that all of her effort was rewarded with a lousy corsage, a pallid white carnation that was cheaply adorned with a bit of baby's breath and a single fern, which is already wilted and in the trash can. I noticed that Aia's attitude was so sour today that I could not handle any more negativity. Ruby and Echo resounded in full agreement with my feelings and Echo kindly re-echoed my sentiments. To avoid hearing any more, we removed ourselves from listening to Aia's complaints describing how she had been unscrupulously treated like a bargain-basement organist by being tricked into being "easy on the pocketbooks" of Joleen and Spencer.

Ruby and I lost our appetites tonight and did not want to travel to the parsonage. Perhaps tomorrow evening we will be interested in a snack when an aura of positivity returns at the Osterhagens. Ruby and I spent the evening delving into a lengthy discussion regarding two bad habits, smoking and jingling change in your pocket. These concerns came up today after Checkers, a continually curious mouse, revealed to me observations he has made concerning parishioner Winston Cunningham. Checkers has been monitoring Winston's behaviour at church every Sunday. He noted that when it is time for the choir to sing their anthem, Winston gets up from the pew and goes outdoors for a smoke in order to satisfy his nicotine craving. After that, he returns to his spot. Checkers said that it is understandable behaviour as Winston is highly addicted to smoking. But, according to Checkers, a second behaviour has been added. Winston smokes with one hand and jingles the loose coins in his pocket with the other hand.

Ruby added a third subject to our discussion, the new quest to keep the church fragrance-free, in consideration of those with sensitivities. When Winston returns to the sanctuary, he reeks of cigarette smoke which is way worse than any perfume, scented body wash, shave cream, or body lotion. Some of the mice have observed that these lovely scents bother some people. We began to discuss John 12:1-3. It goes like this: "Six days before the Passover, Jesus therefore came to Bethany, where Lazarus was, whom Jesus had raised from the dead. So they gave a dinner for him there. Martha served, and Lazarus was one of those reclining with him at table. Mary therefore took a pound of expensive ointment made from pure nard, and anointed the feet of Jesus and wiped his feet with her hair. The house was filled with the fragrance of the perfume." After reading that passage, Ruby and I agreed that we enjoy the aroma of the wide variety of sweet-smelling fragrances that occur every Sunday morning at St. Pete's. We hope that the idea of the church becoming a fragrance-free zone is never brought forward in our lifetime.

At 11:30 p.m. Ruby and I went to bed hungry.

– F.N.

Wednesday, April 22

Several weeks ago Ruby and I invited Cricket Pickett to join us for dinner. While we were eating supper we heard sounds coming from the Osterhagen's living room television. The three of us peeked through the slit in the parsonage dining room wall and caught a glimpse of their living room TV where they were watching an old black and white Tarzan film. We got to see Tarzan in the jungle holding on to sturdy tree vines while swinging and yodeling at the top of his voice. Ever since then, Cricket has been trying to teach himself to yodel. That is a fine activity to pursue, except that round-the-clock he bursts into song vocalizing various trills and warbles. It would not be so bad if he yodeled a sweet-sounding, easy-on-the-ear tune like "A Little Old Log Shack I Can Always Call My Home." Instead, Cricket is not interested in learning the Alpine or North American type of yodeling, but embraces the Tarzan-style yodel, which sounds more like a yell, a screech, a shriek, a real whoop of a holler. Cricket is so obsessed with imitating Tarzan that he has become a threat to our safety, being unable to stay quiet. He has even gone so far to practice swinging on the ancient Weeping Willow tree that is located on the northwest portion of St. Peter's property. He even persuaded his friends to help him drag a fallen weeping willow branch into the building and rigging it up in the church basement so he could practice swinging and yodeling indoors during unpleasant weather. Last night Cricket joined us again for supper, but I told him as kindly as I possibly could that he cannot yodel when people are at church, as it might lead to our village being discovered. He agreed and promised me that he would be quiet and only practice his Tarzan yodeling at appropriate times. I guess that he took my words seriously because today ended yodeling-free.

At 11:30 p.m. Ruby and I hurried to the parsonage and found an almond sliver. The parsonage smelled like almonds all afternoon as Aia made a buttery, flakey, and rich Scandinavian coffee Kringle for tonight's dessert.

– F.N.

The Fourth Sunday of Easter ~ April 26

CHURCH ATTENDANCE WAS VERY LOW THIS MORNING. MOST OF THE RESIDENTS IN THE county must have been attending the Oswald County Air Show at the airport instead of going to church. The air show was scheduled from 9 a.m. - 4 p.m. today. Last week Ruby and I heard some of the members talking about the interesting activities on the air show's schedule. Activities included an open house, vintage aircrafts on view, touring the airport, plane rides, basically everything that is related to aviation. Concession stands were advertised as well as a play area for children. One highlight on the afternoon schedule was the performance of the parachute demonstration team. Everyone seemed to look forward to seeing them in action.

Our mice village decided to take the Sunday off so that we could enjoy the air show. Two of our mice, Quill and Daffodil Mountainside, who possess the gift of being completely organized, volunteered to get the word out about today's air show. They asked everyone in our mice village to gather in the church bell tower no later than ten-fifteen this morning while HSP's church service was in progress. The entire village was thankful for all of the hard work and time that they put into notifying everyone, even though they are often occupied with their sturdy newborn set of twins, Burr-Oak and Brewer's-Oak.

Most of the mice residents in our village viewed the air show from the bell tower. We enjoyed seeing the fast, twisting airplanes do elaborate tricks. The crowning moment of the day was when one small aircraft made numerous twists and turns while towing a banner with an easy-to-read message in the sky that said, "Jesus Loves You." The airport is several miles away from Historic St. Peter's, yet each one of us clearly saw and read the message. Most of the mice wondered how many people got a glimpse of the "Jesus Loves You" message, too. Instead of keeping the Christian message hidden inside a church building, or tucked away in people's hearts, someone took the opportunity to display to the general public a message, the most important news of all that "Jesus Loves You." We do not know if St. Pete's actually was responsible for the skywriting in some sort of way, or if all of the churches worked cooperatively on this project. Everyone who saw it was reminded that Jesus loves them. It did bring to remembrance a Bible verse that I once heard, which said: "The heavens declare the glory of God; the skies proclaim the work of his hands." This, the first verse of Psalm 19, was the first thing that came to my mind when I saw the message in the heavens today.

The Osterhagens were quiet for part of the afternoon as they mentioned they would lie down for a catnap. By just saying or hearing the word "catnap," it makes me jittery and weak-kneed because it includes the word "cat." So do any other words that pertain to cats, especially the word "mouser," which is a word about cats catching mice. It makes me feel nervous and nauseated.

Tonight there was a council meeting and Clement mentioned at supper that he cannot estimate just how long that will drag on. He said that it all depends on if Bill Tiederman, the chairman, can stick to the agenda and keep it moving. It also could be a late evening if Herman Jenkins, AKA the church bully, has gotten a council member's undies in a wad about something, even just some little bit of tittle-tattle. I hope they keep in the forefront of their minds tonight the most important message that was written in the sky today: "Jesus Loves You."

At 11:30 p.m. Ruby and I travelled to the parsonage and snacked on a dropped smidgeon of a deep fried mushroom.

– F.N.

DRIZZLE, SPRINKLE, AND RAINDROP ARE THREE MICE IN OUR VILLAGE THAT ARE intrigued with the physical and emotional well-being of human beings. Perching themselves on one of St. Pete's basement window ledges that looks out on the front sidewalk, they have spent dozens of the early evening hours observing the actions of humans. When I bumped into Raindrop today, I asked him to tell me exactly what they are monitoring. He explained to me that they are closely scrutinizing the behaviour of people that live in St. Pete's neighbourhood. He relayed that the investigation came about in early April after Sprinkle heard the words "Spring Fever" mentioned by one of the parishioners who had caught the fever. The three mice are probing and deliberating over their findings in order to discover the type of symptoms this fever produces.

Raindrop revealed to me that they have not seen a single person whose appearance looks as though they might have a fever. They were expecting people with the fever to have high body temperature, low energy, weariness, decreased energy, or an overall loss of vitality. In fact, no one appears unwell. Their investigation has seen much evidence suggesting just the opposite of a fever. Noticing that the grownups and children in the neighbourhood are enjoying spending time outdoors, they were thunderstruck at this discovery because they surmised that people stay indoors when they are stricken with a fever. Raindrop said that they see enthusiasm and energy in the people that they have observed. The longer springtime days with warmer temperatures have made it possible to wear shorts and a lightweight spring jacket. The grownups either are walking or jogging with a spring in their steps. The children have been skipping, hopping, bouncing, leaping, and jumping with their bodies in constant motion. There are even sweethearts that hold hands, hug and gently caress each other, showing budding signs of romantic affection. One conclusion is that the longer days provided by the change of season seems to be beneficial for human beings. Raindrop remarked to me that the three of them have been perplexed and totally baffled by this, basically more confused than ever as to what spring fever is as they are not noticing any feverish symptoms in anyone.

Raindrop continued on by telling me that the three of them thought about it logically and began to figure out what spring fever is. They concluded that the word "fever" combined with the word "spring" is a misnomer, an inaccurate terminology that is wrongly applied, a simple error in the English language, which was the most intriguing revelation because, prior to this discovery, they thought the English language was unblemished. They unearthed that spring fever is really all about the feel-good emotions like enthusiasm, thrills, zeal, exhilaration, and excitement. Those emotions cannot be measured by a thermometer device as it is not an actual body temperature fever at all. People who caught spring fever probably would register a normal human body temp of 98.6 degrees if their temperature were taken.

Raindrop declared that the term spring fever is nothing but a misnomer, much like the word hamburger. Hamburgers do not contain ham, similar to how a peanut is not actually a member of the nut family, but a legume. The term king crab is comparable to that, too, as everyone is aware that crabs cannot be sovereign rulers of a country, nor are they suitable to become a king of country music. Besides, crabs cannot wear golden crowns with embellished gemstones in the ocean as the crowns would slip off their heads and drop down to the scary depths of the sea where pink-coloured Australian coffinfish reside, spending most of their time resting on the ocean floor awaiting their prey. Additionally, Rain mentioned that they asked for help from Dr. Simonsen, the head librarian, to research where hamburgers originated, assuming it was either Hamburg, Germany, or Hamburg, New York. Raindrop admitted that this was just a little-bitty detail, but perhaps it will be of interest to the many mice in our village that enjoy learning information, no matter how teensy it is.

Drizzle and Sprinkle have put effort into correcting the term "spring fever" in the English language, as they thought it was their obligation to do so. Urging them not to bother with it, Raindrop told them that it would involve too much red tape and paper shuffling to correct the inaccurate word, perhaps requiring a lawyer who could take it as far as the Supreme Court. Drizzle kept thinking about it anyway, suggesting that "La Primavera Fest of Zest" would be a far better term for spring fever because it showed emotional gleefulness. Sprinkle's idea was to call it "Primavera Jubilation" because it has gusto and a passion for life. Raindrop told me that both Drizzle and Sprinkle had excellent suggestions and that their ideas should be brought to the next mice village meeting. After Raindrop heard their suggestions, he thought perhaps it would be worth all of the red tape to get the term "spring fever" corrected. Raindrop revealed to me that after much thought on the subject, he personally thinks that both names should be adopted and enhanced by renaming it "La Primavera Festivity of Zest and Jubilation," a much more accurate replacement for the misnomer "spring fever."

At 11:30 p.m. Ruby and I travelled to the parsonage and snacked on two morsels of an old-lady salad recipe that contained kidney beans, green and yellow string beans, and sliced red onion that are mixed up and marinated in vinaigrette. Aia told Clement that she made a huge quantity of it, a gallon-sized container, claiming that it will stay fresh for several weeks in the refrigerator. Clement didn't look or sound too happy about that because he told her that she didn't ever have to make that recipe again. Ruby and I liked it, but we wondered if Clement would have enjoyed it much more if it contained the legume called the peanut.

— F.N.

Due to an open window in the Bungard's bedroom this morning, the mice underneath that window formed an audience and heard Darla's first words of the day: "This is the day that the LORD has made, let us rejoice and be glad in it." With all preparations made well in advance for hosting the Von Engelberger Singers at St. Pete's today, Darla Bungard must have had nothing left to do this morning except to get decked out for church.

In preparation for today's Bavarian theme, the Bungards made a trip to Frankenmuth, Michigan, to purchase a classically fashionable Bavarian dirndl for Darla. Ruby and I thoroughly enjoyed listening to the many details of the Bungard's trip as told by the mice who reside underneath Darla and Will's wrap-around porch. One evening last week the Bungard mice came to visit us as they were certain this information needs to be included in my journal. I listened carefully and jotted down notes with so many particulars.

Because Darla is the hostess of today's event, she carefully looked over the various dirndl selections that were hanging on a boutique clothing rack. Inquiring of the sales clerk if there were any other options, she was given a special order catalogue from underneath the checkout counter. This "wish book" contained a wide selection of dirndls, various fabrics and colour choices, which all happened to be very costly. Having studied the catalogue a short while, Darla inquired of the salesclerk if there was a place she could comfortably sit down and concentrate on selecting the most suitable dirndl. In one corner of the boutique, Darla sat down at a small round "VIP" table and fixated on her goal. The perceptive sales clerk brought her a cup of steaming cranberry pomegranate herbal tea in a hand-painted English tea cup adorned with pink and red country roses. This insightful sales clerk realized that she might be in for a hefty commission.

Darla's eyes caught the attention of a traditional blue and white checked dirndl that looked crisp and fresh, youthful, and especially striking. She later told Will that she had to skip over that one because she had already ordered blue and white checkered tablecloths from A-1 Linen Supply and Rental, Inc. Darla said the very last thing she wanted to do was to blend into the tablecloths, or worse, to look as though she had hired a seamstress to fashion a dirndl for her out of two of the checkered tablecloths. There was a second favourite that she preferred which was made of forest-green velveteen fabric that was embroidered with flowers speckled here and there in colours of cobalt blue, amber yellow, vibrant pink, and red. This fabric provided old-world beauty and charm. After that she discovered the jewellery section located in the back of the catalogue and choose a fitting ensemble to complete the look that she was after – a handcrafted necklace featuring a large heart medallion carved out of authentic deer antlers, centered with an attached Edelweiss image that was cast out of pewter, along with matching drop earrings.

Will patiently waited for Darla, as he always does, and watched people. Darla needed to try on one of the dirndls from the floor sales rack for a size check. Modelling a size 46 European, or a size 12 U.S., she walked over to Will and twirled round and round in front of him. He attentively and deliberately checked her out. When she came very close to him, the mice later heard that he whispered in her ear something about being his Bavarian Biergarten babe.

Darla's wardrobe worries vanished after the dirndl, blouse, apron, and jewellery were special ordered. She was promised that her order would be ready in three weeks. Both of the Bungards left the store satisfied with their purchases and celebrated by going out to dinner at one of the famous chicken dinner restaurants in Frankenmuth. Will was very happy that Darla found just what she was searching for, and was also happy to return to Frankenmuth in three weeks to pick up her special order, because the food there is so delicious. The second time they stayed overnight in a hotel and went out for breakfast the next morning simply to find out if the breakfasts in Frankenmuth are anything as delicious as the food served at dinnertime.

The Von Engelberger Singers presented incredible music today, the type of music that had a cozy feeling about it, all sung in an unhurried style. Everyone seemed to cheer up by watching a family tradition like theirs carry on for over twenty-five years. The songs sounded so hopeful that some people even cried when the singers asked them to join in on singing "Edelweiss." Darla took for granted that the songs would be from the old-world tradition, but one of the mice heard her tell Will that they sounded more like, "Blowin' in the Wind" or "Gentle on My Mind."

Darla wore her Bavarian ensemble to this morning's worship service. Unfortunately Darla assumed that the Von Engelberger Singers would be outfitted in dirndls and lederhosen. But, instead of that, the females wore bright blue dresses, and the men wore black suit coats and slacks, white shirts, and bright blue plaid ties. Some of the mice noticed that Darla seemed a bit self-conscious wearing her dirndl, being the only one in the room, the county, or maybe even the state, dressed in that type of attire at that precise moment.

When Pastor Osterhagen asked if anyone would like to make an announcement, the Von Engelberger Singers all looked in Darla's direction expecting that she would come forward to speak in the microphone. The singers noticed her dressed in an authentic dirndl, noting that it was anything but a cheap one found on some costume rack. They expected that she was a very special guest, someone with a title, perhaps an aristocrat from Germany or Bavaria, here to bring Christian greetings to everyone. Darla, prior to this awkward moment, was planning to make two announcements, but she was now mum and quietly stayed put in her pew. Pastor was obviously confused as to why Darla was silent, but he quickly covered up this brief moment by inviting everyone to fold their hands for the dinner prayer that was spoken first in German, followed by English.

Following the dinner prayer, it was time for the hungry parishioners to proceed to Woolcox Hall to feast on a catered meal prepared by the noted Axel O'Gara, Chef-in-Residence at the Elkridge Mansion that is located on Lake Harvey. The dinner featured Schnitzel, hot potato salad, sweet and sour red cabbage, pretzel buns, and apple strudel. Elke, a likable and observant mouse who resides at the Elkridge Mansion, decided to treat herself to a day trip today by coming along with Chef O'Gara, unbeknownst to him. Positioning herself behind two of the massive insulated catering containers, she kept a keen eye on Darla as she was certain Darla was a VIP, perhaps a dignitary. Noticing that Darla was painfully timorous during dinner and that her behaviour appeared to perplex her husband, Elke later told Ruby her observations. She said that her husband must understand his wife very well as he probably expected to discuss her feelings later on, to root out what was bothering her. That discussion must have happened at five o'clock this afternoon while the Bungards enjoyed the contents of an over-sized wine glass containing their favourite Spanish Merlot as they sat on two of the six hardwood rockers that are located on their front porch. It is there that they replay the day's happenings. Elke concluded that Darla must have felt self-conscious at St. Peter's today, behaving nervously, as though she was preoccupied and embarrassed, socially ill at ease. Ruby told Elke that those behaviours are not at all reflective of the strong and confident woman that Darla is. Ruby suggested that Darla might have felt overly self-conscious in her dirndl, being dressed up even more than the famous performers. I think that Ruby's speculation might be spot-on as she has a remarkable gift for noticing womanly things like that.

After parishioners left the building today, the mice at St. Pete's assembled in Woolcox Hall for our own Bavarian party. We consumed tiny morsels of Schnitzel along with all the other choice food presented at today's gathering.

– F.N.

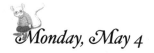

THE DISCUSSION AT SUNDAY NIGHT'S VILLAGE MEETING CENTRED ON HSP's RECENTLY published monthly newsletter called, "St. Pete's Olive Press." A few of the mice were absorbed reading the contents of a newsletter that they found underneath the sofa in the Fireside Room. Most of the fascination with this particular newsletter was due to a new column entitled, "My Favourite Things." The newsletter stated that one parishioner per month will be featured in the upcoming editions so that members of the parish will become more familiar with each other, just like in a family. The mice read that the person selected will be asked to fill out a form answering questions about their "favourite things," like music, sayings, food, or places. The first member of HSP singled out to be featured in the "Olive Press" just happened to be Darla Bungard. The mice agreed that Darla was the first because the entire concept must have been her idea. Bendt, the most muscular mouse in our village, observed that before worship yesterday, Darla presented each musician of the Von Engelberger Singers with a copy of "St. Pete's Olive Press." The mice at the village meeting were so quieted when Darla's responses were read. They went like this:

My favourite music: Classic Country and Alpine Yodeling
My favourite bird: The Bald Eagle
My favourite place: The Outer Banks, North Carolina
My favourite food: Seared Sea Scallops with Orange Saffron
                         Aioli
My favourite saying: "This ain't my first rodeo!" and "That's as
                         common as cornbread."
My favourite flower: The Yellow Rose of Texas, also the Blue
                         Hydrangea
My favourite colour: Aubergine, a dark and deep purple
My favourite book: *How to Handle a Cowboy* (a romance novel)
My favourite memory: Our trip to Iceland, time spent in the
                         geothermal water
My favourite game: Canasta

My favourite pastime:	Time spent at the nail salon. (Currently my nails are painted "Tiffany Blue" and are accentuated with "Seafoam" beads.)
My favourite person:	My red-blooded and devoted hubby, Will Bungard

After enjoying Darla Bungard's responses to "My Favourite Things" there was a suggestion made at the mice village meeting that we should do something similar. We will not write down the info and turn it into a column, but we all agreed that it will be impromptu and done verbally. We began by interviewing two mice last night, Boone and Crockett. I didn't know if it was necessary, but I wrote down their responses anyway in my journal. I just volunteered to do this until we can get organized and it is clear what we are getting ourselves into.

Brothers Boone and Crockett Scott prefer to reside in their remote, rural, backwoods setting instead of being pent up in the church building, even though St. Pete's is an aesthetically attractive church. They are good-natured, independent, and self-reliant, but would prefer to be away from the hustle and bustle of the mainstream. No one in our village knows them very well because they are partial to living in the shed at the back of the church property where the riding lawn mower and the snow shovels are stored. They spend an exorbitant amount of time foraging the ground underneath the white pine forest located in the back property of St. Pete's. They are looking for dropped pine cones for the purpose of harvesting the bodacious wild pine nuts. Despite that, both are faithful members of our village and come into the building to attend the village meetings.

I asked Boone and Crockett if they would enjoy being the very first members of our community to reply to several "My Favourite Things" questions. They responded positively and it was clear that they felt honoured to be selected. Their responses to the questions have already made us closer as a mice family, as they are not just members of our village, but part of our extended family.

Here were their responses:

	Boone Scott	Crockett Scott
My favourite music:	Banjo songs	Harmonica tunes
My favourite bird:	The Acadian Flycatcher	Quails
My favourite place:	A log cabin	The Smoky Mountains
My favourite food:	Cajun boiled peanuts	Deep-fried okra

My favourite saying:	"Well butter my biscuit!"	"Well shut my mouth!"
My favourite flower:	Jack-in-the-Pulpit	Mountain Witch Alder
My favourite colour:	Periwinkle blue	Bittersweet orange
My favourite book:	*How to Make Moonshine*	*How to Find a Good Wife*
My favourite memory:	My first Christmas	Watching fireflies
My favourite game:	Hide & Seek	Marathon races
My favourite pastime:	Watching butterflies	Napping
My favourite mouse:	Finley Newcastle	Miss Feather

I especially felt honoured that Boone selected me as his favourite mouse! But, more importantly, jubilation walked right into our mice village when all of us became better acquainted with the distant mice Boone and Crockett. This was especially true when Crockett responded that his favourite mouse was the fine Miss Feather. From the hushed sound of the room, it was apparent that all of the mice enjoyed observing both Crockett and Miss Feather after their wedding engagement was announced. Within seconds of their announcement the blush of their cheeks changed from light to dark to light in this order: rare wild cherries, common ripe raspberries, Italian blood orange, Brandywine tomato, to resilient red current, and finally returning to the common shade known as "faint blush wine." Now our entire village is aware that Crockett Scott will soon call it quits to his backwoods, mountainous ways, and leap into his future by marrying the delicate, lovely, and ever-so-cheerful Miss Feather. When that happens, he will move in among us and become an actual church mouse instead of an unattached country mouse that prefers to reside in the shed.

Ruby and I stayed home tonight, skipped our snack, and flopped into bed. We decided that we have got to cut down on our calorie consumption as I noticed tonight that even my slippers were snug on my feet. For all one knows, our snacks have been a bit too salty lately and as a result I might have dropsy, an unfortunate condition due to fluid retention.

– F.N.

Thursday, May 7

DIRECTLY ACROSS THE STREET FROM THE PARSONAGE IS A WELL-TAKEN CARE OF MODEST home that is up for sale. During the last few weeks there has been a "House for Sale by Owner" sign posted in the front yard each weekend, but for some reason the owner removes it on Monday mornings. The Osterhagens have not met the owner, but know that she is a widow who lives alone with her poodle and cat, rarely leaving her home. Occasionally they have seen a visitor or relative arrive to check on her every few weeks, a good-looking man that is well-dressed with a head of striking black hair.

Aia is delighted that she might get the opportunity to finally meet this neighbour. She has decided to go over there with Gretchen after lunch and ring the doorbell. Aia has met so many wonderful neighbours on both sides of their street, but when she attempted to meet this neighbour last fall, no one answered the door. Aia mentioned to Clement that she might have a chance to meet the last neighbour on the street, as she doesn't want them to be strangers.

Ruby's two sisters, Topaz and Jade, were outside after lunch today enjoying the sunshine and experiencing "La Primavera Festivity of Zest and Jubilation" as they sat among the blooming daffodils in HSP's garden. Just as they were taking a little breather from talking about some of the goings-on in the mice village, they noticed that Aia and Gretchen were walking hand-in-hand across the street. Because they were curious about where the two of them were going, they made a snap decision to follow them. As they were leaving the daffodil patch, they came upon a garter snake, which was utterly frightening, so they ran full-speed ahead to escape from danger. While running, they mistakenly risked their lives by heading into the street without looking left or right, nearly escaping death by an oncoming stainless steel milk transport truck. After this close call, their fear continued as they came face-to-face with a miniature poodle that was incessant-ly yapping at their presence. Being tied up in the front yard, the poodle could not attack them, but yelped at them with ear-splitting aggression. The two mice rapidly ran to the front porch of the "House for Sale by Owner" and were able to climb up a lattice-work trellis enabling them to land on the nearby kitchen window ledge. This safe spot, for now, would give their rapidly pumping hearts a chance to calm down and return to a normal thumping rhythm. It wasn't but a few minutes before Topaz and Jade discovered that this location on the window ledge was a prime spot to eavesdrop on the intriguing conversation taking place in the kitchen. The window was open and they could clearly hear the conversation.

As they shyly peeked in the window, they spotted Aia and Gretchen sitting at a 1950's square kitchen table with an older lady who Aia referred to as Pleasant and Gretchen called Mrs. Lerwick. Pleasant was preparing a serving tray which held a teapot and a plate of pink strawberry-flavoured wafer biscuits. She was wearing a house-dress that she topped with an old-fashioned cobbler's apron made of fabric printed with pink miniature roses. Aia explained to Pleasant that even though they live in a parsonage, someday they hope to own their own home, and told how grateful she was to have received a complete tour of Pleasant's home.

As they were visiting, Pleasant's white cat entered the kitchen wearing a pink rhinestone necklace and settled into her cat bed stationed in one corner of the small kitchen. Mrs. Lerwick asked Gretchen to guess the name of her cat. Gretchen thought about it and said that she thought the name might be Snowball. Admitting that her guess was an excellent one, Mrs. Lerwick revealed that her cat's name is Coconut.

Aia asked Pleasant why she was selling her house and where she was planning to move to. At this point, Pleasant asked Aia to keep a silly secret for her. She divulged that she has no intention of moving. It's because she has felt extra lonely lately that she posts the for sale sign in the front yard. This leads to visitors who knock on the front door and ask to view the house. She gives them a tour of the house followed by serving them tea or coffee and a treat. Pleasant said that she has a loving son who is extremely handsome and kind, but that he lives too far away from her to see her frequently. She said that her son is the only person she has left in the entire world. If she waited for him to visit her so that she could enjoy a conversation with someone, she said she might completely forget the English language due to lack of use. Pleasant told Aia that she has an intensely quiet life.

Aia invited Pleasant to come to Historic St. Peter's where there are lots of wonderful people who would love for her to spend time with them. After mentioning several groups like the Coffee Fellowship, the Sewing Group, and the Seniors Group, Aia invited her to be a part of these activities that many people enjoy. Pleasant thanked her for the invitation but she said that she would rather attend the worship service on Sunday, just starting with that. Gretchen got so excited about that news that she jumped off of her chair and hugged Mrs. Lerwick telling her that she picked the very best group to be a part of, the worship group. After that Gretchen invited Mrs. Lerwick to sit with them on Sunday.

Before Aia and Gretchen returned home, Aia asked Pleasant what she does when someone gets seriously interested in purchasing the house and presents her with an offer. Pleasant said that it was quite simple. All she has to do is to give them a second tour of the house and point out all of the flaws and deficiencies. She points out the shortcomings, the things that are broken, places that creek, expensive repairs gravely needed, stressing the extent of renovations just to fix the problems. After a second tour of the house, everyone, so far, has become instantly uninterested in purchasing her home.

Clement later heard the encouraging words about their afternoon visit, most of it centering on how happy she and Gretchen were that Pleasant plans to attend church on Sunday. Aia is confident that the warm and loving people at St. Peter's will welcome her and be glad to get to know her.

Clement also heard an earful about Pleasant's cool nostalgic-styled kitchen. Aia noticed the 1960s flashback decor as she studied the pink floral wallpaper and the Sherwood green kitchen appliances. An antique regulator clock with a swinging pendulum hung on one wall. Underneath that was a small counter where a pedal-pink two-slice toaster was sitting. The countertops were cluttered, but clean, and very pink. Several small appliances looked crowded on the counters as though they yearned for a spot of their very own, but there was no room left to put anything away, so they permanently remained on the linoleum counter, almost as though they were homeless.

Later on Topaz and Jade returned to Historic St. Pete's and told Ruby and myself everything that they had seen and heard while across the street. Ruby was upset and perturbed at her sisters as they had not put "Safety First" in several ways. After giving her sisters a piece of her mind, Ruby hugged them both and told them how precious they are. After that, all was forgiven and they sang "Safety First" in a special three-part harmony. Topaz sang the soprano part, Jade, the alto line, and Ruby filled in as tenor.

At 11:30 p.m. Ruby and I travelled to the parsonage and snacked on a tiny dropped morsel of a pink strawberry wafer biscuit. After meeting Mrs. Lerwick this afternoon, Gretchen asked her mother if they could purchase some of those fancy wafer strawberry biscuits like they had at Mrs. Lerwick's house. That is just what they did because they came home carrying a grocery bag from Grocer Dan's.

Ruby mentioned to me that she wished her first name was Pleasant, noting that it has a cheery sound to it and is perhaps of French origin. I told her that her name, Ruby, is a perfectly beautiful match just for her. She thought about it for a few moments and said that she decided it was just plain easier to continue going by Ruby. She did say, however, that she is going to try very hard to be in a pleasant mood as much of the time as she can. No longer will she gripe about the little upheavals, the trivial bits of chaos, and minor oddities that happen in normal everyday life. From now on she will be tranquil, calm, and peaceful, where everything is pleasantly pink.

    – F.N.

Sunday, May 9

TWO VILLAGE MICE, CHABLIS AND HER CURRENT BOYFRIEND, ROMANO, ENJOY SPENDING time throughout the week in the church sacristy, the place where Holy Communion vessels, the supply of monastery wine, and various items, like candles and such are kept. While hanging out there one day last week they witnessed a burglary. Together they saw a man enter the sacristy and pick up a full case of communion wine. After that, he carried it out of the building via the side door. Chablis and Romano quickly reported this to me, after which I called an emergency village meeting.

Clement, Aia, and Gretchen arrived home this evening around eight o'clock. It was then that an animated discussion took place about the wine served this evening at the home of Mel and Mindy Martin. The Martins served the wine in an elegant hour glass decanter instead of straight from the bottle. Aia revealed to Clement the reason as to why that was done. Ruby and I watched through the slit in the dining room wall as Clement listened intently to Aia's words. Aia said that she needed to throw away a tissue at the Martins and headed toward the kitchen cupboard located under the kitchen sink. It was at that moment that she spotted several empty monastery wine bottles in the recycle container, bottles that have the exact same paper labels as the monastery wine used for Holy Communion at St. Pete's.

The discussion centered on the quandary that they are in after discovering this burglary. They could call the police, but then the Martins would be in trouble. Then again, putting the best construction on it, perhaps they have wine specially ordered and delivered from a distributor of church monastery wine. At this point, it was far too late to make a decision as to what to do with this information as Gretchen needed a bath and to be put to bed. The Martins are faithful members of HSP, kind and loving, combined with being good supporters of all that goes on at church.

At 11:30 p.m. Ruby and I travelled to the parsonage. No snack could be found tonight. So, we went back home and crawled into bed hungry, but we reminded each other that we are experiencing only short-term hunger, not long-term hunger that is sadly so prevalent in many parts of the world.

– F.N.

PLEASE NOTE: For many days I have found myself in a stew and have not known what to do. Perhaps it might seem to you to be a simple dilemma, but to me it is a predicament that will require help from the entire mice village in order to be solved. Right now almost all of the pages in my journal are completely full of handwriting. In fact, these very words are being written on every speck of the margins of the last page. Until another journal or notebook is found at St. Pete's, I cannot continue to record the goings on at church. Tomorrow afternoon I intend to convene a meeting of the village in order to ask for their help to locate more paper so that I can continue my journal. I do not want to quit now as so much of the church liturgical year is ahead of us and the news is in full blossom.

I have decided that the first part of my tale needs to be distinguished by giving it a name. What you have read so far is *Finley's Tale: In the Beginning*. This was done in honour of the first person of the Trinity, the Father our creator. It is dedicated to Aia, Her Ladyship of St. Pete's, who is a heartfelt fan of anything Trinitarian, a Trinity College graduate. Because of Aia I have become a fan of anything Trinitarian, too, opening up my awareness of the deep mystery referred to as The Holy Trinity.

Originally I had not intended to list names in my journal, but Gretchen inspired me to do so as I listened to her sing a Sunday School song that touched my heart. Gretchen sang about the church not just being a building, but about people. So, as I wrote, I added each person or mouse to a list, and I have included all of them in an appendix, as each one is very special and I don't want any of them to be forgotten or overlooked. I hope that when you read their many names it will bring about a little smile on your face, a memory about them, and you will be delighted that you had the opportunity to learn a bit about what makes them tick.

So, dear reader, you are near and dear to me since you have stuck in there and reached this page in my journal. It feels like we are now family. But, for now, I have to conclude *Finley's Tale: In the Beginning*. *Finley's Tale: Heaven on Earth* will take up where the first part of my trilogy leaves off as soon as more paper is found. And, if I may, I will conclude with *Finley's Tale: The Bond of Love*. You have shown love to me by following my tale and I express my thanks to you by saying, *Uqqw weoi* (Mouse), *Mange Tusen Takk* (Norwegian), and *Vielen Dank* (German).

Happy tears are falling from my checks as I send you a kiss (X) and a hug (O), and wish all of you, Godspeed! I now sign off with hopeful thoughts that one day our paths will cross again. Remember that I have more tale to tell, and you are invited to follow my tale.

Your "not-so-new to you anymore" friend,

Finley Newcastle (F.N. for short)

Appendix

Characters included in *Finley's Tale: In the Beginning*, are:

Finley Tweed Newcastle, Church Mouse and author of *Finley's Tale: In the Beginning*

Lilje Morgenstern-Newcastle, Finley Newcastle's Norwegian mother

Ellis Newcastle, Finley Newcastle's English father

Ruby Newcastle, Finley's precious gem of a wife

Clement Osterhagen, Pastor at Historic St. Peter's, a real keeper

Aia Osterhagen, pregnant and practical pastor's wife, mother of Gretchen, fan of anything Trinitarian

Gretchen Osterhagen, cherished daughter of Pastor Clement and Aia Osterhagen

Dirk Klanderman, fill-in organist with zero knowledge of organ stops

Silver-Birch, mice village's most genuine and graceful mouse

Bishop Fillmore, seeker of Clement's advice and support about a district couch potato

Agnes Toppler, primary church blabber

Vern Moore, constantly in need of therapy but not in need of prayer

Annette Dixon, Aia's dear and helpful friend

Prairie-Rose, a mouse who hides behind the Lost & Found box

Chuck Brownton, hard-working church janitor who keeps HSP spotless

Herman Jenkins, ever-steady church bully that perpetually hurts others' feelings

Miss Jeanette Grey, HSP's Sunday School Superintendent

Winter & Green, two village mice who enjoy Christmas pageants

Cookie Grey, Miss Jeanette's mother

Eldon Grey, Miss Jeanette's father

Tonya Lorenzo, M&M's President who leads the Ladies' Guild based on advice from the former president

Kallie Sauer, M&M's former president who got sour and transferred to another church

Gooseberry, tender-hearted and compassionate mouse who witnessed events at the Ladies' Christmas Gathering

Esther & Elsa Baldwin, elderly twins who were turned away from the Ladies' Christmas Gathering

Sharon Nash, proclaimed guilty by the potluck criticizer of being a lazy-lady potluck contributor

Lenore Norris, criticizer of the lazy-lady potluck contributor

Jonquil, mouse who observed the winter picnic in Clement's office

Kiks the Donkey, (kiks is the Danish word for biscuit) who carried Mary in the town Christmas parade

Trish Guttermann, Mary in the Christmas parade, who frequently chews bubblegum

Jeremy Abrams, Joseph in the Christmas parade

Gigi, the mouse who nicknamed Trish Guttermann "HSP's Bubblegum Prima Donna"

Mayor Art Heddwyn, awarded the first, second, and third place winners in the lighted Christmas parade

B.Y.O.B.B.A., Bring Your Own Binoculars Birding Association, eight committed birdwatchers who won third place again this year in the town Christmas parade

Pinkie Weston, fan of the Third Sunday in Advent, especially the pink candle on the Advent wreath

Rainbow & Fiddlehead, mice who spotted Justin Severin in his work clothing and got to hear him sing

Justin Severin, self-employed trucker, former professional singer

Josie Johnson, regular church organist with a "problem"

Lloyd Woolcox, head of the long-standing Woolcox clan, philanthropist of Woolcox Hall

Cadence Davis, hand bell director

Stephanie Zeiler, "Bridal Gown for Sale: Worn once, by mistake."

Desiree & Raine, two mice intrigued by wedding attire

Sid Slavik, skinflint who split from HSP and who is continually looking for the "right" woman

Dr. Theodore Simonsen, mice village librarian and intellectual expert

Thunder, Norwegian Elkhound, lover of cold weather, dances in the snow

Palma Evenson, Historic St. Peter's oldest member

Alice Olewig, lady with her cataracts removed, AKA "Inspector Olewig, the Anti-earwig Bigwig"

Dacus Brown, church alligator

Alan Smith, certified electrician, also known as "Big Al"

Marsha Smith, "Big Al's" wife, a bit big in her own way

Mary Walden, annual "O Holy Night" soloist

Evan, Sarah, & Zoya Parker, Christmas Eve Holy Family

Blaze, village's most watchful mouse

Char Reynolds, cigarette lighter owner and Christmas Eve balcony usher

Herbert Lindenlaub, Christmas Eve complainer

Stickley, woodcarver mouse who carved a small totem pole for his girlfriend, Windy

Teak, woodcarver mouse who carved a small wooden heart with the word "Love" on it for his girlfriend Velveteeny

Windy, girlfriend of Stickley and recipient of a small hand-carved totem pole

Velveteeny, receiver of a "Love" hand-carved wooden heart from her boyfriend, Teak

Nimble (given name of Jim-Bob), the wide-awake morning mouse, who once spotted a Wild Indigo Duskywing

Bonnie Blue Habberstadt, in need of Confession & Absolution

Milla Van Camp, gossiper and card club attendee

Norma Lind, card club attendee and Milla's partner in gossiping

Wheeler, Christmas Day scorekeeper of mice running games

Bill Tiederman, Chairperson of St. Pete's

Cherelle, chosen as this year's Christmas Mouse, an honoured title to be graced with

Darla Bungard, the "git-r-dun" girl, Chili Competition Chairperson, and overall St. Peter's cruise director

Wilder, willing and strong leader in the mice village, financial status reporter of Historic St. Peter's financial health

Bertie Koche, laziness checker

Lance & Holly Steinman, parents of newly baptized Andrew

Posey, creator and owner of "Posey's Petals," specialty potpourri

Magnolia Brown, fourth "new" church cookbook editor

Susan Hayes, third church cookbook editor

Dash, mouse with the shortest tail, able to hide faster than any other mouse when danger is near

Robin Brooks, registered nurse who presented a community workshop for women on healthy living

Hunter & Joel Brooks, Robin's sons, who are excellent helpers

Amber & Ember, mice who are sisters that are completely terrified of cats, even scared stiff each time "Cat's Cradle" is mentioned

Lewis & Clark, mouse village explorers

Will Bungard, husband of the fashionable and organized Darla

Penny Larson, hemorrhoid cushy-cushion user

Gwyneth Leszenski, ditto

Bethany Reed, Penny Larson's daughter and helper

Liza Jackson, Gwyneth Leszenski's granddaughter and helper

Simon Thompson, church treasurer, photocopy machine disabler

Sally Swanson, person who fled from changing the copy machine toner

Liz Thompson, wife of Simon Thompson

Marie Schmidt, deceased Rosette Queen and dishcloth knitter

Lillian Hansen, made rosettes for Marie Schmidt's funeral

Twelve Chili Contestants:

Paula Adamson, featured "Prospector's Tasty Chili"

Effie Richardson, featured "Chuck Wagon Chili"

Rita Grant, featured "Rita's Quick Chili"

Tina Bailey, featured "Michigan Avenue Chili"

Carmen DeVault, featured "Suzie's Chili"

Auntie Patti Deibert, featured "Crow's Nest Chili"

Dan Bradley, featured "Thunderbolt Chili"

Joan Matthews, featured "Take a Chance Chili"

Marti England, featured "Classic Texas Chili"

Heidi Wisener, featured "Zesty Chili"

Lynne Boettcher, featured "Ring of Fire Chili"

Chester Dunn, featured "Creole Chili"

Granny Sullivan, mother of four banjo player sons

"The Nitpickers," banjo group that supplied the music for the chili competition

Marvin Clarke, parishioner that consumed twelve different bowls of chili with some repercussions

Kipp, mouse who overheard Marvin Clarke boasting about his iron-clad stomach

Snack, Kipp's pal

Bently, Harmony, & baby Linwood, friends of Finley and Ruby

"The Cobblers & The Coopers," Appalachian folk singing group

Little Lady Slipper, wonders if people in heaven listen to concerts performed on earth

Earl & Gwyn Wright, attend events but not worship

Miss Sassafras, Ruby's close friend

Fitz Woolsey, usher and promoter of Oil of Oregano

Virginia Deerfield, upset at her husband for keeping his cancer news to himself

Andy Deerfield, cancer sufferer who kept the news from his wife

Flaxseed, village nutritional coach

"The Ricochet Trampoline Club," practices often to sharpen their trampoline skills

Jilly Micklewhite, popular trampoline mouse performer who adopted the stage name, Destiny Skye

Chef Axel O'Gara, Elkridge Mansion's Chef-in-Residence

Cy Henderson, avid art glass collector who lost one of his marbles

Gypsy Madame Luminista, village clairvoyant

Esko, Luminista's overworked and sad boyfriend

Christine, Gretchen's babysitter

Zuzanna, owner of Zuzanna's Polish Bakery that specializes in paczkis

Granny Selena, Clement's grandmother who had no interest in viewing the Grand Canyon

Griffin, mysterious person who steals items from HSP

Yolanda, Utility Company employee with other things on her mind

Paulette Paulson, HSP's one-day-a-week secretary

Fakeer Singh & Ramneek Singh, brothers and Sikh Community leaders

Twiggy, Dandelion & Clover, three female mice that overheard Pastor speaking with Fakeer and Ramneek

Daphne Archer, "The Limey" and big-time fan of Indian food

Lester (Pop) & Lloyd Labreque, daily thrift store customers

Skat, village mouse who solved the mystery as to what exactly is the "B" word. It stands for budget.

Will Anderly, St. Pete's Property Chairperson

Lemon Drop, newest mice village member who we all hope does not have a sour attitude

Flip (formerly named Percy), skilled gymnastic mouse who invented three new flips

Butter & Tart, two mice that observed the disappearance of Pastor's eyeglasses

Wistful & Wisteria, knowledgeable female mice intending to obtain a liberal arts education, life-long learners

Finn Larssen, State Historical Society Representative

Mylo Kraemer, church candy man

Bryndle, collector of infant hair bows and a mouse line dancing instructor

Mona Wigstrom, owner of an instructional line dancing video

"The A Capella Cowboys," mouse quartet consisting of Flint, Bart, Logan, and Ash

Bronson, mouse infatuated with Bryndle

Montana, former mouse resident at the Sportsmen's Club who swiped shot glasses

St. Urho, Patron Saint of Finland

St. Philycis, Patron Saint of All Micedom

Aidan Brannigan, Clement's St. Patrick's Day name

Meara Brannigan, Aia's St. Patrick's Day name

Bridget Brannigan, Gretchen's St. Patrick's Day name

Peggy Larssen, Finn's wife, a ladies' guild president in another church

Eldon Johnson, husband of organist Josie Johnson

Aubrie Willington, disturbed about wide runs ruining three pairs of her panty hose

Palma Evenson, 100 year-old member whose birthday fell on Palm Sunday

Jennie Ekstrom, 86 year-old Swedish Happy Birthday soloist, first cousin of Palma Evenson

Stan, Palma Evenson's taxi driver

Bonbon, new member of the mice village who lacks a sweet tooth

Patsy, Stan the taxi driver's wife, potential choir member

Candy & Cane, two mice that witnessed cupcake theft by John Overby

Debra Brinkman, Palma Evenson's daughter

John Overby, gourmet cupcake thief

Mabry Montgomery, sole witness to cupcake theft

Hella Summerfield, dutiful bulletin folder gal

Geraldine Greenmeyer, Easter porcelain figurine collector

Lynda Gallway, HSP's former organist

Emma Woolcox, founder of St. Peter's Ladies' Guild

Kyle Woolcox, pallbearer who suffered an asthma attack from the copious aroma of abundant funeral flowers

Brady, mouse known for acts of kindness whose name was changed to Wade because of his fondness for wading in rain puddles

Blanche Browne, HSP member who originally hails from Eufaula, Alabama, who favours the song, "Just a Little Sunshine"

Willard Blankley, substitute organist whose favourite colour is green

Milton Braxton, piano page turner

Phylum, mice village botanist

Ozzie & Beverly Strong, complainers about the substitute pianist

Crystal & Claudia, daughters of Stan, the taxi driver, and Patsy; trying to determine if their parents are being lured into a cult

Patchwork, village mouse who heard about the cult possibility

Napoleon, "Nap," older mouse that suffers with narcolepsy

Morning Glory, a thoughtful and kind mouse who invited Nap to move with her to Loving Arms Nursing Home by mentioning the fancy Napoleon desserts served there on Sundays

Slippers, wild rabbit that Gretchen observes

Alaina Carter, teenager who told Gretchen a rabbit riddle

Giada Carter, owner of the "Ooh-La-La Beauty Salon"

Joey Cabot, engaged to Jocelyn Murray

Jocelyn Murray, engaged to Joey Cabot

Ian Murray, son of Jocelyn Murray

Maisie, daughter of Jocelyn Murray

Echo, Finley's good friend that often re-echoes Finley's opinions

Joleen Webb & Spencer Radcliffe, wedding couple that swindled Aia

Checkers, continually curious mouse

Winston Cunningham, smokes and jingles coins simultaneously

Cricket Pickett, trying to be like Tarzan, learning the Tarzan-style of yodeling

Drizzle, Sprinkle & Raindrop, three mice investigators of the misnomer term, "Spring Fever"

Quill & Daffodil Mountainside, two mice who possess the gift of being completely organized

Burr-Oak & Brewer's Oak, sturdy newborn twins of Quill & Daffodil

Von Engelberger Singers, featured guest musicians

Elke, observant mouse from the Elkridge Mansion who took a day trip adventure to visit Historic St. Peter's

Bendt, the most muscular mouse in the mice village

Boone & Crockett Scott, mice brothers who prefer to live away from the mainstream

Miss Feather, Crocket Scott's favourite mouse

Topaz, sister of Ruby and Jade

Jade, sister of Ruby and Topaz

Pleasant Lerwick, keeper of a silly secret: "House for Sale by Owner"

Chablis & Romano, two mice who hang out in St. Peter's sacristy

Mel Martin, suspected burglar of monastery wine

Mindy Martin, wife of Mel

About the Author

Greetings! My name is Sandra Voelker. Originally I hail from the United States having grown up in Austin, Minnesota, a mid-sized city that is known worldwide as "SPAM Town, U.S.A." Taking up residency more than twenty years ago in Canada came about when my husband, a Lutheran pastor, accepted a call to a parish in Windsor, Ontario. In 2004 we took the oath of Canadian Citizenship. For the last thirty-three years I have held church organist positions in three different locations, Michigan, Minnesota, and Ontario. A published composer of hymn tunes and settings, I have also worked in church offices, banks, an art gallery, and Hormel's corporate office.

We have four daughters, and God has also blessed us with two granddaughters and two grandsons. Topping my daily delights of favourite things includes breathing God's fresh air, selective types of music, spending evenings at home, my Northern attempts at Southern and international cooking, reading, popcorn and movie nights watching British murder mysteries, word search, daily tea or coffee at four p.m., being a friend, home wine-making, growing flowers and herbs, thrift store shopping, writing and painting.

My daily prayers are thankful to God for the many people I love, but included also are those who are far from loveable. I know that one day Christ our Saviour will take me home to heaven, but I hope that He procrastinates that for a while yet.

The side-splitting groundwork of *Finley's Tale: In the Beginning* springs from actual "church" experiences during my lifetime. Being a P.K. (pastor's kid) and a P.W. (pastor's wife) are blessings that have provided me with a fragrant potpourri of priceless encounters and experiences, a panorama of parish life that only those on the "inside" witness. *Finley's Tale: In the Beginning* exists because I was in seventh heaven writing about that which I know best of all, "church musings."

Soli Deo Gloria

Follow Finley's Tale online at

finleystale.com

where you can find:

• discussion questions for a book group or Bible study

• periodic blog articles about Historic St. Peter's

• recording of "Safety First," the mouse anthem and more!

The next two books in the **Finley's Tale** *series*

978-1-4866-1666-4

Heaven on Earth, the second book in the *Finley's Tale* series, brings to light more amusing adventures and further intriguing developments at Historic St. Peter's, recorded by church mouse Finley Newcastle.

Finley and the entire mice village perpetually observe the anything but boring church people, some odd shenanigans, an underground discovery, church vandalism, and much, much more—and their top priority, as always, is Safety First.

Pastor Osterhagen and his family walk by faith through the church year by doing what they do best: confidently proclaiming and trusting in Jesus Christ, their Lord and Saviour, for the forgiveness of sins, and relying on God's daily gifts of abundant grace and protection.

The Bond of Love, the third book in the *Finley's Tale* series, completes Finley Newcastle's journal of experiences involving church people and church mice. Highlighted are the state-sponsored Underground Railroad tours, the eye-opening discovery by the mice that Historic St. Peter's is a "Lutheran" church, a sheep-stealing debacle, and umpteen other developments. At last, Finley says farewell to his journaling days, turning his attention to another goal on his bucket list.

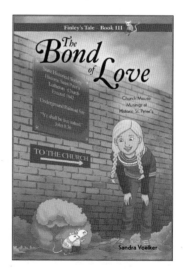

978-1-4866-1668-8

Years later, his journal is rediscovered by a new generation of church mice who are riveted to learn of St. Pete's past. Finley Newcastle becomes a hero in the mouse world, the only mouse who has picked up a pen and written a journal about the most important place on earth: Historic St. Peter's Lutheran Church in Oswald County.